DEBORAH

Prophetess of God

OTHER BOOKS AND AUDIO BOOKS
BY H.B. MOORE

Out of Jerusalem: Of Goodly Parents

Out of Jerusalem: A Light in the Wilderness

Out of Jerusalem: Towards the Promised Land

Out of Jerusalem: Land of Inheritance

Abinadi

Alma

Alma the Younger

Ammon

Daughters of Jared

Esther the Queen

The Moses Chronicles: Bondage

The Moses Chronicles: Deliverance

The Moses Chronicles: Exodus

Ruth

Anna the Prophetess

OTHER BOOKS BY
HEATHER B. MOORE

Women of the Book of Mormon: Insights & Inspirations

Christ's Gifts to Women

Divinity of Women: Inspiration and Insights from Women of the Scriptures

Athena

Ruby's Secret

Tying the Knot

a novel

DEBORAH

Prophetess of God

H.B. Moore

SHADOW
MOUNTAIN

Visit us at shadowmountain.com

PROPER ROMANCE is a registered trademark.

Printed in the United States of America
First Printing: September 2019

32 31 30 29 28 27 26 12 11 10 9 8 7 6 5

ISBN 978-1-52440-999-9

Character Chart

*Deborah
Father: Tobiah
Brothers: Chaim, Abner
Husband: *Lapidoth
Sons: Young Tobiah, Abram

*Barak
Father: *Abinoam
Sister: Kiva
Wife: Evie
Son: Gilad
Daughters: Hannah, Rachel

*Sisera: captain of the Canaanite army

*Jabin: king of the Canaanites

*Heber the Kenite
Wife: *Jael

Nathan: tribal warrior

Vania: matchmaker

Reuben: elder of the village

**Denotes historical figures*

Part One

Then sang Deborah and Barak the son of Abinoam on that day, saying,
Praise ye the Lord for the avenging of Israel,
when the people willingly offered themselves.
—Judges 5:1–2, KJV

Chapter One

Laughter echoed against the hillside where Deborah crouched as she watched the two dozen Canaanite soldiers set up camp. Soldiers had passed through her village before, demanding food and water, then discarding half of it—wasteful in their ways—but they'd never camped so close to her home.

The evening sun had set, and the boulders on the hillside reflected gold and orange, making Deborah's deep-orange tunic blend in with the landscape. She twisted her dark hair into a plait, then tucked it into her neckline to prevent it from blowing in the wind. She didn't want to be spotted. Not out here. Not alone. A seventeen-year-old Israelite woman wouldn't receive much mercy at the hands of Canaanite soldiers. Those men used Israelite women as sport, then abandoned them, broken.

Deborah had noticed the soldiers just in time. She had started down the hillside to refill her goatskin with water from the stream. She'd been focused on picking her way through the rocks, oblivious to the proceedings below, until she'd heard the laughter. She'd immediately taken cover, and fortunately, it seemed she hadn't yet been spotted. She knew her flock of sheep wouldn't follow her down the craggy hillside, so for a short time, she was safe from being discovered. Unless . . .

One of the soldiers broke away from the others and strode toward the stream Deborah had been headed for that flowed at the north end of the hillside, which put him in direct eyesight of her location.

The soldier stripped off his tunic, left only in his underclothing, and splashed into the stream. The spring season lent itself to gushing streams, plenty of grass, and blankets of small flowers. In a couple of months, everything would be dried up, including the stream.

Deborah should make her escape now, but she couldn't. Any movement might attract attention. Out of modesty, she closed her eyes, but the sound of the soldier splashing and bathing still reached her.

Then the sound she feared most resonated above her—a pitiful bleating from one of her sheep. Deborah turned her head slowly. *Oh no.* One of her flock had indeed made its way to the crest of the hillside. Then another.

She could not even command them to move away now, not when there was a companion, and not when a third appeared next to the first two.

When the sheep started down the hillside, coming toward her, Deborah knew something was terribly wrong. By the way the hairs on the back of her neck prickled, she also knew the bathing Canaanite soldier's attention had been caught.

A shout went up from below, and the sound pierced like a knife through her breast.

She'd been seen, and the sheep would either break their necks coming down the rocky hillside or be stolen by the soldiers.

Deborah no longer had a choice. She stood and rushed up the hillside, picking her way through rocks and moving around boulders. Her thighs and calves were strong from years of hiking the hills of the Ramah valley surrounding her homestead, and she was a fair match against her two older brothers in running. She could out-climb and possibly outrun any Canaanite soldier, but to lose her flock would cast her family into poverty.

"Get back! Get back!" Deborah hissed to the stubborn animals. She reached the first bleating sheep, and adrenaline spiked through her as she urged it over a boulder, then shoved its rump to set it going the other way. But the sheep refused to move farther.

Deborah looked toward the top of the hill, and her stomach dropped. The entire flock had now joined the first few.

"No," she gasped. *O, Lord, my God, protect my flock. Turn them around.* "Get back!" she shouted, desperate enough to ignore her own safety.

She pushed, carried, and prodded the sheep, trying to make them change direction. Despite the commotion of the bleating animals, she heard men shouting at each other from below, speaking in their Canaanite tongue. She understood enough words to know that today might be the last time she'd ever see her family.

Suddenly, her breath left her body as she spotted another animal crest the southern ridge of the hill. The predator had tawny brown fur, its rounded ears laid nearly flat against its head, its teeth bared.

The shouting behind Deborah stopped. No longer did the wind blow, and even the bleating of the sheep faded to nothing.

The very earth seemed to still.

Moving closer, the lioness gracefully trod over rock and dirt as if she were merely walking on water. The muscles in her shoulders and neck bunched and flexed with each step, and her golden gaze shifted from the sheep to the bigger target—Deborah.

A single rivulet of perspiration moved along Deborah's hairline, traveled down the side of her face, then dripped off her chin and landed on her collarbone.

Heart thumping, she ever-so-slowly reached over her shoulder and took ahold of her bow. The lioness continued forward, not breaking its focus, taking one measured step at a time. Steadily, Deborah retrieved an arrow from her quiver strapped to her other shoulder.

Then she nocked the arrow and raised it to eye level. She was a good aim and had been hunting with her brothers and father many times, since she had no mother to argue against it. Deborah had hit many a target, but never had one counted so much as this one.

She bit down on her lower lip as another round of perspiration began a new track down her face. Her chest ached with the effort to minimize her breathing, and her hand started to tremble, but she forced herself to hold steady.

O, Lord, my God, please . . .

She released the arrow, and the *whoosh* cut through the still air.

In the split second before the arrow struck the lioness, the beast turned its head. Instead of hitting the lioness's neck, the arrow sank between its shoulder and heart. The beast flinched, then staggered. Her golden eyes widened only a fraction, and then she released a moaning growl. The lioness turned and moved in the opposite direction it had come, her steps now listing and unsteady.

Deborah lowered her bow and arrow, her perspiration mingling with tears she hadn't realized had fallen. The lioness wouldn't make it very far before it bled out, but Deborah doubted the soldiers below would let her keep such a prize.

Slowly, she turned, her heart sinking at the sight of the advancing soldiers. The soldier who'd been bathing, as evidenced by his wet tunic that he must have pulled back on, was the closest. Behind him were two others. A handful more had already come halfway up the hillside.

The sheep had started to move again as well, but this time, they were going up the hillside, not down. A small miracle.

Deborah kept the bow clutched in her hand as she moved back until her legs hit another boulder. If she turned and scrambled up the hillside, she might be able to outmaneuver the soldiers, unless they were agile knife throwers. But running would leave the sheep at the soldiers' mercy.

"Who are you?" the nearest soldier asked in a rough voice, his Canaanite dialect like pebbles scraping against her skin.

Deborah's throat felt like she'd swallowed sand. If she pretended not to understand, things would only be worse. Canaanites had been known to kill Israelites who refused to speak their language.

"I am Deborah, daughter of Tobiah," she said in a halting tone.

The soldier didn't sneer or laugh like she'd expected him to at her feeble attempt at his language.

"Who taught you to shoot an arrow?"

"My brother Abner."

The soldier nodded, his study of her appreciative in a way that made her heart race. "You are a good shot for a woman."

At least that was what she thought he'd said; it might have been more of an insult.

Someone laughed, and Deborah looked over at the other soldiers who had joined the first.

"You must be a woman of many talents," one of the others said. More of them laughed.

At least she thought he'd said *talents*.

Deborah wanted to aim her next arrow at these arrogant Canaanites. Instead, she exhaled, and said, "My father, Tobiah, is a hospitable man. In his name, I will bequeath you three of our sheep for your supper tonight." She held up three fingers so her meaning was clear.

The soldiers smiled; some laughed. Evening's twilight was fast approaching, and if she didn't return to her family tent soon, her father and brothers would know something was amiss. Although, soon, it would be too late.

"We will take your three sheep," the first soldier said with a grin.

They had understood her, she thought with relief.

A high-pitched whistle sounded, and Deborah's knees nearly gave out. She'd know her brother's whistle anywhere. Abner was here. He'd discover what was happening at any moment. Then a new fear shot through her. What if the soldiers fought him and killed him?

She wished she could warn Abner.

The sheep moved faster, following Abner's more compelling command than they ever did hers. He whistled again, and then she heard horse hooves on the ridge. Most Israelite herdsmen didn't own horses, but Deborah's father had been given several horses by a Canaanite he'd nursed back to health. The man had been on the run from the king and had taken a bad fall. No one ever came to reclaim the horses, so they'd been put to work on the homestead.

Deborah turned to look up the ridge just as her oldest brother came into view, riding atop the black horse. Abner was an ox of a man. His broad shoulders and muscled chest made him a match for any man or beast he might have to contend with.

Three more men appeared on the ridge, and Deborah's heart both soared and sank at the sight of her second brother, Chaim; their friend Barak; and Barak's cousin Lapidoth. Four men, all on horses. All looking formidable. This could be a real battle if peace could not prevail.

Deborah stepped around the boulder, as the Canaanites' attention was diverted.

"What is this?" Abner called in his better Canaanite dialect, his voice gruff.

"Brother, these soldiers are camping in the valley below," Deborah said in her rougher version of the language, "and I have given them three sheep."

Abner's dark eyes shifted to the soldiers downhill from her. She could practically hear him calculating the odds of getting into a skirmish with these men. Four men to their twenty-four.

Deborah scanned the faces of Chaim, Barak, and Lapidoth. Out of the three, only Lapi was watching her. He was always watching her, it seemed, and she wouldn't be surprised if he'd been the one to demand they all come looking for her in the first place.

Somehow, she felt comforted at the look of concern in his eyes. Concern mixed with something else . . . fierce determination. Her brothers were herdsmen, and Barak and Lapi were farmers. None of them was a warrior—at least by trade. It was illegal for Israelites to form an army. But Deborah had witnessed these men training in battle moves late into the night. Barak and Lapi were on order from Shamgar, the Third Judge of Israel, to travel from village to village to train Israelite men in the skill of combat.

An Israelite uprising was forming, and certain numbers of their men traveled about the countryside, secretly teaching and training other young men in preparation.

"Only *three*, sister?" Abner said at last. "I am sure Father meant we should give the soldiers *four* sheep."

Deborah waited, hardly daring to breathe.

Her brothers waited.

Finally, the first Canaanite said, "Your family is very generous."

Abner nodded. "We live in the next valley over should you need anything more." His voice was still hard, and his invitation did not include his sister.

It was Lapi who slid off his horse and motioned for Deborah to come up to the ridge. She didn't hesitate for an instant but scrambled up the rocks, passing a few stray sheep that had been too skittish of the horses to follow the others of the flock.

Lapi stood like a sentinel, as if he were forbidding any of the Canaanites to come forward. His broad shoulders were only emphasized by the tunic he wore. His shoulder-length hair blew against his neck from the wind that had cropped up again.

When Deborah reached Lapi's horse, her adrenaline dissipated, and she wanted to burst into tears. But she gritted her teeth together and let him give her a boost onto the horse's back. Seconds later, he swung up behind her, and his strong arms surrounded her as he gripped the horse's reins. Only then, surrounded by the safety Lapi provided, did she dare look down the ridge at the Canaanites.

Four of them had already captured a sheep each, and everyone except for the first man had started down the hillside. The first Canaanite continued to gaze at Deborah and the men with her.

Lapi clicked his tongue and turned his horse around.

Now Lapi was between Deborah and the Canaanites.

"Hold on," Lapi said.

Deborah braced her hands on the horse's neck, grateful for the warmth and solidness of something safe to hold on to.

Lapi urged his horse into a gallop, and without turning to look, Deborah heard the thunder of the other horses' hooves following. She was safe, and she was going home. She closed her eyes and breathed in and out, catching the scent of earth and sage from Lapi as his arms cocooned her. It was soothing somehow, deterring her resolve not to cry, and the tears came hot and fast. Lapi said nothing as she sagged against his torso and let the tears fall.

She would have some explaining to do, but the most important thing was that she was safe. For now.

Chapter Two

"SHE NEEDS TO MARRY AND dwell under the protection of a husband," Barak said, his deep voice hushed on the other side of the tent wall. "She should be spending time raising children, not defending sheep against roving Canaanite soldiers."

Deborah blinked her eyes open. The darkness was thick, and she guessed the hour to be sometime in the middle of the night. She turned her head and winced at the pain—a headache from the adventures of the evening before.

A faint glow came through the tent wall. The men were often up late, training for battle in secret, and Deborah had spied on them more than once. When she was alone with her flock, she tried some of the maneuvers, although they weren't easy in her long tunic.

"You think Deborah should marry?" her brother Chaim scoffed. "She's still a child."

"She's not a child," Barak cut in. "Most women marry by age fifteen. Deborah is . . ."

"Seventeen." It was Lapi's voice.

Why it surprised Deborah that Lapi knew her age, she didn't know. And why did any of them think she should be married off before her brothers? Neither of them was married.

"Our father has not approved a marriage match for Deborah," Abner said. "There have been offers, of course, but none with the right bride price. One man from a traveling caravan offered double the bride price, but he was not of our tribe."

"And Father has kept her isolated to this valley on purpose," Chaim added. "Many Israelites have fallen into sin and idolatry. He wants to keep Deborah safe and pure."

"Your father's motivation is noble, yet Deborah's no longer safe minding the flocks," Lapi argued, his voice authoritative. "Your homestead is not far from the village. Even if the soldiers leave in peace tomorrow, you can bet they'll tell the story of the woman who shot the lioness right before their eyes."

Deborah's neck heated at the way Lapi was speaking about her . . . As if he were a male relative and not an outsider. Was what he said true? Would the Canaanites speak of her to others?

"Lapi's right," Barak said. "You can't let your sister run wild about the hills anymore. She's . . . an attractive young woman. Soldiers are less motivated to detain a woman if she's married."

Deborah moved to a sitting position on her mat. She'd never been called "attractive" before. When they went into the village for festival days, she wore her best tunic of pale blue. She had never scented her hair or used henna to paint her eyes, but it was the only time she felt like she wasn't a mountain goat. Even then, no one had complimented her appearance.

Now her neck and shoulders ached, her skin felt gritty, and her mouth was parched. What she wouldn't give for a wash in the stream.

The men had been silent for several moments, and she wondered if they'd moved to another part of the tent. Then she heard the faint approach of horse hooves. Her father had returned from his errand of reporting the Canaanite camping site to the village elders.

Deborah found she was holding her breath as she listened to her father come into the main tent. She wondered if he would agree that she must marry soon.

The couple of village men who'd offered for her in the past had not lived up to her father's scrutiny. He'd told her they were too young and not established yet, so this was the first she'd heard of them not meeting the bride price. Was her father so concerned about wealth? Abner and Chaim had never shown interest in marrying, and she assumed they'd marry before she did.

Deborah's brothers were quiet and moody. Nothing like some of the pleasant-tempered men she observed at the village festivals. She'd once told Abner that if he smiled once in a while, maybe a young woman would want to marry him. She'd never heard Chaim laugh so hard before.

"Still awake, I see," her father said, his deep voice unmistakable as he came into the tent.

Hearing his voice made her feel guilty all over again. If she hadn't gone down the hillside, beyond the grazing border, the sheep wouldn't have followed her, and the Canaanites wouldn't have been alerted to her presence.

"What did the elders say?" Abner asked.

Her father sighed, and she heard a rustle as he settled into the circle of men. "They're sending out a few village men at dawn to keep an eye on things. They'll observe from the ridge."

"I suppose we'll have to feed them," Abner grumbled.

"That's the least of our worries," her father said. "Those soldiers clearly saw that we have horses and strong men and resourceful women and healthy flocks."

Deborah wanted to curl into a ball.

"We pay our taxes," Chaim protested.

"Greed doesn't have a threshold," Abner said, his tone bitter. "We all know that. No matter how much we give the Canaanites, they always want more. King Jabin will never be satisfied."

Deborah rose to her feet. This was her fault. If the village elders were sending out more men to protect their property, more men's lives would be in danger. There had to be another option. But what? She squeezed her eyes shut, thinking of all the scenarios that might send the soldiers on their way without any more backlash or loss.

Oh, Lord, my God, she prayed in a whisper. *Give us the knowledge to protect our lives and animals. Guide my father in the knowledge he must have.*

The prayer had barely left her lips when an idea struck her—something she would have never considered before—so it could only be from Elohim.

"I will go to the ridge right now," Lapi was saying on the other side of the tent wall. "If their fires are burning, we'll know they are strategizing as well."

"You can't go alone," Barak cut in. "I'll come with you."

"No," Abner said. "This is not your fight. Both of you have much work to do in training others. If something happens to you, the work will be delayed. You cannot risk your lives for my family."

"The risk is well-calculated," Lapi insisted. "I know what I saw in that first soldier's eyes when he looked at your sister."

The men began to argue in earnest, and Deborah couldn't wait any longer. She hurried to the main part of the tent and stepped through the separating tent flap.

The small, single oil lamp kept most of the area in darkness, and the men had risen to their feet in their arguing. Although their faces were mostly in shadow, she was able to pick out her father's form immediately. He was the one she had to appeal to. The one she had to convince.

When her father noticed her, he said, "Do you need something, Deborah?"

"I have an idea," she said to the suddenly quiet audience.

Lapi spun to look at her, and she ignored the awareness that prickled along her skin at his gaze.

"Father," she said, trying to keep her voice steady. She shouldn't have trouble speaking to a group of men, half of whom were family, but her palms had grown damp, and she felt as small as a rodent. "I have a solution to get rid of the soldiers."

Abner folded his arms, not making her interruption any easier.

"I've been trying to come up with a way to deter the soldiers from creating any more . . . turmoil." She took a breath. "What if we tell them disease has visited our home? And we believe the water sources are poisoned. I can approach their camp, looking pale as death, and tell them that a plague has reached the entire village. People are dying, and I've been infected as well. I'll warn them to move on because we fear the disease has infiltrated all beasts and all water in the valley."

None of the men spoke for a moment.

"So, you would be the sacrificial lamb?" Chaim said at last, doubt in his voice.

"No, they won't kidnap a diseased woman," Deborah said.

"It's too risky," Abner said, his tone hard. "Anything could happen. They could . . . hurt you, then abandon you."

"You can be nearby," Deborah said. "On the ridge. Hiding. Armed with bows and arrows."

"You cannot sacrifice yourself in this way," her father said. "Abner is right. The soldiers are unpredictable."

Barak spoke next. "If there were only five or six Canaanites, perhaps it would work, but there are two dozen."

Abner nodded. "If it goes wrong, we'd have a much larger battle on our hands."

Deborah bit her lip, trying to hide her disappointment. She had to find a way to convince her father, then the other men would follow. She knew this would work, and they could prevent other much worse things from happening. "I will go at dawn, before they can put any other plan into action,"

Deborah pressed. "We'll agree on a signal of danger, and if I give it, you . . ." Her gaze went to Abner, then Chaim. "You can reveal yourselves and rain down arrows upon their heads. A surprise attack will give us the advantage."

Next, she looked to Barak, then to Lapi. He hadn't contradicted her, yet he hadn't spoken either.

"Flaming arrows," Lapi said.

Everyone looked at him. With his gaze locked on Deborah, Lapi continued, "Arrows lit on fire would chase them away, not to mention lighting their tents on fire and scattering their horses."

"They'd only flee to their city and return with a larger army," Abner said.

"Deborah's plan is worth a shot," Lapi said. "We can take our places along the ridge before dawn breaks. And I'll be the first one to shoot if any of those soldiers touches your sister."

Abner narrowed his eyes. "We put too much at stake if we're the aggressor."

Lapi's jaw flexed. "We have *more* at stake if we sit and wait for them to make the first move."

The tension only thickened when her father stepped between Lapi and Abner. "Let us strategize as if we are to take Deborah's suggestion. And if by the end of the hour any one of us is unsettled, we will change the plan and wait for the village men to arrive."

"All right," Abner said, his tone full of doubt.

Deborah watched the men settle onto their cushions again. She remained on the outside of the circle, wrapping her arms about her knees while she listened to them debate over possible positions they might take on the ridge, how they'd keep a small fire going where they could quickly light their arrows, what Deborah's signal would be, and what exact time they should set out.

After what seemed an hour-long argument, her father said, "Is anyone against this plan?" No one replied, so her father continued. "Who's in favor?"

Each man nodded in turn, and Deborah's heart soared with anticipation when, in truth, she should have been frightened. She wanted only to set the plan in motion then and there.

Her father rose to his feet. "Come with me, Deborah."

She stood and followed him outside the tent. The night was deep, and the waning half-moon and numberless stars gave off enough light to pick their way to the pen of goats.

Her father stopped when they reached the gate of the pen. "Are you sure you want to go through with this, daughter?"

"I do," Deborah said despite her drumming pulse.

Her father studied her for a long moment. "One of the young goats died tonight," he said. "You will carry it to the camp and place it at the feet of the Canaanites. Tell them that the Israelite god has brought a curse upon our village."

"She should discolor her face so that she looks diseased," a man said from the direction of the tent.

Deborah turned to see Lapi approaching. He carried a pouch, and when he reached her, he held it out.

She took the pouch and opened it.

"This is an herb my mother used to heal wounds," he said. "But if you rub the pale-yellow powder on your face—"

"It will make you look diseased," her father finished, his voice triumphant. "Thank you, Lapi."

Deborah brought the pouch to her nose and inhaled. It smelled of wildflowers, so nothing pungent. "All right," she said in a quiet voice.

"I will find my cloak with a hood," her father said. "That will make you look frailer." Her father strode toward the main tent.

Deborah watched him depart. The interior still glowed as the other men made plans, yet Lapi had come outside to bring her the herbal powder.

She looked up at him. His dark eyes were on her, and standing this close, she could smell the spice that was uniquely him. He had the stoic expression of a warrior, but she'd seen the worry and concern in his eyes when he was around her, and she knew his heart was softer than he let on.

"Here, let me show you." Lapi took the leather pouch. As he bent his head forward to open it, some of his hair escaped the leather strap that held it back. He dipped his fingers into the leather pouch, then looked up at her. "Hold still."

He brought his fingers to her face and swiped on the powder. His touch was warm and gentler than she'd expected from a man who looked like he could best Abner in a fight. She wanted to close her eyes so she wouldn't be caught staring at the way his forearms flexed or how she'd noticed the scar along his collarbone. But she didn't dare do it because she was too aware of the warmth of his skin and the scent of sage upon it.

Lapi dabbed powder along her forehead, then his gaze moved to her exposed neck.

"You should put the powder wherever your skin is showing," he said in a low voice. He took a step back. "You don't need a lot. The powder will flake, but the stain will remain."

She nodded because she didn't trust her voice.

The edges of his mouth lifted, and Deborah wondered if she'd ever seen Lapi smile.

"I think your plan is good," he said. "Strange, perhaps, but that might be why it will work."

Deborah swallowed. "Thank you for supporting it. It's hard to talk my brothers and father into anything . . . three against one."

"I can understand that," Lapi said. "They want what's best for you."

Deborah looked away because the intensity in Lapi's eyes was hard to identify, but it was doing crazy things to her pulse.

"Deborah?" he said.

She had to look at him then, and her mind returned to the memory of when they'd been on his horse and Lapi's arms had surrounded her, strong and steady.

"At the first sign of danger, drop your bow. That will be your signal."

"I will," she said, her voice a whisper.

His gaze didn't waver. "I might have supported your idea, but I still don't want anything to happen to you."

"It won't."

Lapi's brows drew together. "How can you be so sure?"

She could see in his eyes that he was truly interested. "I pray a lot." She expected him to laugh at her, but he only studied her for a long moment.

"Then you seem to have God's ear," he said at last.

This wasn't the response Deborah had expected. "I don't know if I can claim that privilege."

He moved closer, and Deborah swallowed. She wasn't exactly nervous at his close proximity. More . . . intrigued.

Lapi rubbed the back of his neck, and Deborah tried not to notice his movements and wonder why it would make her heart fluttery.

"You were alone," he said, "and facing two dozen Canaanite soldiers, who would have liked nothing better than to claim you for a prize. Did you pray for help then?"

"I did."

He nodded. "I haven't shared this with anyone because . . ." He hesitated. "Well, because I didn't know how it would be received. But yesterday evening, just before we found you, I heard someone say, 'Find Deborah.' I looked about but saw no one around who could have spoken those words. I heard it only once, but the urgency was unmistakable."

Deborah released her breath. "You heard . . . a voice? Did God speak to you?"

Lapi didn't answer for a moment as he seemed to be thinking of a response. "I am not sure, but I must believe it is so because when I acted on the impression, I discovered that you were, indeed, in danger."

Deborah stared at him. Was it possible that God had prompted Lapi to come to her aid? "What did you tell my brothers and Barak?"

"Nothing," Lapi said. "I got the horse ready, and they asked where I was going. So they decided to come along."

Deborah tried to imagine what Abner and Chaim had thought when Lapi had announced he was going to find her. And what if Lapi hadn't heard that voice or whatever had spoken to his mind? She likely wouldn't be standing outside the goat pen on her homestead right now.

She owed this man her very life. "Thank you," she said. "Whatever the source of the voice, thank you for listening."

Chapter Three

The deep gray of dawn melted into violet as Deborah crept soundlessly down the rocky hillside. With one hand, she clutched her father's cloak close to her body, and with the other, she balanced herself so she didn't send any rocks skidding downward. She didn't want to attract attention before it was due. Over her shoulder, she'd slung her bow, ready to be used as a signal. It would not serve as a weapon today since she'd be too close to the soldiers to fight.

Without looking behind her or up on the ridge, she knew that five men hid, watching her proceedings. Her father and Abner were on the south end of the ridge. Chaim and Barak were on the north. Lapi was in the center. She'd strategically placed the dead goat near the top of the ridge so she could point it out to the Canaanites. Everything had been planned, and everything was in place. The knowledge that she wasn't carrying out this bold plan on her own brought her comfort.

Yet, as she descended, she second-guessed her decision, even though she'd been quite certain that the inspiration had come from God. In the wee hours of the morning, she'd been fully convinced she could pull this off. But now, as she drew closer to the sleeping Canaanite camp, she remembered the piercing gazes of those men and the way they'd pursued her.

The soft bleating of a sheep sounded from the camp, and Deborah paused in her step. Somewhere within the camp, the sheep were awake.

And then she saw the guard—just as she suspected there would be. A Canaanite army wouldn't ever leave their camp unguarded, no matter how small the company.

The guard straightened from his crouch, and he withdrew a dagger from his tunic belt. He held the blade loosely in his hand because he could see she was a lone woman. Not much threat.

Deborah continued to descend, making her movements seem feeble so when he saw that she was diseased, it would be more believable. By the time she reached the base of the hill, three other Canaanites had joined the guard.

Deborah ignored the pounding of her heart and the dryness of her throat as she clutched the cloak and kept her gaze lowered. One step, then another, until the command came.

"Halt!"

Deborah looked up into the eyes of four soldiers. One of them she recognized as the man who'd bathed in the stream.

"It's the lioness-killer," he said, his mouth broadening into a smile. He made no secret of scanning her from head to toe.

A shiver ran through Deborah. "Beware," she rasped in her broken dialect. She lifted her hand that had been stained with the yellow powder. "Disease has come to my village."

The soldiers all stared at her hand, as if mesmerized. Then three of them took a step back. The guard didn't move, his expression turning into a frown. "What disease do you speak of, woman?"

Deborah shuffled a step closer. This time, the guard moved back. "It has no name," she said. "Our skin is rotting, and we cannot eat." She pointed to the ridge. "Our flocks are dying where they stand."

The men's eyes shifted to the form of the dead goat upon the rocks.

Deborah pulled off her hood just as the sun crested the horizon.

All the men gaped, and Deborah knew her yellowed face looked garish in the early light. She pulled at her hair, and a lock came free—a bit of hair she'd already cut, but the soldiers didn't know that. "Save yourselves." She dropped the hair on the ground and backed away from it.

"My father sent me to warn you," she continued. "He is too ill to walk. The illness came upon us suddenly." Deborah took another step back, wondering if they would detain her. But the men continued to stare at her as if she were part of a strange dream. "Go, or stay," she rasped. "It is your choice." Then she acted as if she'd been suddenly overcome with pain, and she gripped her stomach and moaned.

The guard stepped forward, but she held up a hand. "No, don't touch me. The disease is spreading to everyone." She pulled the hood over her head. "Save yourselves," she said in a quieter voice. Then she turned and shuffled toward the hillside.

She could not see them and didn't know what their reaction was. Perhaps they'd follow and capture her. Perhaps they'd charge her homestead, seeking to gather flocks that were not protected by strong men. Or . . . perhaps they'd leave the valley.

She weaved and stumbled as she walked, reaching for various boulders as if she had to steady herself.

One of the Canaanites said something, but it wasn't directed at her, and she didn't dare chance looking back. She made the slow climb up the ridge, knowing that if they were still watching, they'd be suspicious if she appeared too agile.

More conversation echoed against the rocks, and Deborah recognized some of the commands. Her heartrate quickened as she realized they were breaking up camp. Did that mean they believed her? She forced herself to keep climbing, around the boulders, past the dead goat, and not look back.

A form moved above her on the top of the ridge. Deborah knew it was Lapi, and she hoped he wouldn't reveal himself too early. If the Canaanites saw they were being watched by a healthy man, they might become suspicious. But by the time she reached Lapi's post, the Canaanites had bundled their bedrolls onto their horses and released the sheep. Deborah would have to call them later, but for now, the creatures would wander aimlessly, prey to wolves, lions, or other predators.

"You did it," Lapi said in a low voice as she crouched beside him behind the rocky ledge.

She looked over at him, and for a moment, their gazes connected. His deep-brown eyes were lighter in the dawning light, with flecks of gold in them, the color of frankincense. "Let's hope they don't return," she whispered.

Lapi made more room for her, and she settled in beside him, their arms brushing. Deborah was about to inch away when Lapi placed a hand over hers. "I'm glad you're safe."

He did not linger in the pose; he lifted his hand from hers almost instantly, and all that was left was the brief warmth his touch had brought. She didn't know why she was so aware of Lapi every time he was near. She was used to being around men. She had no mother, no sisters, and only her father and brothers for company.

Yet, around Lapi, she felt more . . . womanly. And for some reason, she didn't want him to view her as a girl but as a woman. He'd been in the discussion with her brothers about her need for a husband, and the thought now made her feel conscious of every action and word from Lapi. He could be married, for all she knew; although she'd never heard his wife mentioned. Barak had a wife and two children.

All Deborah knew was that she shouldn't be thinking of such things now.

She shifted her gaze to the other end of the ridge, but she couldn't see her brothers or her father or Barak. She knew they were still there, watching.

Trying not to think about Lapi's touch or the relief in his eyes when she'd joined his station, she focused on the activity at the base of the hill.

The soldiers had awakened their remaining companions and had packed almost everything they'd brought within moments, and then they started north. Their horses weren't really galloping, but they were moving quickly. The Canaanite soldiers were truly leaving.

Deborah found she was smiling as she watched their departure.

"Great work," Lapi said, his voice no longer a whisper.

She looked over at him. He wasn't exactly smiling, but one side of his mouth was turned up as he watched her.

"I was worried our plan would fail," she said.

"*Your* plan," Lapi corrected. He shifted to a sitting position and crossed his ankles in front of him. "You came up with it, and *you* executed it."

Deborah let her eyes stray over the shape of his shoulders, the strength they so obviously exuded, and she had to refocus her thoughts again. She untied the cloak at the base of her neck. The dawn had already given way to the morning heat, making the weight of the heavy cloak stifling. She lifted it and bundled it into a tight ball. "We were blessed. We owe our gratitude to God."

Lapi nodded. "Yes."

A triumphant shout went up from Chaim on the other end of the ridge. He stood and raised his hands over his head. "They're gone!" he called out.

Next to him, Barak laughed in that deep voice of his.

Deborah looked to where she'd last seen the Canaanite soldiers. They were well out of earshot, their forms upon the horses looking like carved toys for children.

Relief cut through Deborah. Success felt sweet, and despite not having slept for many hours, she wanted to prepare a huge meal in celebration. Perhaps the men the village elders had said they'd be sending would join them as well and celebrate the fact that they would not be engaging in battle today.

"Praise the Lord!" her father's voice echoed along the ridge.

Deborah looked in his direction and saw a rare smile on Abner's face as father and son embraced. They began to walk toward Deborah.

Lapi stood and held out his hand to help Deborah to her feet.

She hesitated, knowing he was only offering to help her, but she knew that any touch from him would again stir her blood.

Lapi's gaze remained steady on hers, questioning, and she decided she would stop acting the stubborn woman.

She placed her hand in Lapi's larger hand. His fingers were calloused, as all desert men's were. She wasn't surprised that his grasp was sure. He pulled her to her feet with little effort, and for an instant, his grip tightened over hers.

"You are favored by God, Deborah of Ramah," he said in a quiet voice.

Then he let go of her hand, and she was still trying to comprehend what he'd meant when her father's voice broke into her thoughts.

"You wash up, daughter, and we will kill the fatted calf in celebration," her father said, his tone jovial.

She turned to see her father's grin. He closed the distance between them in a few more strides and pulled her into an embrace.

His thick beard tickled her face, and his chest rumbled as he chuckled. "You are a wonder. I can't believe how fast those soldiers broke camp. It was like they were running from God's fiery wrath."

Abner grinned, and soon Chaim and Barak joined their group. The men clapped each other on the back, talking about how gullible the soldiers had been.

"You will be a legend, little sister," Chaim said, turning toward her. "You'll be known as the girl who can kill a lioness and chase away an army of Canaanites in the same day."

Deborah laughed then. "Already, your tale has grown large. I can't wait to hear what you'll say tomorrow."

"It will be a lioness and a bear by tomorrow," Chaim said with a wink.

Barak rested a hand on Chaim's shoulder. "And the army will have grown to fifty men."

Chaim shrugged. "Twenty-five or fifty—the number doesn't matter."

Lapi hadn't joined in with the joking; in fact, he seemed to be in deep thought.

Deborah handed the cloak to her father. "I am going to wash off this yellow stain." She made her way toward the edge of the ridge and climbed down to where the stream pooled before meandering down the hillside. The water would be cold this time of morning, but she wouldn't mind. She wanted to cool off.

The men's voices faded as she slipped off her dusty leather sandals at the edge of the small pool and dunked them in the water. They'd still be wet when she walked back, but at least they'd be clean for a few moments, and she could walk mostly on wild grass.

With a glance toward the top of the ridge and the men, she saw that they'd started out for the homestead. She tied the hem of her tunic so that her legs were exposed from the knee down. Then she waded into the pool. The hem would get wet, but it would be less than if she hadn't tied the ends.

She scrubbed at her hands, then she washed her face. Last, she submerged her head because surely the yellow powder had found its way into her hair. By the time she climbed out of the pool, she'd started to shiver, and goose pimples had covered her body like a rash. But she felt refreshed, and her heart was filled with gratitude. She sat on a nearby boulder and pulled on her leather sandals, then wrapped the straps around her ankles to secure them.

The sun was well on its way to ascending the blue sky, making everything around her green and golden. Early-morning insects inspected the water droplets that had fallen onto the boulder. A sheep's bleating attracted her attention, and she stood and made the climb to the ridge.

Lapi was coming up the far end of the hillside, leading the sheep abandoned by the Canaanites.

Deborah watched him maneuver among the rocks, his footsteps steady, his form moving with easy confidence. She marveled at how effortlessly he led the sheep, without a word or command. It was like they considered him their new master.

At that moment, he looked up, and her face heated when he caught her watching him.

She couldn't turn away now and pretend she hadn't seen him. So she waited for him to crest the ridge.

He stopped at the top, his breathing rapid with the exertion of climbing the hill so quickly. Next came the sheep, and Deborah bent to scratch their heads. "You are very lucky sheep," she said. "Either that or very, very foolish."

She felt Lapi's gaze on her, but she refused to look at him because even though she'd untied her tunic and put on her sandals, her wet hair made her feel somehow uncovered.

"I'll walk you to the homestead," Lapi said. "I don't like the idea of you being out here alone."

Deborah straightened, glanced at him, then looked toward the valley. "The Canaanites are well and gone."

"Canaanites soldiers aren't the only danger to a woman," Lapi said.

True. She kept her focus on the valley as the wind picked up and threaded through her hair. The warming day would dry the strands in no time, and then she could plait them. "Is that what you told my father and brothers?"

"I told them I'd fetch the sheep," Lapi said, moving beside her and casting his own gaze over the valley. "I did not want them to know that I thought you should still be watched over. Or think I was showing special interest in you. At least beyond what a brother might show."

She exhaled. This turn in the conversation made her feel off-balance. "Yet, you are not my brother."

He gave no response. Deborah could not understand this mysterious man with his observant ways and his tendency to never be far from her sight.

She looked at him then, and he turned his head to look down at her.

"You are not my brother, Lapi," she said again. "So why are you always . . . watching me?" Deborah hadn't expected him to smile, but his upturned lips made her feel like her breath had just been stolen. She rested her hands on her hips. "Why are you smiling?"

His brows lifted. "You make me feel like smiling."

Oh. She exhaled and tried to calm her racing heart. "I don't understand why you're so interested in what I do."

"Do you not understand?"

Apparently, he was a man of riddles. She sighed and looked away again. She should probably start walking back to the homestead. She was a woman now, but interacting with someone like Lapi was beyond the depth of her experience.

"Deborah," he said, his voice nearly as quiet as the wind. "I came here on a training assignment ordered by the Judge of Israel. I did not expect to find you."

"You did not expect my brothers to have a sister?" Perhaps she was giving him a hard time, but she also deserved some answers. She didn't need to look at him to know he had that intense look in his eyes. She smoothed her half-dry hair back from her face and neck and twisted it around her fingers.

"I did not expect *you*," Lapi said, his voice remaining soft.

His quietness did strange things to her pulse.

"You are an intriguing woman," he continued. "And I cannot stop thinking about you."

She dropped her hands to her side, and she turned to face him then.

He wasn't smiling anymore. "If you will consent, I would like to ask your father, Tobiah, to give you to me as a wife."

Chapter Four

Surely Deborah had not heard Lapi declare he wanted to marry her. But here he stood, looking down at her, his dark eyes earnest. Deborah's mind spun, and she tried to comprehend how this had come about. She'd heard the conversation between him and her brothers—talk of bride prices and tribes. Had Lapi not heard a thing they'd said? Besides, when she'd considered marriage, she'd assumed it would be to another herdsman, someone like her father. A man content to live on the same homestead year after year; content to walk the same hills.

The morning sun grew hotter and made her skin prickle with perspiration between her shoulder blades. One of the sheep butted against her, and she absently patted its head, using the distraction to think of how to reply to Lapi. She guessed him to be about eight years older than she, but she knew little else about him.

"You are not of my tribe," she said at last, knowing that her words might bruise him. But she wanted only the truth between them. "My father turned down an offer by another man for that reason."

Lapi remained silent for a moment, and she wondered if he'd stride away now, put this conversation behind both of them. When he spoke, his voice was low. "And you would not defy your father's wishes?"

"No." Deborah breathed out.

He gave a short nod. "You are a devoted sister and daughter, Deborah. And I would expect nothing less from a woman like you."

She was a woman of marriageable age, yes, but she also felt young, naïve, and perhaps a bit fearful to face a man such as Lapi and discuss such a serious and life-changing topic.

"Perhaps your father has rejected other suitors because they were not the right one, despite your tribe and despite his expected bride price," Lapi said at last. "I do not mind waiting and getting to know your family better. Perhaps then your father will see my intentions are pure." He didn't sound angry. But would waiting really convince her father to go against centuries of tradition? Not only would marriage to Lapi take her from her home, but it would also taint their tribal line should Abner and Chaim never have children.

Did she want him to wait? She looked out across the valley at the green landscape made gold in the morning sun. She had many questions, but would those questions be too complicated?

"It is not fair to ask you to wait when my father has not agreed to others before you. It is not like you can change your tribe." She felt confident in her answer, but for some reason, tears burned her eyes. She blinked them away and glanced over at Lapi. He focused on the valley, and Deborah sensed he was a good man, an honest man, and he would be a faithful husband. She didn't know why she felt these impressions about him so strongly, and if they were true, why did she not say yes to his offer?

Her words would not come, and the two of them remained locked in silence until Lapi stepped away from the ridge and clicked his tongue. The sheep readily followed after him.

Deborah knew he meant for her to follow as well. And she did, walking a few paces behind. As the heat of the day increased, she watched the line of his shoulders and the ease of his stride. She found him interesting . . . and attractive . . . but to marry would mean defying her father's wishes and most likely her brothers'. It would go against generations that had come before her. She would leave her family, her tribe, and become part of his.

Where would he take her? How would it be to live amongst another tribe, with their own traditions and expectations?

Warmth tingled in her limbs as she thought about what it might be like to live as husband and wife with Lapi. But she could not let her thoughts go there. Deborah lifted the hair from her shoulders and neck and determined she could now plait the long tresses in order to keep cooler.

By the time they reached the homestead, she had let her mind wander too far, including what it might be like to have Lapi's arms about her and what it might be like to kiss him. She should not be thinking these thoughts about him. Especially if she were to remain in the valley of Ramah and marry another.

Once the staked opening of the main tent came into view, Deborah saw that her father had visitors. Two pairs of sandals she didn't recognize had been placed outside the entrance. If her father had guests, surely they were in need of refreshment.

She stepped into the dim interior, following Lapi's entrance, and she immediately stopped.

Two village elders had arrived, recognizable by the sand-colored tunics they wore. The older man was Elder Reuben, but at the moment, she couldn't conjure up the name of the younger one.

She bowed her head and lowered her eyes as her father welcomed her.

"Are you in need of refreshment?" she asked, keeping her eyes respectfully lowered.

Lapi made some excuse and left the main tent. Deborah couldn't very well ask him to stay, not in front of these men.

"Daughter, come and sit," her father said, surprising her. "The elders have come to hear the story of the Canaanites. They want to hear from you, in your own words, how you bested two dozen soldiers."

Deborah lifted her gaze. She hadn't expected this. "I have been blessed."

Her father chuckled. "She is modest, as all good daughters are." The pride in his voice was plain, but for some reason, it made her uncomfortable.

Deborah did as she was told and sat on the cushion next to her father, across from the two elders. Elder Reuben was older than her father, his beard white, and the other a good ten years younger. The younger man was watching her with undisguised interest. The intensity of his eyes reminded her a bit of how Lapi looked at her, but the elder's scrutiny made Deborah want to check the brass mirror to see if there was something wrong with her appearance.

Granted, her hair was dry and plaited and covered with a scarf. But she'd slept little, and her adventures were many. She did not quite feel herself. No, the Deborah of today was different from the Deborah of yesterday.

"Your father says you are watched over by the Lord," Elder Reuben said. "Is that the secret behind your fortune?"

"I am . . ." Deborah said. "I am blessed. Perhaps the Lord has restored me to my family so that I might continue serving them."

The nods among the circle of men told her that she'd given the right answer.

"Tell us of these Canaanites," the younger elder said.

So, Deborah told them of how she'd come upon their camp the day before and how they'd advanced on her. When she recounted the tale of the stalking lioness, she mentioned Lapi and how he'd shown up at the most crucial moment.

Her skin warmed at these recollections, and she hoped the elders wouldn't notice her flushing. It was strange to have so much interest from the elders, men who'd never paid her attention before. And she hadn't quite processed all that Lapi had told her.

Once her tale was completed, her father asked her to fetch refreshment, and she gladly did so. In the cooking room, surrounded by all that was familiar, she could almost believe that the events of the last day hadn't occurred. But as she prepared tea and sliced honey cakes, her hands shook.

Before returning to the visitors, she took several steadying breaths. When she entered the tent section where the men sat, her brothers had joined the circle. She wondered where Barak and Lapi were, but she didn't feel that she could inquire with the extra company present.

Deborah served the men quickly, then brought more date-palm wine. Her duties fulfilled, she escaped the tent, but not before she overhead the younger elder say, "Is your daughter betrothed?"

Her father murmured a "No," and Abner said something she couldn't decipher.

But the younger elder's next words were clear. "She is comely and obedient. Surely there is a man in the village who is worthy of her hand."

Deborah hurried away, not wanting to hear her father's response. Outside the tent, the heat was nearly at its zenith, and she wished she could find rest in the cool interior of her tent chamber. But she could not bear to listen to such conversation about her.

Besides, she was curious to know what Barak and Lapi were doing in the heat of the day. Deborah walked to the goat pen and decided to refresh their water. She made the short trek to the well and brought up fresh, cool water, then she returned to the pen and dumped the water into the goats' trough. Their happy bleating made her smile.

If only life were so simple for her.

The arrival of the Canaanite soldiers had brought many complications.

She looked beyond the goats' pen to the grove of pomegranate trees where the sheep lazed throughout the day until it was time to set off for the hills again. It was then that she saw Lapi moving about the sheep, touching each one as he went. What was he doing?

She headed toward the grove. He must be counting the flock. They both knew very well the Canaanites had left the sheep they'd been given, so why was counting necessary?

Lapi looked over at Deborah as she approached. And perhaps she might have felt awkward at their encounter, especially since she'd stalled his offer of marriage, but her curiosity was too great.

"One of the sheep is missing," Lapi said before she could question him.

"Are you sure?" She looked across the grove, counting as she located each sheep. Minus one? When she met Lapi's gaze, the concern in his eyes mirrored her own. "What do you think happened?"

"I hope it only means the sheep went astray," Lapi said, moving to join her where she stood in the shade of a pomegranate tree, "and that we don't have to worry about raiders or another lioness."

Deborah swallowed against the dryness of her throat. A sheep going astray would be the best scenario. The last thing her father and brothers needed was to deal with Israelite sheep raiders. Those types of desert dwellers were cunning and fierce. At least the Canaanites traveled in groups; whereas, a raider might travel alone and prey upon herds completely undetected.

"I will collect your father and brothers so that we might start the search," Lapi said, turning toward the main tent.

"No." Deborah hadn't intended to contradict him.

Lapi turned back, surprised. "The sooner we look, the better chance we have of finding—"

"I know," Deborah said. "I don't want to disturb my father's meeting with the elders . . ." She couldn't hold Lapi's gaze any longer.

He took a step closer. "Is something wrong?" he asked in a low voice.

She felt him watching her, but she didn't want to be looking at him when she spoke her next words. "One of the elders, the younger one, has paid me particular attention."

She heard the breath that escaped Lapi's lips.

"Has he dishonored you?"

"Oh, nothing like that," Deborah said quickly. She looked into Lapi's eyes and saw something there that both made her heart flutter and her stomach twist. "He only asked my father if I am yet betrothed."

A muscle in Lapi's jaw flexed. His next words were spoken in a tight tone. "He is a widower. I would not be surprised if he asked you to wife. As an elder, he is one of the wealthier men of Ramah."

Heat flooded Deborah's face. How could it be that she had two men wanting to marry her in the same few hours? "Surely he does not desire me for his wife."

Lapi's chuckle was soft, and it only caused more heat to rise within her. "Deborah." His voice was like a sigh. "You will capture and break the hearts of many men if your father continues in his stubbornness."

She smoothed back a strand of hair from her face. "Do you ever wish you could return to an earlier time?"

Lapi's brows knitted, and his expression turned thoughtful. At least he wasn't laughing at her or thinking she was childish. "I do. My parents would be alive today if I were able to return to the night the Canaanites burnt our fields and my parents tried to put out the fire."

Deborah stared at the man before her. "I didn't know. I am very sorry."

He rubbed his hand over the back of his neck, and for the first time since she'd known him, his gaze faltered. "All Israelites have a tragic story when it comes to our oppressors. No one has been left untouched by the Canaanites. My parents should have let their fields burn. Crops can be replaced; lives can't."

She wanted to reach out to him, find a way to comfort him, but she knew that was impossible, given that they were not related. "Is this why you travel around to train men in the art of battle?"

His brief nod told her all that his lack of words didn't.

Deborah took a step back, feeling heady from her close proximity to Lapi and the personal nature of their conversation.

She didn't know how to soothe the sorrow in Lapi's eyes. She'd lost her own mother, but she still had her father. "I will look for the lost sheep, and if I can't find it, I'll ask for my father's and brothers' help."

"I will help you," Lapi said. "You search the shelters, and I'll search the grove. Perhaps it found shade to sleep in."

Before she could reply, he turned and started to walk through the grove. Deborah watched him until she realized she shouldn't be staring after him. She set off toward the tent designated as the stable, where her brothers kept their horses and extra feed. As she neared, she heard a man's hushed voice—as if he were speaking to someone and didn't want to be overheard. Was it a sheep raider? Her heart thumping, she moved to the side of the lean-to and listened. Then she recognized Barak's voice. She looked around the wooden wall. He was speaking to one of the horses.

The animal had a bundle secured on its back, and at the sound of Deborah's movement, Barak turned.

"Are you going somewhere?" Deborah asked.

Being around Barak was a lot different from spending time with Lapi. Possibly because she knew Barak had a wife and children and his gaze never followed her and his eyes didn't grow intense when they were alone.

"I'm going home to check on my wife and children," Barak said. "I'll remain with them for a time, although Lapi will continue in our training mission to other villages."

"Lapi is leaving with you?"

Barak nodded, his brow furrowing, but he didn't question her.

The horse nickered, and Barak turned his attention back to the animal.

"I've lost a sheep," Deborah said. "Have you seen any strays?"

"Not here," Barak said, glancing over his shoulder at her.

She sensed he wanted to ask her a question, so she moved out of the lean-to. "Thank you." It was then she heard a call, and she moved into the sun.

Lapi was striding toward her, the body of a sheep slung across his shoulders. For a moment, she thought the sheep might be dead, but then she heard it bleat.

Deborah grasped the edges of her tunic and hurried to Lapi. "What's happened?"

"It's been bitten by a predator." He stopped in front of her and knelt, then he lifted the sheep from his shoulders and set it on the ground.

Deborah knelt too and bent over the injured animal. Its front leg was covered in dried blood. "What kind of predator?"

"I'm not sure," Lapi said.

Barak came out of the lean-to and brought a goatskin of water. He knelt with the two of them. "How long has the sheep been missing?"

"At least a day," Lapi answered. He worked to get the sheep to drink the water.

The poor animal swallowed a few times, then gave a pitiful bleat.

Deborah took the goatskin from Barak and poured water on the sheep's leg to reveal puncture wounds. "I'll put a salve on it to help the healing?" Her gaze met Lapi's.

"I'll wait here with the sheep."

Deborah hurried to the cooking room situated near the main tent, deftly avoiding having to walk through the main portion, where her father still met with the village elders. She plucked dried leaves from the hanging herbs alongside the wall, then she crushed them and added a bit of water to make a paste. She found a length of cloth to use as a bandage, then hurried outside, wishing for cloud cover to cool the day.

By the time she reached Lapi's side, he'd moved the sheep to a spot of shade, and Deborah wasted no time setting to work. When she completed wrapping and tying off the bandage, she surveyed the sheep.

Its pitiful bleating had quieted, and she didn't know if that was a good or bad sign.

Deborah stroked the sheep's head. "Do you think it will be all right?"

"I've seen sheep come through worse injuries," Lapi said as he placed a hand on the sheep.

Their hands touched briefly, and Lapi moved his away.

Barak came out of the stable, leading two horses.

Lapi rose to his feet and brushed off his tunic.

"Thank you for finding him," Deborah said.

Lapi looked down at her. She sensed he wanted to speak to her more, but what could she say to him? Yet, she wished he would stay and that she didn't have to say goodbye so soon.

"Take care of yourself, Deborah," Lapi said, then he strode past her and joined Barak.

Barak lifted a hand in a wave before he and Lapi entered the tent, likely to say goodbye to her father and brothers.

Deborah offered the sheep more water, and it took some effort to get the animal to swallow. When Barak and Lapi exited the tent again, she watched them from the shade. They mounted their horses.

Barak took the lead, his and Lapi's forms taking on a shimmering quality as they traveled in the day's heat. The wind tugged at their clothing and hair. The men were in for a long, hot ride. She ignored the way Lapi sat with confidence on the horse and seemed to master the animal well.

Deborah had a feeling their urgency had something to do with her. The sooner Lapi left her homestead, the sooner he could forget about her. It was with both regret and relief that Deborah watched the men leave. Regret that tribal traditions would keep them apart, and relief that at least her life could return to normal.

Chapter Five

"You've been quiet," Barak told his cousin Lapi as they finally slowed their horses to a canter when they reached the outskirts of Kedesh-naphtali. Granted, his cousin was the quiet sort but never absolutely silent. Lapi was prone to commenting or complaining where due, and the two-day ride back to their village had been fraught with a hot, dry wind and little sleep because a pack of wolves had scared the horses.

Barak had insisted they set out well before dawn. Now the sun had crested the horizon over an hour ago, drying out the dew on the desert grass.

Lapi looked over at Barak but said nothing.

"You know Evie is going to question your black mood," Barak said. "So you might as well tell me so you can unburden yourself before my wife gets to you."

Lapi scoffed, then he unwrapped his turban that was supposed to keep the heat off. But the unseasonably warm weather hadn't been their friend these past two days. "Evie should focus on her newly returned husband."

"Is that all you're going to give me?" Barak said. He was no fool. He'd seen the particular interest Lapi had shown in Tobiah's daughter. Not that Barak could blame his cousin. Deborah was a resourceful woman and beautiful in her own way, but she was not of their tribe. And if there was anything Kedesh-naphtali was known for, it was tradition. Just as Ramah.

Not that Lapi seemed to care all that much for traditions. Since the death of his parents, he'd lived with Barak, and Lapi had always had a bit of a nomad streak in him. It was why Barak had been surprised that Lapi had readily agreed to return to Kedesh-naphtali.

But Barak was good at one thing. Waiting. So he brought his horse to a stop and let it graze the spring grass as he waited for Lapi to explain.

Finally, Lapi said, "I don't like how easy it was for Deborah to scare the Canaanites away."

"You saw them leave for yourself." Barak studied Lapi. "What are you thinking?"

Lapi guided his horse a few paces to reach a generous clump of grass. "Tobiah's homestead is isolated, and his daughter is unmarried and vulnerable."

"She has the protection of a father and two brothers," Barak argued.

"You know that any unmarried woman who is of age and looks like Deborah is at risk for kidnapping, or worse."

Barak did know. Tales from far and wide reached their village. The women in Kedesh-naphtali were trained from a young age never to travel alone. Their village was much closer to Canaanite territory than Tobiah's. Yet, Barak could see Lapi's point. His own sister was nearly fifteen—another reason for him to return home and begin the process of finding her a match. His mother had died years earlier in a plague that had swept through their village, and his father was not on good terms with the village matchmaker. Therefore, Barak had to act as the father to his younger sister.

"We can't force Deborah's family to marry her off to someone," Barak said.

Lapi's jaw flexed. And then Barak knew.

"You proposed marriage to her, didn't you?" Barak asked.

Lapi snapped his gaze to Barak.

In his cousin's eyes, Barak saw the truth. "What happened?"

Lapi jerked the reins of his horse and urged the animal into a trot. Barak did the same to keep up with him.

"It doesn't matter what happened or didn't happen," Lapi said. "We're of different tribes. Her father has made that clear to one suitor already, and Deborah told me she would not defy her father's wishes."

Barak shouldn't be surprised, yet he was. "Did you speak to Tobiah? Or did Deborah? Her age is past the usual marrying age, and perhaps if you offered more than the bride price—"

"No." Lapi's tone was clipped. "Her loyalty to her father far outweighs any thoughts of me. Let us forget about Deborah and the Ramah valley. We've enough work to do to focus on the future and not the past."

"All right," Barak agreed. He doubted this was the last he would hear of Deborah or the last Lapi would think of her. Barak was curious to know what type of conversation had transpired between the two, but it was obvious his cousin had been disappointed. How deep could his feelings go? They'd been in the Ramah valley for only a couple of months, training Abner and Chaim. Lapi had no parents to arrange a marriage for him, and Barak had been fortunate in his arranged marriage to Evie.

Although the morning was early when they rode through the main part of the village, Barak was surprised at how quiet the road was. Unusual. Lapi must have noticed it too. He cast a worried glance at Barak.

Barak planned to investigate before he reached his homestead.

A young boy skittered onto the street, chasing a pigeon that had one of its wings clipped—likely a pet.

Barak recognized the boy. "Joel, do you want to earn a bit of silver?"

Joel stopped and gave an eager nod.

Barak tossed the bit, and the boy caught it midair. "Go tell my wife that I'm on my way home, and I'm hungry enough to eat an entire harvest."

Joel grinned. "Yes, sir." He scooped up his pet pigeon, then ran down the middle of the empty road, his bare feet kicking up dust behind him.

If nothing else, Evie would have the morning meal prepared by the time he reached their house. The two men slowed their pace as they approached the blacksmith's hut. The familiar ringing of hammer against metal echoed in the quiet morning. Barak reined his horse to a stop, then swung down from the animal. He walked into the hut to see Yann pounding at a red-hot sword in front of a kiln. The heat inside the hut was like standing beneath the midday summer sun. Perspiration dripped off Yann's square face, and his tan tunic was stained at the neckline and arm area.

When Yann looked up, he didn't greet Barak with a welcoming smile but only nodded.

Lapi came into the hut as well and stood next to Barak, watching Yann work.

Yann turned over the sword and began pounding the other side. The sword was of fine workmanship, one that Barak had never seen in the hands of an Israelite, which could mean only one thing.

"Whose sword is that?" Lapi asked.

Yann slowed his pounding enough to answer. "This sword belongs to Sisera."

The very word sent a chill through Barak, despite the heat of the kiln. "The Canaanite captain, Sisera?"

Yann's nod was more of a jerk as he lifted the sword and plunged it into a vat of water on the other side of the kiln. The steam hissed and rose to form a temporary cloud between Yann and Barak.

"Why in all that's holy is Sisera in our village?" Lapi growled.

It seemed his silent streak was over. There had been no signs of a large army camping near the village when they'd approached.

"Sisera heard of my blacksmithing skills and came to refine his swords," Yann said. "He is taking two of the swords to King Jabin as a wedding gift."

"The king is to take another wife?" Barak asked.

He knew the answer by the look on Yann's face. Barak's gaze moved to the other side of the hut. Several swords leaned against the wall. Their crafted metal gleamed in the light of the kiln, and their jeweled hilts could buy a man's inheritance.

"Fine gifts for a king who already has many riches," Lapi said drily.

Barak crossed to the line of swords and picked one up. He heard Yann's warning scoff. If Barak was caught handling a Canaanite sword, the consequences would be dire. It also reminded him that he needed to get back to his homestead and hide his training weapons before he encountered any Canaanites.

"Has the village shut down?" Lapi asked Yann. "No one's in the roads."

"There was an incident yesterday," Yann said in a grim tone. "The villagers are staying indoors until Sisera and his guards leave."

Barak turned. "What incident?"

Yann picked up another sword and held it over the kiln, heating the metal to a glowing red. Before he started to pound again, he said, "Sisera whipped one of his slave boys to death in the market square."

Barak closed his eyes as a wave of nausea gripped his stomach.

"Was the slave boy an Israelite?" Lapi asked in a barely controlled voice.

"No. Syrian." Yann pounded the sword a few times.

The sharp sound reverberated through Barak's chest like a punch. He could well imagine the Canaanite captain beating a defenseless slave, and he pushed it out of his mind. "A prisoner of war, then."

"Likely." Yann turned the sword over and pounded again.

Barak glanced at Lapi, who was staring into the flames of the kiln. When Lapi met his gaze, he tilted his head toward the entrance of the hut.

Lapi gave Barak a slight nod. They would return to their homestead and eat with their family, and then they would strategize how to get the Canaanite captain out of their village. Too bad Deborah wasn't here to come up with a plan. Of course, Barak would never voice that thought aloud to Lapi.

As the two men mounted their horses and traveled the remainder of the way through the silent village, Barak grew more anxious to see his wife and young children. It had been nearly three months since he'd last been home. Surely his youngest, one-year-old Hannah, was much grown.

Down the road, Barak spotted Joel coming toward them, carrying that lame pigeon of his.

When Joel neared, Barak said, "Did you see my wife?"

"She's awake!" Joel announced. "And your baby was crying."

Barak chuckled. "Thanks for helping me with an errand."

Joel hurried past, intent on some other mysterious errand. The final bend in the road took them down an incline, which bottomed into a stream. That stream led straight to Barak's house.

Barak slipped off the horse and released it to the stream so it could drink. Then he walked the last paces to the yard. Lapi followed, albeit at a slower pace.

Their homestead was modest but something to be proud of. The house had been expanded to several rooms over the years and was surrounded by a walled-in courtyard. Beyond lay their cultivated fields.

"Barak!" Evie's voice sounded from inside the house before he even saw her.

Then she was hurrying out of the house, her dark hair flowing about her shoulders, the babe on her hip. Her round face was all smiles, and before he could get a proper look at her and the child, she'd flung her free arm around his neck.

Barak pulled her close, baby and all, and buried his face in her hair. She smelled as he remembered. Like wildflowers and honeycakes. It was good to be home. He kissed his wife's cheek, then her lips.

But his kiss was cut short because between them, the baby squirmed and whined.

He drew back. "Let me see Hannah."

Evie released the child to him, and he took Hannah in his arms, then kissed the top of her curly, dark head.

"It's Papa," he said.

Hannah wanted nothing to do with him and squirmed away, whining for her mother. Barak handed her back with a sigh.

Evie smiled. "Give her some time to get used to you."

Secure in her mother's arms, Hannah blinked her large brown eyes at him as if she'd planned on always getting her way.

"Where's Gilad?" His son never slept past dawn, so Barak was surprised he hadn't come out to greet him.

"He had nightmares last night, so he's sleeping next to Kiva."

"Nightmares?" Lapi said in a quiet tone, joining them. "Hello, cousin." He embraced Evie, then stepped back to look at her closely. "What's wrong with Gilad?"

Evie's gaze moved to Barak, her face pale now. "Yesterday, at the market . . . something terrible happened."

"The slave boy," a deep voice rumbled. Barak's father, Abinoam, stepped out of the house.

His limp was more pronounced than Barak remembered. At nearly sixty years of age, Abinoam had seen a lot of hardship.

"Father," Barak greeted and embraced the man.

"I trust your travels have been fruitful?" Abinoam asked, turning to greet Lapi as well.

"Yes," Barak said. "We will discuss those matters later. Yann told us about Sisera."

"Gilad saw everything," Abinoam said, his voice grave.

Evie grasped Barak's hand. "I could not move fast enough to get him away."

Barak squeezed his wife's hand, looking from his father to Lapi. Both men's eyes were hard. "I will speak to Gilad when he awakes. How is Kiva? Was she there too?"

"We all were—for market day," Evie said. "We had several jars of honey to sell."

Barak pulled his wife close again. Despite Hannah's whine, he kissed Evie's forehead. "We will rid the village of Sisera as soon as possible."

She drew away, her eyes wide. "Do not confront him, Barak. Sisera is a dangerous man, and he's a Canaanite commander."

"I know very well who he is, and I'll not have him terrorizing our people."

His father nodded, but Evie's cheeks flushed. "I'll not have *you* provoke him, husband."

"The captain is sorely outnumbered," Barak said. "A little show of force will have him backing down and leaving our village. If he is not gone by today, then tomorrow I will do something."

Evie bit her lip, and Barak knew he'd not heard the end of her scolding. The only reason she held back now was because Lapi and Abinoam were with them.

"Come in and eat," Evie said. "Joel warned me—it appears you think everyone should do your bidding."

Barak draped his arm over his wife's shoulder as they walked toward the house. "You haven't complained yet."

"That might change," she said, her tone soft.

Inside the house, Evie had indeed prepared a meal, and though it was simple—cooked barley, sliced melon, and day-old honey cakes—Barak had missed eating at his own table. He had missed his wife's cooking, he had missed her, and he had even missed her scolding.

Evie was as astute as ever. While serving Lapi, she said, "What's wrong, cousin? Surely you're happy to be home with a meal in front of you."

"I am blessed to be eating at your table," Lapi said, but his subtle tone belied his words.

Evie rested a hand on his shoulder but looked at Barak. "He's acting as if he has a broken heart."

Lapi didn't react, but Barak knew his wife had hit the mark.

"We'll speak later," Barak said, not wanting to drive Lapi out of his home on the first day. They were in sore need of some sleep, and tales of Ramah could be told later. Much later.

Chapter Six

Barak woke with a start. He lay in the quiet darkness for a few moments, listening, but heard nothing, save for the sound of Evie's quiet breathing. She'd been up a couple of times during the night with the baby. Hannah still hadn't warmed up to him, or else he would have attempted to comfort the child. But it seemed she wanted only her mother in the middle of the night.

Perhaps Gilad had had another nightmare? Or Barak's father was having leg pains again?

The dimness of the small bedchamber Barak shared with his wife told him that dawn was still a couple of hours away.

He heard a faint cry that sounded like Gilad, so he rose from the bed mat and made his way into the next chamber. His four-year-old son was sitting on his mat, his blanket clutched to his chest as he whimpered.

Without asking what was wrong, Barak settled next to the boy and pulled him into his arms. Gilad leaned against him, sniffling, and Barak ran his hand over his son's curls—curls that matched his little sister's.

Barak had heard enough from Gilad the previous day to know that he was having trouble forgetting what he'd seen in the marketplace. As Barak held his son, he tried to push down the rising anger toward the Canaanites. Oppression was nothing new in his life, nor his parents'. The Israelites had been taxed and controlled for decades. Skirmishes arose, but the Canaanites always came out on top.

Gilad's small body fully relaxed, and Barak realized the boy had fallen asleep. Still, Barak held his son, not wanting to disturb him. Besides, he doubted he'd be able to fall back asleep. His mind was too alert now, and he was already thinking of all he needed to do today. First up was to take the broken wagon wheel to the blacksmith for repair.

"Is he crying?" a soft voice said from the entrance of the chamber.

Barak looked up. His younger sister, Kiva, had changed over the past few months. Not only did she now have a woman's shape, but her eyes had gained wisdom. Which was now evident in her concern for Gilad.

"He was," Barak whispered. "He's fallen asleep now. I'm sorry he woke you up too."

Kiva smiled in the dimness. "I don't mind." She sat cross-legged at the end of the mat. "I went to bed early last night. Maybe it was because I knew you were finally back and all was well."

Barak nodded. It was hard on both him and his family for him to be gone, but it was necessary to get as many Israelite men trained as possible.

"How are you doing, Kiva?" he asked. "I didn't get a chance to spend time privately with you."

"Evie and the children have missed you, and Father's been grumpy, as usual," she said.

Barak chuckled softly. "What about *you*, my sister?"

Kiva lowered her gaze and picked at the edges of her robe. "I am doing well."

"Your birthday is soon," Barak said. "Fifteen."

"Yes." Her voice was quiet. Then she looked up. "I don't want to marry, Barak, at least not yet."

He let the words sink in; it seemed that he'd heard something similar from Lapi about Deborah. "Are there no young men you are interested in?"

She exhaled. "The young men in the village are fine . . . but I don't want to leave my family."

"You wouldn't be going very far," Barak said. "Perhaps to the other side of the village. And do you not want children of your own?"

Kiva's gaze went to the sleeping form of Gilad. "I do. I just . . . I never thought we'd lose Mother so early, and I'd have to go through this alone."

"You have me and Evie and Father." Barak reached over and patted her knee. "Even Lapi is here."

Kiva lifted one shoulder. "You and Lapi will be leaving again, as you should. Evie always needs help."

"But Evie wouldn't want you to give up your own future for her."

Kiva went silent, and Barak hoped she was considering his words. He wanted to see Kiva happy.

"Is there any young man in particular who's caught your eye?" Barak ventured to ask. "Or should I meet with the matchmaker?"

"No, don't talk to the matchmaker." She fell silent again, and Barak waited. "Perhaps Shalem . . . He's a hard worker."

"Yann's apprentice?" Barak asked. "How old is he?"

"Twenty."

Barak exhaled. He knew the family, and if Shalem learned his trade, he'd be able to provide for a wife. "I will speak to his father today, all right? I'm taking the wagon wheel to Yann's for repair, so I will combine the errand."

Kiva gave him a small, hesitant smile. "All right."

The dimness of the room had lightened, as dawn was on its way. Barak shifted Gilad to his mat and drew the blanket over his sleeping son.

Kiva rose, and Barak followed her out of the room.

She turned to him when they reached the short corridor. "Thank you, brother," she whispered.

"You're welcome." He kissed her cheek, then said, "I'll be in the gardens if Evie asks. I want everyone to sleep as long as possible." Truthfully, he'd check on the gardens when the sun rose, but for now, he'd work on weapons repair in the stable. He didn't want any interference in that task.

Once he reached the stable, he fed the two horses, then saw to the donkey. He located the satchels where he and Lapi kept their daggers and swords, then spent time cleaning them and sharpening the blades.

"I thought I'd find you in here," Lapi said, coming into the stable.

Barak looked up. "Grab a stool and help me."

As they worked, Barak told Lapi of his intention to speak to Shalem and his father that day.

"I'll come with you," Lapi said. "I want to make sure Sisera is out of the village so things can return to normal."

Barak exhaled. "You heard what Evie said."

"I heard."

Barak knew there would be no dissuading his cousin from coming with him. Besides, it might be good to have Lapi around when speaking with Shalem's family. Lapi could give his approval as well.

"I'm leaving tomorrow for Bethel," Lapi said.

Barak frowned. "I thought we'd stay here for a couple of weeks before leaving the homestead again."

"You're staying," Lapi said. "Your family needs you. I'm already feeling stifled, and I'm anxious to begin training the next group."

Barak decided his cousin was trying to stay busy enough to put Deborah out of his thoughts. "There's planting and plenty of repair work—"

"All that can be handled by you, your father, and the hired laborers." Lapi set down the knife he'd finished sharpening. "We can divide and conquer."

Barak nodded. "All right, then. After the morning meal, we'll go into the village to get some things done. Then you can make your announcement during the evening meal. Otherwise, Evie will spend all day trying to change your mind."

Lapi gave a brief smile. "That she will."

Two hours later, Barak and Lapi were on their way to the village center. Barak had hoisted the broken wheel onto his shoulder, and Lapi carried a couple of pruning tools, along with two bows needing refurbishing.

Just as they exited the yard, Kiva came running out of the house, tying on her mantle as she went.

"I need to buy some spices at the market," she said. "Can I travel with you?"

Barak looked his sister over and was glad she'd brought a mantle to cover her lustrous, dark hair and shade her face. He was certain she turned heads wherever she went.

"Can Evie spare you?" Barak asked.

"She's the one who asked me to do the errand since she knows I can travel with you." Kiva fell into step beside them. "If the Canaanites were gone, I could do it myself, but you know Evie."

Barak did know Evie, and he was glad she was so protective of Kiva. "Very well, then," he said.

Kiva grinned, and on the walk to the village, she told them of recent antics of Gilad and Hannah. Barak appreciated hearing the stories of what his children had been up to during his long absence. Perhaps Lapi was right. He was needed at home for longer than a couple of weeks, and then he could rejoin Lapi once the planting was finished.

At the blacksmith's, Yann was nowhere to be seen, and Shalem wasn't around either. "Where are they?" Barak said aloud, although he wasn't expecting an answer.

Then he heard what sounded like a chariot rumbling along the road. Barak walked out of the blacksmith's shop to see three chariots heading toward the marketplace. He couldn't see the driver of the first one, but he had no doubt it was Sisera.

"It looks as if Sisera is leaving," Lapi said.

"Or causing more trouble." Barak looked at Kiva. "Stay inside the shop, sister." Then he turned and started after the chariots and their billowing dust.

"Wait," Lapi said. "Where are you going?"

"To make sure Sisera behaves himself." Barak continued walking.

Without a word, Lapi joined him. The two men increased their pace so they reached the marketplace just as Sisera was ordering a vegetable seller to fill a basket for him. There was no doubt who was the commanding officer under the Canaanite king. Sisera wore a red-and-indigo-patterned tunic and a leather band around his forehead. His dark, tight curls fell to the nape of his neck, and he wore his beard cropped.

The other sellers in the marketplace kept to their stalls, fear on their faces as they watched the Canaanites. Thankfully, it appeared as if only men were present, as if the sellers had kept their wives and children away.

Barak stopped by a stall that displayed bracelets and anklets.

Sisera hadn't even climbed out of his chariot, and his horses looked as if they'd seen the thin end of a whip more than once. The whip that had recently killed a slave boy.

Barak's stomach hardened and then did a flip when Sisera turned his head and locked gazes with him.

The commander's expression went from mildly curious to suspicious within the space of mere seconds. Barak sensed that Lapi had noticed too.

The vegetable seller approached Sisera with a bowed head and presented the captain with the vegetables.

"Set it in the chariot," Sisera said, his tone dismissive.

Fortunately, the seller understood enough of the language to do as bidden.

"Well, what do we have here?" Sisera continued, looking past Barak.

What could the man be looking at with such interest? A chill brushed against Barak's neck as he turned to look. His sister, Kiva, stood not far off.

"Kiva, I told you to—"

Kiva shrank against the jewelry seller's stall as if she'd just realized who had spotted her. Barak couldn't fathom why she had thought to follow him when he'd specifically told her to stay at the blacksmith's shop.

Sisera stepped out of the chariot, and the men in the other two chariots climbed out of theirs as well. Just like that, Barak and Lapi were outnumbered, and Barak knew the market sellers would rather run than face a foe.

"What tribe are you from, young lady?" Sisera asked, walking toward Barak and Lapi. Barak knew his sister couldn't understand the captain's words, but Barak understood each one.

There was nowhere for Kiva to escape. Behind the seller's stall was a cluster of huts, out of which some of the residents had come to their doorways to watch the unfolding events.

Kiva didn't answer; how could she? Barak heard her panicked breathing behind him. Lapi stepped closer to Barak until they created a barrier in front of Kiva.

Sisera wasn't deterred but continued toward their group. His men advanced as well. "Does the woman not have a tongue?"

"She has a tongue," Lapi said in the Canaanite language. "She does not understand your language."

"Oh?" Sisera stopped. His eyes were a mixture of green and brown—an unusual color for a Canaanite. "Our king has demanded that all who occupy our lands should know the language. Even if she is a mute, she should understand my questions."

"She's not a mute," Barak said, trying to keep his tone even.

"Tell her to come here," Sisera said. "Perhaps I can teach her a few words."

The sneer in Sisera's tone made Barak's skin crawl. He moved his hand to the knife strapped to his thigh. The message to Sisera was clear.

"Is she your wife?" Sisera asked, looking from Barak to Lapi. "Or is she married to someone else?"

"She's my sister." Barak pulled his knife from its strap. "And she is yet unmarried."

Sisera smiled, but it wasn't a friendly smile. "Wonderful. She has much to learn, then." When his gaze dropped to the knife that Barak held, he frowned. "I don't want any harm to come to the young woman, so I will propose a trade."

Barak exhaled. "There will be no trade. You will go on your way and leave her alone."

One of Sisera's dark brows arched. "And if I don't?"

"You will have to go through me first," Barak ground out.

Sisera stared at Barak as if trying to come up with an answer. Finally, he said, "What is your name, foolish man?"

"Barak."

Sisera scoffed. "You really want to do this?"

Lapi withdrew his knife as well. "We are ready."

Sisera put his hands on his hips, looking from Barak to Lapi. "We will fight for her. The first one who cries mercy will give up the woman."

Barak nodded. "One on one. There's no reason to bring any other into our battle."

"Don't do this," Lapi hissed. "Think of your wife . . . your children. Let me take your place."

Barak ignored his cousin and stepped forward. "Knives?"

"I'll use my whip." Sisera grinned. "It's proven very effective. Within moments, I'll have you on your knees begging for mercy."

Chapter Seven

Barak refused to second-guess his decision as he watched Sisera fetch his whip.

"Let me take your place," Lapi said. "Evie will never forgive me if something happens to you."

"I'll not have my sister dishonored," Barak said. "This is not your fight, cousin. Just keep Kiva out of the way." Barak felt, rather than saw, Lapi's displeasure.

Lapi exhaled, then joined Kiva, where she hovered near the jewelry stall. The girl's face had paled as she clutched her mantle tightly about her neck. With or without her head covered, Kiva was a lovely young woman, which had now proven to be dangerous. The market sellers took refuge behind their stalls, and the soldiers with Sisera formed a group near the other two chariots.

As Sisera turned from his chariot, whip in hand, Barak walked toward him, then stopped in the middle of the market square. The day was early enough that the heat hadn't set in, yet Barak's palms were damp, and perspiration pricked between his shoulder blades. His wish for any sort of breeze went unheeded.

No one in the market square spoke or moved until Sisera said, "Well, Barak, let's see what type of fighter you are." He cracked his whip.

Barak's heart flinched. He went into a crouch, both hands raised for balance.

Sisera lifted his arm and brought the whip down to the left of Barak, missing on purpose in a deliberate effort to intimidate.

But Barak was ready. He sliced his dagger against the end of the whip and cut off the tip.

Sisera pulled the whip back with a sharp tug. "Nice move," he said in a dry tone.

Barak didn't focus on the captain's expression but kept his gaze on the hand holding the whip. Wherever the hand went, the whip would follow.

Sisera cracked the whip again, and the end of it snapped to Barak's right side. He immediately barreled straight for Sisera before the man could draw the whip back. Using the element of surprise, Barak nearly made contact with the man, but Sisera recovered from his shock and dodged.

Barak plowed into the chariot, then righted himself and turned around. He'd banged his knee, but the throbbing was only a small inconvenience. He was now just paces away from the other Canaanite soldiers. And from this vantage point, he saw Kiva kneeling by the jewelry stall and Lapi standing next to her, legs spread, his knife in hand. Lapi's expression told Barak that his cousin was seconds away from taking action.

If Lapi acted, the soldiers would also join in the fray, and the mercy rule would no longer apply.

Sisera smiled at Barak and took a few steps backward, which put him closer to Kiva and Lapi.

Barak watched the captain's arm raise and the whip start in motion again—this time aimed directly at Barak's face. He ducked, and carved his knife through the air, missing any contact with the captain.

Sisera chuckled. "You can only duck for so long."

Barak moved closer to Sisera, keeping his knife in front of him. Sisera raised his arm again, but instead of sending the whip forward, he snapped it behind him.

It was as if time slowed, and Barak watched with horror as the end of the whip struck Kiva's cheek. The impact caused her to topple against the stall, and then in disbelief, she raised a hand to her face. Drawing her fingers away, she saw the blood. And screamed.

Lapi was next to her in an instant, pulling his turban off and pressing it against her bleeding cheek. Kiva continued to scream, and someone else was screaming too.

It took Barak a moment to realize it was him screaming insults at Sisera.

Sisera's grin was triumphant, and Barak realized with a sickening feeling that the captain had maimed Kiva on purpose.

Sisera narrowed his eyes and focused on Barak completely, then lifted his arm again and brought the whip toward Barak's chest.

Barak knew that what he was about to do would maim himself as well, but if he didn't stop Sisera, he was not worthy of being Kiva's brother. Barak raised his left hand and grabbed the whip just before it struck him. The end of the whip cut into Barak's hand, burning like he'd placed his hand in the blacksmith's kiln, but he held on. And then slowly, while gritting his teeth against the pain, he twisted his hand, wrapping the end of the whip around his palm. He twisted again, taking more of the whip.

Sisera's eyes widened, and when he realized what Barak was doing, Sisera pulled back on the whip.

Barak jerked forward with the motion and almost lost his balance. Tears sprung to his eyes as he held on and kept twisting and wrapping while pulling against Sisera's weight.

Kiva's screaming had stopped, but others were yelling. Lapi? The Canaanites? Barak wasn't sure. He just kept twisting, ignoring the searing pain in his hand, knowing that the flesh of his palm had been cut to the bone. Tears blurring his vision, he could focus only on using the strength of his arm and torso to continue winding the whip around the palm of his hand.

And then Sisera let go of the whip and ran toward the chariot.

There was no way Barak was going to let the man flee without begging for mercy. Barak lunged toward him and knocked him off his feet. Sisera landed face-first on the ground. With the hand that was tied up in the whip, Barak held Sisera's head against the ground. Barak then pinned Sisera's arms with his knees, and with his right hand, Barak pressed his knife against Sisera's neck.

"Ask for mercy, or I will cut your throat," Barak growled.

Sisera tried to lift his head, but Barak used his adrenaline to overpower the man.

"Don't think I won't," Barak said. "I'd happily be crucified by your king for my actions here today."

Sisera made a gagging noise, and Barak pressed the knife harder against the man's neck, drawing a line of blood.

"Speak clearly so everyone can hear you begging like a dog."

"*Please . . . have . . . mercy . . .*" Sisera gasped. Then his body went limp, and the man closed his eyes.

Barak knew the captain hadn't fainted, but the words had been clear enough. Barak moved off Sisera, then spat in the dirt. The spittle landed a handspan from Sisera's face. Barak looked at the other Canaanite soldiers, who had turned as pale as Kiva had earlier.

As Barak slowly unwound the whip from his bloodied hand, he said, "Does anyone else want to threaten my family?"

The soldiers took a step back, their gazes shifting to their inert captain.

"Good," Barak ground out. "Now, leave my village."

Two of the soldiers climbed into their chariot, while the other two moved toward Sisera. By the time they stooped to pick him up, Sisera had opened his eyes.

"Don't touch me," he said, pushing away one of the soldiers. He climbed into his chariot on his own, dirt staining his fine clothing. He looked over at Barak, who remained standing in the middle of the market square, blood dripping from his hand.

"We will meet again," Sisera said, "and next time *you* will be the one begging for mercy."

Barak lifted his chin. Seeing the soiled and red-faced Sisera brought Barak enormous pleasure. There would be consequences later. For now, he'd won this battle.

"And your sister, there," Sisera continued, "will repel every man who looks upon her."

If Lapi hadn't chosen that moment to reach Barak's side and grasp his arm, Barak might have finished off Sisera then and there.

Sisera's smile was triumphant as he commanded his horses to move forward.

Barak watched the chariots exit the market square, leaving behind their dust and memories. He dimly became aware that Kiva was standing before him and had wrapped his hand in her mantle. The bleeding of her cheek had slowed, and it didn't take a healer's expertise to know she'd have a significant scar upon that beautiful face of hers.

The sight made Barak's anger rise again, molting into pure hatred. He'd welcome a rematch against Sisera. Any time. Any place. And he would be ready.

"Barak," Lapi said, his voice cutting into Barak's imagining of another encounter with the captain. "We need to get your hand stitched."

Barak blinked and looked down at his bound hand. It had already stained Kiva's mantle with blood.

"Come," Lapi said. "I'm taking you to the healer."

"What about Kiva?" Barak looked at his sister. Tears stained her face, and that cut . . .

"We'll take care of her too." Lapi grasped Barak's good arm and led him across the market square.

Barak felt the stares of the villagers as he walked. He didn't have anything to say to anyone, and no one spoke to him. His thoughts were a jumbled mess, but he knew one thing for certain: Evie wasn't going to be happy when he told her they would have to leave their homestead.

Barak and Kiva were now both marked. Barak wouldn't put it past Sisera to take revenge in another way. And the only way Barak would be able to fully protect his family was to relocate them.

"Here we are," Lapi said, opening the door to the healer's house without knocking.

The healer didn't seem surprised at their arrival. Word traveled fast in villages, it seemed.

"Take care of Kiva first," Barak said, wondering why everything was so blurry. And the cushions on the floor seemed to be moving.

"Easy," Lapi said. "You need to sit."

Why did Lapi's voice sound so far away?

Barak's vision went black, and he felt like he was falling. Lapi spoke, but Barak couldn't understand him. Was he speaking another language?

"Barak," someone else said, and Barak had to force his eyes open.

The healer hovered over him. "You should drink this." The healer held a small cup to Barak's lips.

Was he thirsty? He wasn't sure, but he drank the foul stuff anyway. He nearly spat it out, but the healer said in a surprisingly commanding tone, "Swallow it, Barak. It will help the pain."

So he swallowed.

"Now bite down on this," the healer said, holding out a rounded piece of wood that looked like a peg.

Barak obeyed, and moments later, the pain in his hand seared as the healer began to stitch it closed. Barak fought back a scream and tried to think of anything but the work the healer was doing.

"You're almost done," Lapi said from somewhere in the house.

Barak was too focused on not screaming to turn his head to look for his cousin. What had happened to Kiva? Had she been stitched too?

"There, it's done," the healer said again. "You can rest now."

Barak couldn't rest. He had to tell Evie what had happened, and he had to relocate his family before the sun set. But Barak's eyes slid shut, and everything went dark for the second time that day.

The next words he heard were, "You foolish, foolish man."

"Evie?" Barak croaked.

"You're awake," Evie said. "Thank the heavens."

Only Evie would say that, so it must be her, Barak decided. He wanted to open his eyes, but he was afraid if he did, the pain in his hand would return. Right now, it was only a dull throb—something he could live with.

"Barak, what did you do?" Evie said.

He opened his eyes, if only to defend himself and explain.

Evie's face was close to his, her eyes wide, her cheeks streaked with tears. Her hair was not in its usual plait but had come loose and tumbled about her shoulders. The flush upon her face made her look as if she'd been running.

"How . . . did you get here?" Barak asked.

Evie made a strange noise, a mix between a laugh and a cry. "You foolish man. I should be asking *you* the questions. I don't know what possessed you to pick a fight with the Canaanite captain."

Barak swallowed. The taste in his mouth was bitter, likely from whatever the healer had forced him to drink. "He threatened Kiva."

Evie nodded, and whispered, "I know." Tears filled her eyes. Then she kissed his forehead, his cheek, his jaw, his lips. "You could have been killed, husband."

He lifted his good hand and wrapped it around his wife's neck, pulling her closer so he could breathe in her sweet honey scent. "I am fine."

She exhaled and kissed him again. Then she drew away. "Lapi is outside, and he says he has to leave tomorrow. You'd better not be leaving with him."

Barak pushed himself up into a sitting position, wincing at the pain lancing through his hand and extending to his arm. He closed his eyes for a moment as dizziness took over.

"You need to stay lying down," Evie said. "That's what the healer said."

Barak gripped his wife's hand. "I need to tell you something, and you're not going to like it."

Evie's brows drew together, panic forming in her eyes.

"We need to disappear for a while," he said. "All of us. Kiva will bear the mark for her entire life, and Sisera is not going to forget her anytime soon. He won't forget how I embarrassed him."

"Will he come back here?" Evie asked.

"Yes," Barak said. "And the rest of our family is in danger. You included."

Evie tugged her hand from his. "Are you sure? We are a small village, and surely Sisera has had many such encounters when passing through Israelite villages. Perhaps by the time he reaches King Jabin's wedding, he'll forget—"

Barak cupped his wife's chin. "You saw what he did to that slave boy and now my own sister. Surely he's not a man to forget."

Evie blinked back the tears forming in her eyes. "You're right," she said. "What will we tell your father? He can't manage the homestead alone. Who will cook his meals?"

"We're taking him with us," Barak said.

Evie rested her head against Barak's shoulder. "Where are we going? Who will take us in?"

"Our last assignment was in the village of Ramah," Barak said. "We worked with the sons of the herdsman Tobiah, and there was plenty of land to the south of his."

"We'll be *sheepherders*?"

"With God's grace, yes."

Chapter Eight

By the following morning, nearly everything was packed and all Barak had to do was load the bundles onto the horses and into the cart. Specifically, Lapi and Abinoam would do the loading. Barak's hand still throbbed, and he'd already ripped a stitch out of the new wound, about which his wife had berated him.

Barak stood in the early dawn at the edge of the newly planted field—a field he'd deeded to their nearest neighbor for safekeeping. The neighbor could keep any harvest he produced until the day Barak returned. As the sun bloomed over the eastern horizon, Barak knew he was experiencing the last moments of quietude he'd have in a long time.

Looking over the fields of his homestead brought on a nostalgia Barak hadn't expected. He'd plowed every bit of dirt many times over the years. He'd watched plants grow. He'd harvested those plants and partaken of their nutrition at his table. He'd worked side by side with his father and planned to work side by side with his son. Barak would return to this place; he'd make sure of it. But he was convinced that relocating his family for a few months, or perhaps a year or two, was the best choice.

He stifled a weary yawn as the colors of the horizon changed from violet to pale gold. He'd slept poorly again, new worries piling on top of old worries. He'd gotten Lapi to agree to accompany the family to Tobiah's homestead, but from there, Lapi would soon need to travel to his next assignment.

Barak needed Lapi's help for several days at least. It would take a lot of work to establish a home for his family at the new homestead, and until his hand healed, progress would be slow.

However, he could not delay the transition. His family's safety was paramount, so he would press forward, and do whatever it took to protect his loved ones.

"Evie asked me to bring you a warm drink," Kiva said behind him.

Barak turned to take the cup of tea from Kiva. She wore a clean mantle over her head and had draped it so it covered the wound on her face. The healer had not stitched it, since he said that would make the scar even worse. For now, Kiva applied a salve every few hours to aid in the healing process.

His younger sister was still beautiful.

If only he'd been able to save her from such mutilation. Barak blinked back tears. It seemed his emotions had multiplied since his hand injury.

Thankfully, his sister didn't say anything about the redness of his eyes, and Barak sipped at the warm honey tea. The sweet liquid soothed his throat and calmed the turmoil in his stomach.

Evie must have sent Kiva out to him so they could have private time together.

"I am sorry for following you to the market square," Kiva said, her voice trembling.

Barak knew that if he looked at her and saw tears, his own tears would return. "You couldn't have known what might happen, Kiva. You are not to blame for Sisera's despicable actions."

"I am sorry you had to fight for me," she whispered, and her voice broke. "I'm sorry about your hand, and I'm sorry that we now have to leave our home."

Barak set the cup on the ground and pulled his sister into his arms. She leaned against him and started to cry. He didn't say anything because there were no words to comfort her pain, which was his pain as well. The only solace was that they both still had their lives, and they were together.

Several moments passed before Kiva stopped trembling. She took a deep breath. "I will make it up to you. I'll be the best sister ever, and I'll never—"

"Shh," Barak said, kissing the top of her head. "Don't make promises like that. We are all learning. We all make mistakes. We will get through this."

"I just don't understand how there could be men like you and Father, who are loving and good, and then men like Sisera . . ." She shuddered. "When Sisera looked at me, I felt like I was looking into the eyes of the Helel, the evil son of the morning."

Barak released Kiva but held her gaze. "Remember that, sister. Remember that you've seen the difference between good and evil. Always choose the good path. Despite our heartaches and challenges, it is the only way to happiness."

Kiva wiped at her tears. "I see that every day in you and Evie. And someday, I hope to have that too. It is what I've been praying for."

"You can be happy now, Kiva. You can be happy always." Barak picked up the cup from the ground and took another swallow of the tea his wife had made for him. The tea had cooled, so he drank the rest of it down. He handed the empty cup to his sister. "Today, we might be leaving our home and starting anew, but we will be together, and that's what's important. It is counsel for me as well."

"Thank you, brother," Kiva said, rising on her toes to kiss his cheek.

"Hello there," someone said, and both Barak and Kiva turned.

A woman walked toward them, her indigo cloak flapping behind her as she strode with sure steps. Barak recognized her as the village matchmaker, Vania. He stiffened, wondering what the woman could possibly want. Surely she'd heard of Kiva's misfortune.

"Good morning," Barak said, his tone guarded. "It is early yet for visitors."

"If I had waited until after the morning meal, I feared you would have left," Vania said, her blue-gray eyes surveying first Barak, then Kiva. Her gaze missed little.

"What brings you here?" Barak knew he was being curt, but he had no time for a matchmaker's gossip.

"I've come with a warning," Vania said. "I heard from someone in the village that you are leaving and going to Ramah with Kiva."

"Yes." Barak was irritated. He'd told only a handful of people who had sworn to keep the location secret, but now Vania apparently knew. Who had told Vania? Perhaps Barak would have to make one more stop before leaving their village. "What is your warning?"

"You should not take Kiva with you," Vania said.

Barak scoffed. "And leave her here to be another target should Sisera return?"

Vania held up her hand—her many bracelets clinking together. "No, I suggest you put her in hiding for a few months, or at least a few weeks. Sisera could easily track your family to Ramah, but when he learns there is no evidence of Kiva living with you, he'll find something else to focus his time on."

Barak wanted to dismiss the idea right away, but something in the back of his mind made him ask, "What do you suggest?"

Vania looked at Kiva, then back to Barak. "I know a woman who has helped other women in delicate situations before. She lives on the plains of

Zaanaim with her husband, and they do not take political sides. They are Gentiles, yes, but they have taken compassion on young Israelite women in need."

Barak narrowed his eyes. "Explain."

Vania clasped her hands together. "Last year, they took in my cousin. She'd been assaulted by a Canaanite passing through her village and became with child. My cousin stayed with them until the child was delivered and could be adopted by another family."

Barak stared at Vania. "Now where's your cousin?"

"She returned home and is living out her life," Vania said. "No one in the village suspects what happened, so there is no ostracism or persecution."

As much as neighbors in small villages were willing to help each other, they could also turn on each other.

Kiva spoke next. "Where is this man and wife you speak of?"

"Jael and her husband, Heber the Kenite, live on the plains of Zaanaim, near Jabneel," Vania said. "You could make the distance in a day. Leave Kiva there, then travel to Ramah."

Barak needed to speak to Evie and his father, but Kiva had more questions. "How do we know that Jael will take me in? I am a stranger to her."

"Tell her I sent you." The matchmaker pulled off one of the many rings on her fingers and pressed it into the palm of Kiva's hand. "Give her this, and she will understand."

"I can't take this ring," Kiva said.

"It is a token that I want Jael to have in thanks for taking care of my cousin," Vania said.

Kiva looked down at the ring in her hand, then she looked at Barak. "I don't want to bring any more danger to the family. Perhaps this is the best way."

Barak exhaled. "Perhaps. We will discuss it with Father and Evie." He looked at Vania, unsure of her motivation. "If we decide not to take Kiva to Jael's, we will return the ring to you before we depart."

"Very well." Vania placed a hand on Kiva's shoulder. "May the Lord God watch over you."

After Vania left, Kiva returned to the house, and Barak had even more to think about. Despite his reluctance to admit it, the matchmaker might be right. Hiding away Kiva for a few weeks or a month might be the best way to protect her in the long run. They could travel to the plains of Zaanaim and make the final decision once he met Jael and Heber. Leaving Kiva in the care of someone else would be hard, at best.

His mind made up, he left his field behind and walked back to the house. By the look of the gathering in the cooking room, it appeared that Kiva had told everyone. Lapi was there, leaning against the wall, his arms folded. Evie had busied herself with meal preparations, Hannah perched on her hip.

Everyone looked at Barak as he entered.

"I will take Kiva to the plains," Lapi said, straightening from his slouch. "Traveling as a large group would only bring more attention and alert others to our plight."

Barak opened his mouth to respond, but his father cut in. "Lapi's right. I would do it if I could travel as fast as those two can together."

Barak looked between the men. "What do you suggest? Share a horse?"

"Exactly," Lapi said. "We'd travel faster, and I'll meet you at Ramah in three days' time to help you establish your homestead."

Barak hated that he had to depend on Lapi, but with his injury, there was no choice. He met Evie's gaze, and he saw that she'd reconciled herself to this turn of events. Kiva had already made her choice clear. "All right," Barak said with a sigh. "Let us pray, then eat. I'll help you reorganize the bundles so you and Kiva can travel lightly and swiftly."

Lapi offered a curt nod, affirming the finalization of their changed plans.

Gilad came into the room, and they began their meal. They were relatively silent while they ate, save for Hannah's babble. Once the meal was finished, the men went out into the courtyard to reorganize the bundles. One-handed, Barak did as much as he could, but he found himself wincing in pain more than once.

"Go easy on yourself," Lapi said, coming over to take a heavier bundle from Barak. "In a couple weeks, you can do a lot more. You don't want to risk further damage."

"I know." Barak flexed his wounded hand. His fingers would only curl halfway before pain lanced through his palm.

Lapi lowered his voice. "I will make all haste, and if Heber and Jael don't seem trustworthy, I'll keep Kiva with me."

"Thank you, cousin," Barak said in an equally quiet tone. "I owe you a great debt."

Lapi shook his head. "You owe me nothing."

"I wish I had two good hands so you could go straight to the next training assignment." Lapi looked away, so Barak added, "I hope it won't be too painful for you to encounter Tobiah and his family again."

Lapi looked sharply at Barak. "I am not worried about seeing Deborah again, if that's what you are referring to." He swallowed. "It's not as if there aren't other marriageable women in Israel."

Barak hid a smile. "Of course not."

The women came out of the house just then, and before Barak knew it, he was bidding farewell to Kiva.

Evie linked arms with him as they watched Lapi's horse leave, with Kiva riding behind him, holding on to his waist. Barak could only pray that Kiva would reach her destination safely and that Heber and Jael would lavish hospitality upon her.

"Come, we'll see them soon enough," Evie said.

Barak looked down at his wife. "You seem so sure."

"I've been praying for our safety," Evie said, "and when Kiva told us what the matchmaker said, it rang true." She squeezed his arm. "I believe it's a solution from God."

The women in Barak's life had a humbler and more spiritual perspective than he did. It was a good thing his wife had just said what she had, because Barak wanted to run after Lapi and tell him he'd changed his mind. That the family should all stay together. But he focused on his wife's hand on his arm as Lapi and Kiva's forms upon the horse grew smaller and smaller with each moment.

"Papa, can I ride with you?" Gilad said, his small voice interrupting Barak's thoughts.

He looked down at his son. "Grandfather is riding the horse, and Mother and I want you with Mother in the cart so you can help with Hannah."

"Because Kiva's gone?" Gilad asked.

"Yes." Barak crouched before his son and rested his good hand on Gilad's shoulder. "During travel to our new home, we aren't to tell anyone about Kiva. Do you understand?"

"Because of the bad man?"

Barak nodded, his throat feeling tight. "Yes, son. We don't want the bad man to find her." He leaned forward and kissed his son's forehead.

"I'll be Mama's helper, then," Gilad announced, pride in his voice.

"Of course you will, my boy." Barak straightened. Lapi and Kiva were out of sight now, and it was time to start his own journey. He bent to kiss Evie's cheek, then the sleeping face of Hannah. "Time to go."

Chapter Nine

The snake was nearly as long as Deborah was tall. Its black scales gleamed gold as it reflected the orange of the setting sun. She'd been waiting in the same spot for almost two hours for the thing to appear. And now she'd been rewarded at last.

Yesterday, one of her sheep had been bitten. She'd been swift to tie off the sheep's leg and drain the venom, followed by a pleading prayer for the sheep's healing. The sheep was walking around this morning, acting as if it was completely recovered, but Deborah knew she couldn't be so fortunate twice. She feared the snake would attack again, and the outcome wouldn't be so favorable.

She determined not to let something as preventable as a snakebite kill her sheep. Canaanite soldiers were a little more difficult to get rid of, but these snakes were predictable. They hid in their holes or rocky crevices in the heat of the day but came out as soon as the air cooled when the sun sank behind the western hills.

Deborah shifted her position atop the large boulder and adjusted her cramped legs. She moved very slowly so as to not startle the snake, though she knew the creature could smell her. It slithered slowly around the rock, and Deborah watched as it made its way to the edge of the stream. It wasn't a water snake, but it needed water all the same.

And then it would spend the better part of the evening heading to the area where the sheep grazed. But Deborah didn't plan on letting it get that far. She licked her dry lips and wished she could scratch the itch on her nose. As if sensing her distress, a fly buzzed around Deborah's head. She clenched her jaw to stop herself from reaching for it.

The snake had started its forward trek, and Deborah waited another couple of moments before she withdrew the arrow and nocked it against her bow. It would be a challenge to hit a creature so long and narrow, and Deborah knew if she didn't hit close to its head, it might continue to live. Snakes were durable like that.

She exhaled, licked her lips again, then took aim. She held steady, watching the snake's ambling movements through her half-slit eyes. Then she released the arrow. It whooshed through the air and struck . . . right in the dirt next to the snake's head.

She blew out a breath of frustration, then withdrew a second arrow. The snake had started to move again, faster this time, and soon it would be out of target range. Deborah stood, took aim, then let the arrow fly.

She missed again.

And now the snake had gained too much ground for Deborah to hit it with an arrow. All she could do was meet up with the sheep and usher them to the other side of the stream. Before nightfall, she'd have to bring the sheep to the homestead for the added protection.

She hopped down from the boulder, feeling that she'd just wasted hours for nothing, and fetched her two arrows. But before she could pick up the first one, a hissing sound made her stop cold. She looked at the ground. It was a different snake, and she'd apparently stepped on its tail.

Before it could retaliate, Deborah turned and ran for the boulder, not daring to look behind her.

She scrambled onto the rock, scraping her knees and hands in the process. She hoped she hadn't drawn blood since it would only make her more of a target. When she turned to survey the position of the snake, her skin went cold.

A third snake had been aroused from its nap, and it slithered into the evening light. The boulder must be the entrance to a snake nest.

How many more snakes were there, and how long would it take for them to leave their nest? Deborah reached for the knife she kept strapped to her calf. She gripped the handle and held the blade in front of her as she moved to the far edge of the boulder, away from the third snake.

Its head turned toward her, eyes like dead, black holes on each side of its head.

With her other hand, Deborah scraped up some dirt and bits of rock from atop the boulder. If the snake moved, she'd toss the dirt and try to stall its advance.

But the creature seemed perfectly content just watching her.

She took a step back and another step until she reached the edge of the boulder. Then she leapt backward, hoping she didn't land in an awkward position and hurt her ankles.

Her feet made contact with the hard ground, and she was able to keep her balance. She scrambled onto the next boulder. This one was higher, and hopefully, this one didn't house a snake nest. She stood and surveyed the ground beneath her on all sides.

Then she looked toward where the sheep grazed. If the first snake didn't slow, it could reach the sheep in a few minutes. Deborah's heart was thumping so hard she decided to herd the sheep home early tonight, and maybe she could come up with some traps by tomorrow morning.

She was about to climb off the boulder and take a new route to her flock so she could avoid the snake nest when she saw someone riding a horse toward the homestead. The evening light made it hard to tell which of her brothers it was—Abner or Chaim. But why would they be coming from the direction of the village? They'd both been working on the homestead when she'd left with the sheep that morning.

But as Deborah watched, she realized the rider wasn't one of her brothers. The figure seemed familiar somehow, but it wasn't one of the village elders either.

She stared at the man's form and how easily he rode the horse, as if he rode every day. He was also riding rather fast—urging the horse to maintain a steady gallop. A bundle was tied to the back of the horse. Was the man a traveler? A nomad? A friend of her father?

The rider neared the homestead and reined the horse to a stop. She watched him dismount, and then she knew . . . *Lapi*.

What was he doing here? She hadn't allowed herself to entertain thoughts about him since his and Barak's abrupt departure. She hadn't told her father or brothers of Lapi's marriage proposal. In fact, the longer he'd been gone, the more Deborah had talked herself into believing that the conversation had never taken place.

Surely a man like him couldn't have true feelings for a woman like her. She was young and had never traveled beyond her village. Lapi had traveled the entire countryside and knew many people. He was a respected military trainer, like his cousin Barak.

Her thoughts turned from her inner turmoil to curiosity about why Lapi was here, back at her homestead. Then the fear struck. What if something had happened to Barak? Or perhaps her father or brothers? Was there another band of Canaanite soldiers roaming the valley?

She leapt off the rock and hurried toward her sheep, making a wide berth around the snake nest, then she started toward the homestead while she kept an eye on what Lapi was doing. Fortunately, her father appeared, and then her brothers too. They seemed to be in a deep discussion, and Deborah urged the sheep faster. They bleated their displeasure, but Deborah didn't relent.

When she had the sheep close enough to the pomegranate grove, she set them loose and made her way to the men. Lapi turned to see her first, and she was sure she looked a sight. Her hair had come out of its plait, and she was breathing hard. Her hands and arms were scraped from the rocks.

Lapi's dark eyes were unreadable. She'd forgotten how tall he was, how broad his shoulders were, and how intense his gaze was. Her father and brothers were still speaking among themselves when her father noticed her.

"Where are your arrows?" he asked. "And why are you carrying your knife?"

Deborah slowed her step. She looked down at her hand and the knife she still gripped. She looked past Lapi to her father and her brothers, who were both staring at her. "I was . . . hunting down the snake that injured the sheep yesterday. I, uh, tried to shoot the snake with my arrows, but then I disturbed a snake nest."

She felt Lapi watching her, and she hoped her cheeks wouldn't redden.

"Looks like the snakes won this round," Chaim said, amusement in his voice.

Deborah shrugged, pretending she hadn't been scared witless a short time ago. She slipped the knife into the strap about her calf, then realized Lapi probably wasn't used to seeing a woman strap a knife to her leg. When she looked up, he glanced away. Heat stole through her.

"What . . . are you doing here?" she said to Lapi, walking closer to the group of men. Perhaps she was being blunt, but if they considered her a young woman, then she had the right to know.

"He's looking for Barak," her father said. "Have you seen any sign of approaching travelers?"

"No," Deborah said. "Is Barak in danger?"

None of the men answered.

"Well?" Deborah cut her gaze to Lapi. "What's happened?"

Lapi rubbed the back of his neck, and Deborah tried not to notice how the action made the muscled lines of his arm more defined. She shouldn't be thinking of Lapi in any other way than as a friend of their family.

"We had some trouble in our village with a Canaanite captain," Lapi said at last. "Barak uprooted his family and was heading this direction last I knew." Lapi shifted his gaze to her father. "Barak was hoping to work the land nearby and, with your hospitality, begin anew. Or at least until he felt it was safe to return home."

Her father nodded. "Barak and his family are welcome to stay as long as necessary."

Deborah couldn't have been more surprised at this turn of events. She'd told herself she'd never see Lapi again, so she was pleased to see him now. She could apologize to him properly, although not in the presence of her brothers and father. But first, she wanted to know what had happened with Barak.

"Let us go inside, and Lapi can give us more information over supper," her father said. "It will soon be too dark to keep watch, but we can keep a fire burning in the courtyard in case they are traveling at night."

Deborah led the way into the interior of the tent. She'd kept barley soaking all day, and she added vegetables before heating it over a small cooking fire. Then she cut up dates and made a date cake that she formed and set above the fire to bake.

She served the soup, then brought out the date cake, along with some date-palm wine. Her brothers had lit several oil lamps, and the light chased back the darkening shadows. Once everyone was served, she sat next to her father on a cushion. From this position, she was across from Lapi and could see that his shoulders had slumped, and he looked tireder than she'd ever seen him.

Lapi told the story of Sisera, the Canaanite captain, and how he'd confronted Barak over his sister.

Deborah found herself gripping her hands together as she listened to the story and to how Barak had fled the village, Lapi taking Kiva one way and Barak coming toward Ramah. Yet . . . they had not arrived.

"Do you think they stopped over somewhere?" Abner asked. "Perhaps camped?"

"I don't think so." Lapi blew out a breath. "Barak is injured. His wife has a baby. His father has a bad foot. I think they'd travel as quickly as possible to reach the valley." He stared down at his hands. "I shouldn't have left them."

"But you had to take Kiva to safety," Deborah said, not sure if it was too presumptuous of her to contradict Lapi.

He didn't answer.

Abner took another swallow of wine, then said, "We'll begin a search at dawn if they've not arrived. We can split up and inquire along the various roads. There are only so many roads they could have taken. If they've camped, perhaps someone has spotted them."

"Or . . ." Chaim looked at Lapi. "We can also find out if Sisera has been traveling again. Do you know when the king's wedding is?"

Chaim had a good point, Deborah thought. If they could count on Sisera to stay at the king's wedding for all the celebrations, he'd be off the roads.

"I had the impression it was within a few days from Sisera's visit to our village," Lapi said, his tone sounding dejected. "So that might mean the wedding is any day now."

"That's good news for Barak," Deborah said, and again Lapi's gaze fell on her. Her face warmed for a second time. The intensity of his eyes that used to be a mystery to her had now taken on a new meaning after he'd proposed marriage. She couldn't let it affect her now, not after she'd already told him her father would never approve and not when he was so worried about his cousin.

"I hope it's good news," Lapi said in a quiet voice.

Deborah couldn't stand this melancholy from Lapi. She wanted to somehow comfort him, to dispel the heaviness in his countenance. But she was only the daughter of Tobiah to him now; she could never be anything more.

"I will prepare the fire in the courtyard," Deborah said. "It's nearly dark."

Her father nodded, and Deborah rose to her feet. She collected the empty bowls of soup and returned them to the cooking room, then headed outside. When they had overnight visitors at the homestead, her father would frequently talk late into the night, and they'd gather around an outside fire, reveling in both the warmth of the flames and the coolness of the weather.

But tonight's fire would also be a beacon to any lost traveler. She gathered kindling and set the sticks and dried grass inside the ring of river stones. Then she fetched a few larger pieces of wood they kept in the stable. Once she had those arranged, she balled up a bit of dry grass and set it in the middle of the fire ring. She struck a piece of chert against a flat stone multiple times until the grass started to smoke. She picked up the ball of grass and waved it in the air to fan the smoke into flame.

Orange flames burst out of the grass, and she dropped it onto the kindling. Then she bent forward and blew on the small flames until the kindling caught fire. Satisfied, she straightened and gingerly arranged the other kindling, making sure she didn't burn her fingers.

"Thank you," a deep voice said behind her.

Deborah didn't need to turn to know that Lapi had come into the courtyard. She heard his footsteps as he approached. He crossed to the other side of the fire ring and crouched before the young flames.

The yellow glow lit his square jaw, but his eyes remained shadowed. He wasn't looking at her but focused his concentration on the fire.

Deborah wondered what her brothers and father were doing and why they hadn't come outside as well. It made her nervous to be alone with Lapi. Not that she feared him. But the last time they'd been alone, their conversation had been deeply private, and she knew she'd disappointed him by telling him her loyalty was to her family. Surely no man liked to be rejected.

She closed her eyes for a moment, trying to redirect her thoughts. Lapi's concerns were about Barak right now, not some foolish woman's thoughts about marriage. She wished she could drum up some words of comfort, but she'd said all she could think of inside the tent. She was curious, of course, to hear more about Barak's family, especially Kiva—who was only a couple of years younger than Deborah. She tried to imagine what Kiva must have thought and felt being at that market square and capturing the interest of the Canaanite captain.

Deborah remembered how it had felt when she'd been alone with the two dozen Canaanite soldiers. Only by God's grace had her brothers, Barak, and Lapi arrived in time to dissuade them from mischief.

Feeling Lapi was watching her, Deborah opened her eyes. He was still the only one on the other side of the fire ring. He didn't look away when their gazes connected, and Deborah felt compelled to say something.

"I hope they arrive soon," Deborah said, knowing her words were inadequate, but she pressed on. "I can join in the search. I don't have my own horse, but I'll walk the ridge and keep a lookout."

Lapi didn't say anything for a moment, just looked at her, which only made Deborah's pulse speed up for some reason. "Thank you," he finally said. Then he fell silent and went back to staring at the flames.

Chapter Ten

Deborah's neck hurt from sleeping in a tense position. At any moment during the night, she'd fully expected to be awakened with the news that Barak's family had arrived. But dawn was nearly here. The darkness of her bedchamber had softened to an inky gray, and the first sounds of the birds told her the sun was only an hour from tipping the horizon.

She rubbed the ache in her neck, then cast off her rug. She pulled on her warmest robe and left her bedchamber to start the cooking fire in the kiln. When the men awoke, ready to begin their search, she'd have fresh honey cakes for them.

But first, she'd make sure the courtyard fire had been put out. Soon after Lapi had thanked her again, her brothers had come into the courtyard and put together a plan to keep watch over the fire during the night.

As she stepped into the courtyard, she saw that Lapi was sitting in the same place she'd last seen him the night before. Hadn't he left? As she approached, she knew he was asleep. His arms were wrapped around his drawn-up knees, and his forehead leaned atop them.

The fire smoked, and although no flames could be seen, most of the wood had been reduced to red coals. The gray of the early morning was softening to violet, and a gentle breeze curled the smoke into the air in a slow dance. If she poured water over the coals, the hiss would surely wake Lapi. Deborah stood for a moment, regarding him, knowing she was watching him in a private moment.

But before she could turn away, he raised his head.

"I'm sorry," Deborah said. "I didn't mean to wake you."

Lapi rubbed a hand over his face, then blinked his eyes a couple of times. "I didn't mean to fall asleep."

Deborah stared at him. "You were out here all night?"

Lapi nodded, then he rose to his feet, and Deborah looked away as he stretched his shoulders. She was around men all the time, but every action of Lapi's drew her attention. Her gaze strayed again. His hair had come out of its leather tie, hanging loose to his shoulders, and she watched him absently push it back.

"I was about to put the fire out," Deborah said. "I'll have honey cakes ready soon, so by the time everyone wakes—"

"Deborah." Lapi cut into her monologue.

She looked up at him because he'd walked over to her side of the fire ring. "I can put the fire out. You don't need to do everything."

The deep brown of his eyes was trained on her, and it wasn't its usual intensity that she had come to expect. This close, she saw a lighter, warmer brown within the deeper color. *This close* . . . she shouldn't be standing so close to him because she could smell his scent of earth and sage.

"All right," she said in a whisper. What was happening to her? Her stomach felt fluttery, and she wanted to reach out and run her fingers along his arm. To hold his hand. To tell him she didn't like him so worried and tired. But she did none of those things. She moved away, then walked across the courtyard and stepped into the tent.

Lapi said nothing else, but she could feel his gaze on her back.

It didn't take long to mix up a batch of honey cakes, and moments later, she had them baking in the kiln. She heard the rumbling of the men's voices as she picked up a wooden bucket, then headed out to the goats' pen to fetch goat's milk. She'd start the cheese processing since she hoped they'd have plenty of guests for supper—and she wanted to be able to provide more nourishment than barley and vegetable soup.

When she returned to the cooking room, the honey cakes were golden brown, and she removed them from the kiln. She gathered a bowl of olives and dates, as well as two oranges her father had brought home from the village market a few days ago, a real delicacy.

She carried the dishes out to the main tent area and set them on the low table.

Abner came into the room. "Lapi tells us you're going to watch the ridge."

"Yes, I want to help."

Abner studied her for a moment, and she hoped he wouldn't tell her no. But then he said, "Our signal is three long whistles. I don't want you out of sight of the homestead. The animals still need to be watched over."

Deborah's heart leapt. She was being allowed to help. "All right."

"And if we are too far to respond to your whistles, build a fire in the courtyard," he said. "The smoke will signal that we need to return in all haste." He looked at her thoughtfully. "If *anything* happens, give us the signal."

Deborah frowned. "What else could happen?" When her brother didn't respond immediately, she said, "Tell me, Abner. I'm not a child."

He clenched his jaw, then sighed. "When Father went to the village market a few days ago, he overheard more than one tale of a woman who can fight off lions."

Deborah's eyes widened. "They mean *me*?"

Abner nodded. "I don't know who started the rumor, but it will keep you on the minds of the Canaanites you ran out of our valley."

Deborah didn't know what to think, what to say.

"There's more to that rumor," her father said, coming into the tent with Chaim. "The story of how you escaped two dozen soldiers and then sent them fleeing in fear for their lives has also spread and grown."

"How can anyone know what I did?" she asked. "Was it the elders?"

"The elders or the soldiers themselves," her father said. "We don't exactly know, but what you did has become its own legend. The elders want to pay a visit in the next few days to discuss with you exactly what happened. They are fearing that other people might come to the village, intent on seeing the lioness-woman herself."

Chaim laughed. "Fearing? You mean the elders are *anticipating*. They think trade will increase, and they'll be able to meet their tax obligations to the Canaanites."

Deborah sank onto a nearby cushion. She didn't want any attention. She didn't want her life disturbed.

"Whatever the case, Deborah, your name is being heralded in many circles," her father said, crossing to her and placing a hand on her shoulder. "And I know you don't want to hear this, but the elders might request your presence at the next village festival to tell the tale yourself."

Deborah tried to let the information sink in. She liked her quiet life here in this valley, upon her homestead, with her family. "I'd rather not go to the festival, and I'd rather not become a storyteller."

Her brothers and father exchanged glances.

Deborah straightened. "What?"

"Whether you go to the festival or not," her father said, "interest in your story will continue to grow. The Israelites across the nation are desperate for a story of hope. Which is *your* story."

"It will also draw the attention of the Canaanites," Lapi said, coming into the room.

Deborah looked over at him. He stood in a wide stance, his arms folded.

"True," her father said in a humbled voice.

"Do you think that's wise, then," Lapi continued, "to have her act as a traveling storyteller?"

Chaim stepped toward Lapi. "Father was only suggesting that she share the story at the festival and—"

"I heard the suggestion," Lapi cut in, his voice tense. "And it puts Deborah in a dangerous situation."

Deborah went still. Lapi was outright arguing with her brother and father—interfering in their family business. What was going on?

Her father stepped between the two men and rested a hand on Lapi's shoulder. "Now, my friend, no one here wants to bring any harm to Deborah."

Lapi didn't relax, and neither did Chaim.

"Why are you so concerned, Lapi?" Chaim ground out in a tone Deborah rarely heard from her easygoing brother. "Don't you have your own family to worry about?"

No one in the room moved or spoke.

Lapi merely held Chaim's gaze, not backing down and not apologizing.

Then Chaim looked over at Deborah, and in his eyes, she saw that he was about to guess why Lapi might be protective of her. Deborah felt lightheaded at the idea of Chaim finding out that Lapi had proposed marriage.

Before her brother could speak, her father said, "We should prepare to start our search." He turned to Deborah. "We'll be at the stables."

Deborah nodded, unsure of what to say, if anything. Her father and brother left, and Lapi turned to follow them, except he paused by the tent door, looking back.

For an instant, she thought he might say something, but in the next moment, he disappeared outside.

Deborah exhaled. What had just happened? What was Lapi thinking, interfering in the business of her family? She glanced about the room, trying to refocus her thoughts. The food on the table had remained untouched. Were they really going to leave with no sustenance? She hurried to the cooking room and wrapped the honey cakes in separate squares of cloth.

She left the tent again, and this time, she headed directly for the stables. Abner had joined the other men with the horses. They'd tied waterskins to the horses, which told Deborah they were prepared to be gone all day, if necessary.

"Wait," she said, approaching the men. "Take these cakes with you." She handed the first one to her father, then the next to Abner.

When she reached Chaim, she avoided his gaze, because she didn't want to see the suspicion or knowledge in his eyes. It was hard enough to keep the secret of Lapi's proposal, so if one of her brothers suspected, it would all be brought to light. She didn't know what her father's reaction would be—he'd probably send Lapi away. And Deborah would never see him again.

Lapi was next, and by the time she reached him, he'd mounted his great beast of a horse. She held up the wrapped honey cake, and his fingers brushed hers as he took it from her hand. Deborah was aware that Chaim was watching them closely, so she stepped back quickly and turned to her father.

"I will be along the ridge," she told him, "awaiting any signal that might come."

Her father nodded and thanked her before he mounted his own horse.

Deborah walked toward the courtyard as the men set off, each in the direction they'd already discussed the night before. She paused by the low stone wall. She needed to resupply her arrows, then bring her own sustenance to the ridge. But for the moment, she watched Lapi as he guided his horse up the hill that led away from their homestead.

As she watched him, her heart felt both light and heavy. Light that perhaps he did truly care about her, and heavy that he was a man she could never marry. And if, by some miracle, her father did allow her to marry Lapi, what would her life be like? Lapi had no parents and no permanent home. He traveled like a nomad, moving every few weeks to a new training assignment. What would he expect in a wife? For her to live by herself at the edge of a village? To live with Barak and his wife?

The wind gusted about her, cool and scented with wildflowers. She smoothed her hair back and plaited it as Lapi continued on his way, pausing to scan the ever-lightening landscape as the sun's rays chased away the dawn's violet sky.

Lapi had a stubborn personality. He was a fierce man. He was a loyal man. A protector. And he made Deborah's heart race despite her reluctance to admit it. Was it possible for her own heart to betray her?

She turned from her watch post and made her final preparations. The sheep would have to spend the day at the homestead while she kept watch from the ridge. She replenished the arrows she'd had to leave behind near the snake nest the day before. She'd eventually recover them. She wrapped up her own honey cake, then added some olives as well. Grabbing a mantle from her bedchamber, she tied it about her hair to ward off the sun from her face.

Soon, she was on her way, bow and arrows slung over one shoulder and a waterskin slung over the other. She tried to think of what Barak and his family were doing right now. Had they traveled during the heat of the day, or were they traveling at night? Had they been delayed by soldiers or something else, like illness? Perhaps Barak's injured hand had festered into a terrible disease. She'd heard of men dying from severe wounds.

She hoped for Lapi's sake that his cousin would be found soon, healthy and safe. As she walked toward the ridge, she whispered a prayer, and the words caught in the wind. *Oh, Lord, my God. Glory is Thy name. If it be Thy will, grant us the blessing of finding Barak today. Protect his family and bring him to us safely.*

Deborah reached the ridge. Out here, the wind was stronger, and it pulled strands of hair from its plait. She retied the mantle about her head so the strands of her hair wouldn't blow so much, then scanned the valley from her perch. The early-morning light didn't show any groups of travelers, and beyond the valley, a bank of clouds had moved in.

She watched the muted gray clouds for a moment and hoped it didn't signal rain. As much as rain was always welcome, today the storm would complicate their search. Wadis of rushing water could form in an instant, making travel dangerous for everyone.

Deborah walked from one end of the ridge to the other, keeping her eyes trained on the valley below. At one point, she thought she saw a trail of smoke, but it was quite a ways out and not in an area where people traveled or camped. In the next moment, the smoke had disappeared, and she decided she'd imagined it.

She continued to walk and pace, alternating between watching the valley and the darkening clouds. The wind grew fierce and much colder, so she scrambled down the ridge a few paces. She should have brought a thicker cloak. She hunched against one of the boulders to take some shelter while still watching.

Then she saw another line of smoke. It disappeared almost as soon as it had appeared. But it was in the same spot as before. Across the stream, past the location of the Canaanite soldier camp, beyond a grove of scrubby bushes.

She started down the ridge, keeping her eyes on the spot. The smoke was gone, but Deborah had seen it enough times to know she should investigate. She halted, debating what to do. Certainly, the wind was too strong, and the men were too far away to hear her whistle, but she'd have to do it anyway, just in case.

So she scrambled to the top of the ridge again and released three long whistles. She could only hope that her hunch about the smoke proved to the right. She didn't want to completely abandon the homestead, but what if the smoke was a signal of some sort? What if Barak was in trouble?

Once Deborah reached the base of the hill, she began to run, which proved difficult. The ground was rocky, and the wind seemed determined to slow her down and steal her breath. No more plumes of smoke appeared, but she continued toward the location where she'd seen it rise. The clouds overhead had grown darker and grayer—nearly black now.

Thunder cracked overhead, and Deborah flinched, then ran faster. If anything, she might have to take shelter in a thicket. Her thighs soon burned with the effort of running, and her chest heaved with labored breathing, but she pressed on.

Finally, she reached the bushes where she'd seen the smoke, and she slowed her step. There was no sign or scent of smoke, but when she cleared the thicket, it was plain she'd just arrived at a camping spot.

And not five paces from Deborah, a woman crouched behind a tree, a knife in her hand. Deborah guessed her to be about five years older than she. Nothing in the woman's eyes or body frightened Deborah. First, she was an Israelite, and second, a baby had started crying.

Chapter Eleven

The woman's attention shifted with the sound of the wailing baby, and Deborah took a few steps forward. Even if the woman was an excellent knife thrower, Deborah would be ready to dodge.

Although Deborah couldn't see who occupied the camp behind the woman, the coincidence was too great for this woman to be none other than Barak's wife.

"Evie?" Deborah asked.

The woman's mouth fell open, and confusion marked her face.

"I'm Deborah, daughter of Tobiah," she said. "Are you Barak's wife?"

The woman gave a slow nod, and her shoulders relaxed, but she still gripped the knife. She was a small, slight woman.

Deborah took another step forward, holding up her hands. "I'm here to help. Lapi arrived last night, and we are all looking for you." She glanced toward the camp behind the woman. "Have you had trouble?"

"Yes," Evie said in a half whisper. "Barak is very . . . ill." Tears spilled upon her cheeks. "And his father is crippled. We saw . . . soldiers . . ." Her voice drifted off.

Deborah was afraid the poor woman would collapse where she stood. "We live in the valley on the other side of that ridge. I'll check on Barak now and then bring help."

Evie nodded, her strength seeming to have left her body. Deborah walked toward the woman and took her arm to aid her return to the camp.

Beyond a makeshift lean-to, Deborah caught sight of a small cart and a donkey tied to it. A young boy, who couldn't be more than four or five, sat inside the lean-to, holding the crying baby.

"Why don't you collect the baby," Deborah said, "and I'll check on your husband."

Evie reached for the baby, and the crying quieted. The young boy scurried away from Deborah as she stooped to step inside the half-tent. The wind battled against the tent walls, and she knew the full force of the storm would soon blow the thing apart.

It took Deborah's eyes a moment to adjust to the dimness, and she discovered an older man watching her.

"This is Deborah, daughter of Tobiah," Evie said to the man. "She says Lapi is at her homestead, and they can get Barak there."

The man's lined face softened in relief. "I am Barak's father, Abinoam. Barak is ill with fever."

Deborah swallowed at the sight of the inert form lying on the other side of Abinoam. She crept forward and knelt by Barak's side. The last time she'd seen him, he'd been a healthy, vibrant man. A strong warrior and expert horseman. The Barak before her was pale, his lips chapped, and his breathing almost nonexistent.

Deborah glanced at his bandaged hand and knew the stink she was smelling must be from putrefying flesh. She placed a hand on Barak's forehead and found it hot and moist.

Evie joined her at Barak's side. "When he could no longer walk beside the cart, I knew we had to stop. It was impossible for one donkey to pull both Barak and me, even with our son walking alongside the cart."

Abinoam spoke next. "We spotted some soldiers, and we didn't know if they were on a patrol or looking for a fight. It was my idea to release the horse and send it the opposite way. To distract them."

Evie patted the man's hand. "It was a good idea and likely deterred them from finding us."

Thunder rumbled overhead, sounding closer than before, and the baby whimpered.

Deborah rose to her feet. "I will fetch the others. Our homestead is above the western ridge. Not too far." She wondered if it would be possible to transport this whole family, especially Barak, before the storm was fully upon them.

When she stepped out of the lean-to, she feared the thing would blow over before she got help. But she couldn't very well get anyone in the family to the homestead before she alerted the other men.

Deborah pushed through the wind, gripping the mantle against her neck so it didn't blow away. She moved as fast as she could up the ridge, gasping for breath as she reached the top. A quick look behind her revealed that the dark clouds had multiplied at least three times. The first drops of rain hit her face as she turned toward the homestead. She took another moment to give the three-whistle signal again, then she started to run, ignoring the burning in her calves and thighs.

She almost sank to the ground in relief when she saw two horses heading toward the homestead until they spotted her; then Abner and Lapi changed direction and came galloping toward her. They reined in their horses in front of her, and she told them all she'd found out about Barak.

"He's *ill*?" Lapi asked.

"With fever," she called over the wind. Her mantle slid from her head and whipped away.

"I will hunt down Father and Chaim and lead them to the camp so we can get everyone out," Abner said. "Lapi, you go see what you can do now."

Lapi nodded, his expression grim. His gaze cut to Deborah, and he held out his hand. "Come with me."

It wasn't prudent, she thought, because if she rode with Lapi, that was one less spot upon his horse. She could always walk back to the homestead, storm or no storm.

Without waiting for Abner's approval, she slipped off her bow and arrow set and put them by the courtyard wall. She grasped Lapi's outstretched hand, and he pulled her onto the horse, in front of him. The thunder boomed, jolting Deborah's heart, or perhaps it was Lapi's touch as he wrapped his left arm around her waist and snapped the reins with his right hand.

The horse bolted, spurred by Lapi's command and another peal of thunder.

Deborah grasped the horse's mane, not wanting to rely wholly on Lapi to hold her upright. Still, his torso acted as a solid anchor. Deborah felt bad that her hair was likely whipping against his face as they rode, and she tried to tuck it into her tunic neckline but to no avail.

The journey to the camp was much faster on horseback, even though they had to take a diagonal path down the ridge so the horse would have surer footing with two people on its back. When they reached the bottom of the ridge and Deborah pointed out the direction of the camp, Lapi asked, "How did you find them?"

"I saw smoke," she said, although she didn't remember seeing a cooking fire when she'd encountered Evie.

Lapi didn't comment, but his hold tightened around her waist as the rain increased. The drops stung in sharp pricks against her face as the horse moved faster.

"I don't see anything," Lapi said, his voice rumbling next to her ear.

She fought back a warm shiver. "There." She pointed ahead. "Past the thicket."

Lapi slowed the horse, and after a moment, he said, "Ah. How did you see this from the ridge?"

"It was the smoke."

"There's no fire pit or kiln." Lapi reined the horse to a stop and slid off.

The warmth that had surrounded Deborah immediately dissipated. He reached toward her, offering his hand again. She clutched at his hand as she slid off the horse. Her tunic was nearly soaked now, and Lapi didn't fare much better. She might have laughed about it had his expression not been one of worry for his cousin.

After making sure she was steady on her feet and the slippery ground, he released her hand and called out, "Hello? Evie? Uncle Abinoam?"

Evie appeared at the edge of the lean-to, and it looked as though she was crying, but it was hard to tell in the driving rain that separated them. "Oh, Lapi. You've come!" The emotion in Evie's voice made Deborah feel emotional as well.

Lapi took the remaining strides to the lean-to and grasped Evie's arms. "Are you all right?"

"I am fine," she said. "Barak is very ill. He won't even open his eyes."

Deborah followed the two of them and took in the scene. One of the tent walls sagged with the weight of wind and rain, and she didn't think it would hold much longer. The young boy sat on Abinoam's lap. Miraculously, the baby slept, wrapped in a small rug, beneath the driest part of the shelter.

Lapi immediately crossed to Barak and touched his forehead and face. "When was the last time he drank water?" he asked.

"We can't get him to swallow anything," Abinoam said in a low tone.

The little boy in his arms turned to his grandfather and wrapped his thin arms about Abinoam's neck.

Lapi looked at Deborah as if she had the answer, and instinctively Deborah said, "Let's try to get him to drink while we wait for the others to arrive." She tugged off the waterskin she had slung over her shoulder, then knelt on the opposite side of Barak, opposite from where Lapi was kneeling.

She tilted the waterskin toward Barak's mouth as Lapi lifted his cousin's head and pressed on his chin to open his mouth.

Barak's mouth opened, and Deborah poured in a small measure of water.

It ran out over his cheeks and down to his neck.

"Barak," Lapi said, keeping his cousin's head lifted. "It's Lapi. You need to swallow some water." He nodded to Deborah.

They started all over again. Still, Barak didn't swallow.

A gust of wind rocked the lean-to, and the tilting wall came all the way down.

The baby woke and started to cry. The little boy buried his face against Abinoam's chest. There wasn't much protection for anyone from the wind and rain now.

Deborah reached over Barak and rested her hand on Lapi's arm. "Take Evie and the children back to the homestead. I'll stay here with Barak and his father." The wind caught her words.

"Are you sure?" Lapi said.

"Yes. Go."

Lapi rose and, with a few short commands, had Evie and the two children moving toward his horse. The little boy started to cry, along with the baby, but soon everyone would be warm and dry.

Deborah turned to Barak. There was no way to prevent his feet from getting wet, but perhaps it would reduce his fever. This gave her an idea, and she removed the rug over Barak. She hoped to cool him down using the natural elements of the weather, and she rolled up the rug to keep it dry so they could use it to transport him later.

She opened his outer robe, then took the waterskin and dribbled water along his neck, then patted it on his face.

"Let me help." Abinoam moved to join her. Together they tried to get Barak to rouse and drink. This time, some of the water stayed in his mouth, and miraculously, he swallowed.

"Praise the Lord," Abinoam said, triumph in his voice.

Barak didn't open his eyes, but Deborah felt her own heart soar at their achievement. As the rain continued to fall and the wind whipped through the shelter, Deborah felt none of the cold. The warm feeling of accomplishment made her forget that she was in the middle of a storm, her clothing soaked through.

"Thank you," Abinoam said over the sound of the wind. "Thank you for finding us and then bringing Lapi."

Deborah looked into the man's grateful eyes. His appearance was an older version of Barak; she could see that now.

"How did you find us?" he asked.

"The smoke from your cooking fire," Deborah said. "I saw it briefly, and when I saw it again, I decided to investigate."

The man's brow creased. "We didn't have a cooking fire. Evie was afraid it might draw the attention of the Canaanite soldiers."

Deborah let the information sink in. Surely she'd seen the smoke. She'd seen it more than once. Perhaps Abinoam hadn't known that Evie had been cooking something? Otherwise, what had drawn Deborah directly to this location?

Before she could come up with a reply, she heard Abner's voice, then Chaim's. A thrill ran through her. Help was here. Her brothers would transport Barak to their home.

Abner stepped inside first, his gaze connecting with hers, then shifting to Abinoam and finally to Barak. "Lapi sent us."

"We got him to swallow some water," Deborah said in a trembling voice. She didn't know why she felt like she was about to cry. Her father and Chaim came into view. Both of them checked on Barak, and then Abner and Chaim lifted him between them. They carried him to the cart and loaded him on top of the wet bundles. Then they covered him with the rug Deborah had rolled up.

Chaim hitched two of the horses to the now-heavier cart, and her father helped Abinoam climb atop a horse so he could ride as well. Deborah insisted that she lead the donkey while the men watched over the cart and Barak.

The rain was merciless now, and the dark clouds had completely blocked out all semblance of daylight. The horses were jittery in the midst of the swirling storm, and they had to take the long way to avoid the steepest parts of the ridge.

Finally, they reached the homestead, where Evie and her children were now warm and dry. Evie had even begun to prepare soup for everyone, and her baby, who Deborah learned was named Hannah, was sound asleep in Deborah's chamber.

It was just as well. Deborah didn't imagine herself resting anytime soon, despite having slept little the night before. What mattered was restoring Barak to health. She changed out of her wet clothing quickly, then pulled on a dry tunic. She ignored the wet tresses of her hair since it would have to dry before she plaited it.

She left the sleeping babe in her chamber and found that the men had taken Barak to her father's chamber. She watched from the entrance of the room. Barak was paler than Deborah remembered him being. His breathing was still labored, and she didn't know if that was a good or bad thing.

Her brothers and Lapi had gathered around him, and Lapi had set about changing the bandaging on Barak's injured hand after her father had come in with hot water.

When Lapi removed the whole of the bandage, he cursed under his breath as he examined Barak's swollen hand. "Is there a healer in your village?"

The thunder crackled as if in response.

"Yes, but this weather will make travel there and back difficult," her father said.

Her brothers didn't speak for a moment, and the dull sound of the rain sent a chill along Deborah's skin. How many more risks would be taken today?

"I'll go fetch the healer," Abner said. "I'll take two horses so returning will be that much faster."

"Thank you, my friend," Lapi said.

Abner gave a single nod, then left the room. No one argued his mission, but Deborah knew that even if her brother returned swiftly with the village healer, it might be too late for Barak.

She couldn't be in this room any longer. She couldn't watch as Lapi attended to the festering wound. She couldn't gaze upon Barak's pale, still face. So she left the bedchamber and went to her own for a few moments to compose herself. She sat quietly on the end of her mat, near the sleeping baby.

Deborah's heart ached at the thought of this young child growing up without a father. Was death to visit their valley tonight? All because a good man tried to protect his sister from a terrible fate? No. Deborah couldn't believe it. Yet, what could she do?

She moved to her knees and clasped her hands together, then bowed her head. She'd had many prayers answered in her lifetime, and she couldn't deny that she had blessings to be grateful for.

Once again, she closed her eyes, and prayed. *Oh, Lord, my God. Great is Thy glory. Wise are Thy ways. Pour down Thy blessings upon our friend Barak. He is a father and a husband, a son, and a friend. His life still holds much value, especially to his loved ones and the Israelite people.*

Deborah paused, listening. The surrounding tent walls were quiet, and she could only imagine Evie finishing supper preparations. Lapi cleaning his cousin's wound. The other men quietly discussing what must be done. Abner racing the horses across the rain-swept valley toward the healer's home.

Oh, Lord, my God, Deborah began again, tears pricking her eyes. She would pray as long as it took, as long as it was needed. Barak could not die today.

Chapter Twelve

DEBORAH LISTENED ON THE OTHER side of the tent wall as the healer spoke in low tones to Lapi and Abinoam. The healer had wrapped Barak's wrist with palm leaves soaked in water. Then he'd mixed a paste and told Lapi to put it on every hour to draw out the redness. The healer said he would return in a day's time, but it was important to make Barak drink liquids. The healer lit incense in a clay bowl and said the pungent smoke would draw out the illness from Barak's body.

Deborah shifted away from her spot when the healer left the room. She didn't want to be caught listening. The healer's words had brought her relief since prayer was the only contribution she had made.

Her father and Abinoam spoke with the healer in the main room, and Evie asked him a few questions as well. From all that Deborah could hear, the healer's words were positive. At least, he didn't seem to believe that Barak was about to die.

Deborah believed that too. All her praying had brought her comfort, and she couldn't exactly explain why, but she felt peaceful. Even the storm had somewhat subsided. The thundering had stopped, replaced by a calmer, steady rain.

Abner would travel back to the village with the healer and bring another supply of herbs they'd need for more poultices.

When her brother and the healer left, her father and Abinoam settled down to eat. Deborah had no desire to eat, and she hovered in the entryway to her father's chamber, where Barak lay. Except for Lapi, the others were in other parts of the tent.

Lapi looked up as she entered.

"How is he?" Deborah asked, kneeling on the opposite side of Barak from Lapi.

Lapi told her what the healer had said, most of which she already knew from listening, but then he said in a low voice, "Abinoam said there was no cooking fire at their camp."

Deborah swallowed. She sensed the question that was coming.

"How did you find them, Deborah?" His gaze was intent on hers, and she didn't know how else to explain. She *had* seen smoke. She'd gone to that location because of the smoke, and that was where the camp was.

"I'm not sure," she said in a quiet voice. "I know what I saw, but I can't explain it."

Lapi nodded. "Abinoam thinks it was a sign from God, leading you to their location."

Deborah exhaled. Hearing Lapi's words confirmed it in her heart. "That's what I think too."

Lapi didn't speak for a moment, and the only sound in the chamber was the steady rain, joined by Barak's labored breathing. His color had warmed, and Deborah considered any small sign an improvement.

"He's looking better, is he not?" she said, wanting to take the attention away from herself, although she could still feel Lapi watching her.

"He is," Lapi agreed. "You may very well have saved his life."

Deborah shook her head. "I cannot take that responsibility."

"I've seen a lot of things in my life, Deborah," Lapi said slowly. "I've been a lot of places. And I've heard a lot of tales. But this gift you have . . . it's not common."

Deborah's neck felt hot. She didn't want to be different; she didn't want to stand out. She looked down at her hands. "We were all looking for him. One of us would have found him."

"Perhaps," Lapi said. "But it would have been too late."

"I still might have been too late," Deborah whispered. She didn't want the burden of this—the burden of being responsible for whether a person lived or died.

Lapi didn't agree or disagree. "Help me get him to drink again."

Deborah reached for the waterskin. Lapi lifted Barak's head, and miraculously, Barak took two swallows of water, his eyes remaining closed.

"I can watch over him if you want to sleep," Deborah said. "You look as if you're ready to collapse."

"I hope I'm stronger than that," he said, laying Barak's head down.

"There's no doubt you're strong, Lapi," she said. "But you are still human." One side of his mouth lifted as his eyes connected with hers again, and Deborah couldn't help but smile at him. "At least I think so."

"I am very human," Lapi said.

The chamber suddenly grew warmer, and before Deborah could respond, Chaim entered the room. "I will take a shift," he said, looking from Deborah to Lapi.

His look was stern enough that Deborah didn't dare argue with her brother. She knew there were still unspoken words between Chaim and Lapi, and she didn't think an argument would help matters any. Their focus should be on Barak's recovery.

She rose, saying nothing to either of the men, and left the room.

Over the next few hours, she worked in the cooking room, spoke to Evie, held the baby, and learned that the young boy's name was Gilad. As the evening hours approached, she went with Evie to check on Barak. Chaim had traded places with Abinoam, and Gilad sat curled in his grandfather's lap.

Barak's wife knelt by his side and took his hand in hers. "How are you, husband?" she said.

Barak's eyes fluttered, and Deborah's breath caught. Would he wake up?

"Father," Gilad said. "Wake up!"

Deborah smiled, tears filling her eyes. If only it were that simple. Her chest swelled with the emotion of seeing mother and child hover over their ill husband and father. Deborah wished there was something she could do, more than praying. Alas, there was not. So she began to pray again, silently, in her heart.

And then it happened. Barak's eyes fluttered again and finally opened.

Evie gasped. "Barak, you're awake."

"Father! You're awake!" Gilad's small voice echoed loudly.

Tears streaked Evie's cheeks, and she leaned forward and kissed Barak's forehead.

The other men in various areas of the tent had heard Gilad's exclamation and came to see Barak and witness the event.

"Where am I?" Barak rasped, lifting his good hand.

Evie grasped it and squeezed. "We're at Tobiah's home," she said. "You've had the fever for a couple of days."

Barak turned his head ever so slowly, blinking to focus on those who crowded the room. "Abner?"

He nodded. "We're glad you're awake."

Barak spoke the names of the other men in turn, and Deborah was sure that no one's eyes were dry. It was clear Barak still needed plenty of sleep and rest, but it seemed the worst of the fever had passed.

Deborah moved out of the chamber, wanting to give Barak privacy with his wife and son, and the other men soon followed. She continued walking until she was outside, needing some space from the tenseness of the day.

Twilight had descended, and with it, the rain had reduced to a drizzle. Deborah didn't mind the wet, even though her feet were sure to get muddy. She checked on the goats in the pen, then she went to the sheep. She ran her hand over their damp wool, soothing and talking to them as she moved among them. The rain eventually stopped, but it had left fallen branches and rivulets of small, muddy streams throughout the homestead. The wind sighed about her, more of a breeze now.

She thought about what Lapi had suggested. Did she have the ear and eye of the Lord?

Many of her prayers had been answered, and she couldn't explain the smoke that had led her to Barak. But what did it mean? Of course God answered prayers, as long as they were according to His will and desires. So, she concluded that it had been the Lord's will that Barak be found and his family spared his death. Deborah had merely been the instrument that had connected Barak to her family.

She couldn't deny the unusual character of it all.

She walked beneath the pomegranate trees that dripped with leftover raindrops. The moisture had brought out the sweet scent, and she closed her eyes as the cool breeze floated around her. Words of gratitude came to her mind, and she began to pray, thanking the Lord for restoring Barak to his family and allowing her to have a small part in it.

The next week passed swiftly as Barak made great strides in his recovery. Soon, he was sitting up and eating a full meal. At week's end, he was walking about the homestead, a bit grumpy in his manner as he trudged through the pain, but he was full of plans.

Deborah's father had allotted him a portion of land to the south of their homestead. Barak would establish a home there, and once he was fully healed, he'd continue his traveling to train others in the military strategy. Deborah overheard many discussions among the men about the exact location where he'd establish his home, how his family would be provided for in his absence, and Lapi's plan to leave in a few days' time.

Whenever Deborah heard something about Lapi's departure, she felt an ache in her chest and a hollowness in her stomach. And there was nothing she could do about it, so she spent more and more time with the sheep. She'd had no opportunity to speak privately with Lapi, and even if she had, she wouldn't have known what to say. Who was she to convince him to stay around longer? He had a job, and it was his livelihood.

The closer the date to Lapi's departure became, the more Deborah found that she was avoiding him. So she was surprised when he rode up to her on his horse while she was lazing by the stream on a warm afternoon. The sheep had nearly eaten their fill, and she planned to usher them back to the homestead in about an hour. But for now, she was enjoying the warm breeze, the scents of new wildflowers floating about her, and the coolness of the stream where she soaked her dusty feet.

Out of the corner of her eye, she saw that Lapi was the rider and not one of her brothers. She kept still, not wanting to show her surprise. She didn't feel alarmed, but that didn't stop the fluttering in her stomach as she heard every movement of his dismount and his subsequent command to the horse to graze.

She hid a smile at that because one couldn't really command a horse to graze. They'd do it any time they weren't moving. She didn't turn her head as he approached and settled on the bank a few paces from her. He plunged his hands into the water, then splashed his face. Next, he leaned back on the grass and stretched his legs out so that his feet were in the water too—upstream from hers.

Deborah kept her eyes forward so she didn't look over at his tanned calves and feet. She wasn't sure why she was feeling so stubborn, but she waited for him to speak first.

"I leave tomorrow," he said at last.

Tomorrow? The word jolted through her. She'd known he'd depart soon—but now that it was here . . .

He was waiting, and she had to look at him then. The sun glinted off the moisture of the stream water on his face, and she again noticed the scar along his collarbone. "We will help Barak get settled," she said, "if that's what you've come to ask."

"That is not what I came to ask." His gaze on her was all-encompassing.

Deborah's heart raced. Would he renew his offer of marriage? Ask her to defy her father? As soon as she thought it, she berated herself for thinking such a thing. He had respected her decision, and he was hardly a young man mooning after a girl. He was loyal, hardworking, and had many concerns that had nothing to do with her.

"What did you come to ask?" she said.

Again, he didn't say anything right away. Deborah didn't know if she could stand this waiting any longer. Perhaps she would be glad when he left tomorrow. She could tend her sheep in peace.

"Do you want to come to the knife training tonight?" he asked.

Deborah raised her brows. This, she hadn't expected. "To watch the training?"

"To practice throwing knives with us," he said.

Deborah stared at him for a moment. Nothing in his earnest gaze said he was teasing her. "My brothers wouldn't like it. They consider military training a man's duty only."

Lapi tugged a bit of grass from the ground, then tossed it into the stream.

Deborah watched it float toward her, then ebb its way around her soaking feet.

"It's not up to your brothers to decide," Lapi said. "*I* invited you."

Deborah swallowed as her heart soared with his declaration. She continued watching the bits of grass meander along the stream, floating farther and farther away from her. "All right. I will come."

She heard the lightness in his voice when he answered, "We're meeting after dark behind the stable. I'll see you then."

She nodded, not looking at him because she was afraid he'd see the excitement in her eyes. A thrill ran through her because he'd asked *her*. Because he'd sought her out.

He rose to his feet and crossed to his horse. She listened to his every movement as he remounted the horse, clicked his tongue, then slowly cantered away.

Deborah tipped her head back and closed her eyes, allowing the sun to bathe her face. Tonight, she'd learn how to throw knives. The snakes had better be on their guard.

Chapter Thirteen

Hours later, when the moon was high in the sky, bathing the homestead in silver light, Deborah was ready. Knife sharpened, hair tied back, and pulse thumping, she made her way to the stable, where the men trained. As she neared, the men's voices grew more distinct and the occasional knife blade reverberated as it struck a target. She'd waited awhile after supper for the men to organize whatever the training entailed. But she didn't want to delay too long and make Lapi think she'd forgotten his invitation.

She crossed the courtyard, then headed toward the stable. Once she rounded the back corner, she caught sight of her brothers, along with Barak. He wasn't participating, but he had plenty of instruction to offer.

Chaim saw her first, and he immediately said, "Is everything all right, sister?"

"Yes," Deborah said.

Lapi turned. "I invited her to learn."

His words warmed her from the inside out.

Chaim frowned. "She should be inside with Evie. That woman is overworked."

"All of us are overworked," Abner said, his tone much more conciliatory than Chaim's. "Do you think it wise to turn our sister into a warrior, Lapi?"

Chaim scoffed. "Is that what he's doing?"

"I'm not turning anyone into a warrior," Lapi countered. "I can only teach skills, and what you do with them is your decision." He walked toward Deborah, which she thought was fairly brazen, considering her two brothers were watching his every move. "Did you bring your knife?"

"I always have my knife," she said, pulling it from the strap about her calf as if to prove her statement.

Lapi's gaze followed her movement, and she decided not to be self-conscious. "Good," he said simply.

"Is no one going to ask us for *our* approval?" Chaim said. "Deborah's our sister, not your trainee."

"Enough, Chaim," Abner said, his voice sharp.

"Abner's right." Lapi turned to face Chaim. "If you have a problem with me teaching your sister to protect herself, let's settle it now. Between us."

Chaim eyed Lapi. Both men were equal in stature and strength. Deborah didn't doubt that Lapi's advanced skills in military training would give him the edge over either of her brothers.

"Do you have intentions toward my sister?" Chaim said in a low voice.

Deborah released a soft gasp.

Abner and Barak didn't move, but the tenseness among everyone was evident.

"Is something going on that we should know about?" Abner asked, his tone changing from its earlier ease to full alert. He looked from Lapi to Deborah, then to Barak.

"I've merely invited your sister to learn how to throw a knife properly," Lapi said. "Whether she is fighting off snakes or warning off a Canaanite, every woman of the desert should be taught this skill."

Deborah didn't dare look at her brothers because, although what Lapi said was true, she knew there was more . . . She felt it . . . There was something between them, something she could no longer deny.

"All right, then," Abner said, dispelling the tension. "Teach her."

Barak nodded his agreement, and Chaim seemed appeased as well.

"You should watch us first," Chaim grumbled. He pulled his knife from one of the wooden targets and took up position to throw again.

Deborah watched the men throw a few times, then she stepped forward while the men were gathering their knives from the targets.

When Lapi turned around, his gaze filled with approval.

The men gave her a wide berth as she readied herself to throw, mimicking the stance and position she'd watched the men take. On the first throw, she missed the narrow wooden target.

"Use your other hand to aim," Lapi instructed. "Once you have that method down, you won't need your second hand."

Deborah threw again, this time hitting the edge of the target.

"Keep your eyes straight ahead, focused directly where you want to hit," Lapi told her.

She did so, and her next throw hit nearly in the middle.

"Good work," Barak said. The praise was simple, but it spurred Deborah on to make another throw. This one hit dead center.

"You're a quick study," Abner praised.

It was disconcerting to have so many watching her and offering advice. She ignored the fact that Chaim withheld any encouragement or praise. It didn't bother her. She'd never thought the day would come when she'd hold another man in esteem over one of her brothers, but apparently, it had.

She lost count of how many times she threw her knife, retrieved it, and threw again. But she continued, each time imagining a coiled snake or a narrow-eyed Canaanite as she released the blade.

An hour or more had passed when she realized she was the only one left throwing. The other men had finished and returned to the tent . . . all except Lapi.

He remained, leaning against a tent poll, arms folded, no longer instructing her.

She looked over at him. "I could do this all night, but my arm's getting sore."

"You're a fast learner," Lapi said, straightening from the wall and walking toward her. "But you're right. You should take a break so you don't strain your shoulder."

She watched him grow closer, and her heart thumped with each of his steps. When he stopped in front of her, she wondered if her heart was beating so loud that he could hear it.

"Thank you for inviting me," she said. The moonlight cast silver across his face and shoulders but left his eyes too shadowed to read. Her gaze moved to the pale scar on his collarbone. As if her body had control over her mind, she lifted her hand and brushed a finger along his scar.

He drew in a breath but didn't move.

"What happened?" she asked.

"My first hunting trip with my father," he said, his voice a low rumble in the stillness of the night. "I tripped and fell and landed on my arrow."

"That sounds painful." She lowered her hand, but he reached up and grasped her fingers.

Heat surged through her at his touch, and when he kept her hand in his, holding it against his chest, she felt the rapid beat of his own heart.

"It *was* painful," Lapi said. "But my father also found it funny. He laughed after he made certain I was all right. He also took great delight in recounting the story to our neighbors. Now I consider the scar a cherished memory of spending time with my father."

Deborah nodded. Her heart and mind were racing too fast to come up with a reply. She realized then that she wanted to be with this man, above all else. To be truly his. Joined in marriage and tied to his future. Even if it meant leaving all that she knew behind. Her brothers, her father, her way of life. Looking into Lapi's dark eyes, she saw the future she wanted.

She felt the warmth of Lapi's breath on her cheek, and she wanted to lean into him. To have his arms wrap around her and . . .

"Deborah," he said. "Are you still opposed to marrying outside your tribe?"

Her breath stalled. Lapi still wanted to marry her. The realization sent a flood of emotions through her. She closed her eyes for a moment, feeling the rush of her pulse and smelling his scent of earth and sage. "I am not opposed," she whispered.

He squeezed her hand, and she opened her eyes. This time, the shadows on his face didn't mask the desire in his eyes. She felt it to the very pit of her stomach.

"I will speak to your father tonight, then," Lapi said. "And God willing, your father will see the wisdom in our union."

"Tonight?" Something like panic shot through Deborah. "So soon?"

"I must leave and fetch Kiva," Lapi said. "That might take a couple of weeks. Too long to wait."

He touched the edge of her jaw, and goose bumps raced along her skin. "Pray for me, Deborah. For us."

Deborah felt the breath leave her. Lapi lowered his hand, then turned from her. She said nothing as she walked around the stable. Tonight . . . he was going to speak to her father. Now.

She hurried around the corner in time to see Lapi enter the tent. If they met in the gathering room, she'd be able to hear them from her bedchamber. Would Lapi speak to her brothers too?

She waited a few more heartbeats, then silently moved across the courtyard space and entered the back of the tent. Once she was in her bedchamber, she crept to the place where she'd overheard many a conversation.

The voices belonged to two men—her father and Lapi. It appeared her brothers weren't inside the tent. Deborah closed her eyes and whispered a prayer as she heard Lapi speak her name.

"Thank you for meeting with me, Tobiah," Lapi said.

"You said this was about Deborah," her father said. "Have you heard more rumors about what the Canaanites are saying about her?"

"No," Lapi said. "I've come with a personal request."

Deborah closed her eyes, focusing on every word Lapi spoke.

"You know that I have no parents, no home, and that I work on commission under the direction of Shamgar the Judge," Lapi said.

"Yes." Her father's voice sounded confused but curious.

"I have traveled and worked in many villages," Lapi said. "I have met Israelites all over the land, and I have never found any woman, or person, to be so remarkable as Deborah."

Her father's next words were definitely wary. "You are not telling me anything I don't already know. Deborah has a gift. That is undeniable."

"Yes," Lapi said. "Deborah has a life in store for her that none of us can imagine."

Her father was quiet for a moment. "Have you been speaking to the elders?"

"Not exactly," Lapi said. "Deborah needs protection. That of a husband."

"You've brought this up before," her father said. "Deborah will not be given to just any man."

"That is good to hear," Lapi said, "because I have come to ask you for her hand in marriage."

Deborah held her breath. Her father wasn't responding, and she wished she could see his face.

"I know I am not of your tribe," Lapi said. "But a woman like Deborah should not be confined to one tribe. She is a woman who represents all of Israel. Gives us all renewed hope. She stood up to Canaanite soldiers with no thought for her own safety. She values her family above all else. She is loyal, generous, and faithful. I believe she has the ear of God. And because she does, she will need extra protection. Someone who can devote his life to her."

"And you are offering to be that person?" her father said in a faint voice.

"I am," Lapi said.

Deborah's heart was thumping so loud it echoed in her ears.

"You want to marry her to protect her," her father clarified.

"I want to marry her because I love her," Lapi said. "And I will put her life before mine."

Deborah didn't move as tears formed in her eyes and trickled down her cheeks. Lapi *loved* her.

Her father had gone quiet again, and Deborah squeezed her eyes shut. Praying. Pleading. Promising.

"Have you spoken to Deborah?" her father asked.

"I have," Lapi said. "She is not opposed to marrying me."

Deborah felt a smile tug at her lips. Would a miracle happen? Would her father relent?

"If you can meet the bride price for Deborah, you may have her hand in marriage," her father said.

Warmth filled Deborah's chest and expanded to the rest of her body. She covered her mouth with her hand so she wouldn't cry out. She heard nothing else of the conversation. Her heart was soaring; her body felt like she could rise up in the air and fly like a bird. When her thoughts refocused, she heard Lapi telling her father he'd be leaving tonight. To begin his journey to fetch Kiva.

That meant . . . She left the tent through the back way and made her way to the barn. Lapi would have to fetch his horse, and she would be waiting.

It wasn't long before she heard him crossing the courtyard. And her rapid pulse had nearly made her faint in anticipation of seeing him. When he came into view, his brows rose in surprise at seeing her waiting.

"You're still here?" he asked.

Deborah took two steps and flung her arms about his waist.

Lapi didn't move for a moment, then his arms slowly came around her. Deborah closed her eyes and breathed him in. She memorized his solid chest, the warmth of his arms, the touch of his hands on her back.

"You overheard."

She nodded.

Lapi chuckled. "I should have known you'd be listening."

She only held him tighter.

He lifted a hand and smoothed his fingers over her hair. "Does this mean you're happy?"

She exhaled and gave a little laugh. "I do worry about how you'll come up with the bride price."

Lapi drew away from her and took each of her hands in his. "Have faith, Deborah. Do not doubt that whatever your father asks, I will provide."

Chapter Fourteen

Two moons. It had been two months since Lapi had left Ramah. Deborah had stayed busy, and in the quiet moments, her hands stilled and her heart ached with worry. What if something had happened to Lapi? What if he'd been injured or worse . . . ? What if he'd changed his mind about marrying her?

Her mornings were filled with caring for the sheep, and she spent her afternoons and evenings helping Barak and Evie in their new home. She and Evie had woven rugs and made mats of reeds. She'd watched over the children from time to time, and they'd found a place in her heart. Deborah didn't know how long the family would stay, but she would miss them when they left.

Barak's hand had fully healed, though he said it didn't have the strength it used to. But Deborah believed improvement would come with time.

The day after Lapi had left, Deborah's father had pulled her aside and told her he'd given Lapi his blessing for their marriage. She'd given him a fierce hug. Then she'd told him not to tell her brothers until Lapi returned with the bride price.

This afternoon, Evie was at Deborah's home as they baked together. In the heat of the summer, it was better to cook in the same kiln and to bake several batches of flatbread at once.

Hannah slept in a bundle in the corner of the cooking room, and Gilad was dividing his time between the cooking room and the goat pen. One of the goats had adopted Gilad and wanted to follow him everywhere. Deborah had put her foot down at letting the goat come into the tent. Once a single allowance was made, others would follow.

"Someone's coming!" Gilad shouted, running into the cooking room, the goat right behind him.

Deborah's heart lurched with hope.

"Is it Lapi?" Evie asked, forming Deborah's own question.

"I don't know," Gilad said. "There are two men, and they're walking."

Deborah didn't take the time to add her questions but hurried out of the tent instead. Her father had come out of the stable and was watching the approaching men. Deborah recognized the cloak of the elders upon each man, and she wondered why they'd come all the way to the homestead. Her father traveled to the village every market day, and that would occur tomorrow.

She looked south, toward Barak's homestead. Her brothers and Barak were coming as well, from where they'd been working to dig a well. They must have seen the approaching elders too. What if . . . she wondered . . . what if they had news of Lapi and what had befallen him? Surely their appearance could only mean the news was not good.

Behind her, Evie stepped out of the tent with Gilad, holding fast to his hand. They remained by the entrance.

"Who are those men?" Deborah heard Gilad ask his mother.

"They are the village elders," Evie said in a quiet voice. "We must stay out of their way and let them speak to the men."

The skin on Deborah's neck and arms prickled as her father spoke with the elders. She was curious about the purpose of their visit, but it wasn't her place to approach unless she was invited.

"What is going on?" Abner said when he reached Deborah's side.

"I haven't heard," she said. "I came out of the tent after Gilad alerted us."

Abner nodded, but he didn't seem in too much of a hurry to join the conversation. Deborah looked over at Barak. He simply greeted his family as if there were no worries that the elders might be bringing news about Lapi.

Then Deborah found that both elders were looking at *her*.

Her father motioned the elders to come into the tent. The three of them approached the courtyard where Deborah waited with her brothers.

After everyone greeted each other, her father said, "Deborah, these men have come with a message for you."

Deborah's throat felt dry, but she nodded, steeling herself for whatever news they brought about Lapi.

Elder Reuben stepped forward, his hands clasped in front of him. "Shamgar, the Third Judge of Israel, has requested an audience with you."

Shamgar . . . she'd heard of him, of course. He was the spiritual leader of the Israelites, and he was also the one who had commanded that Barak and Lapi conduct secret military training.

"Why?" she said, but her voice was more of a whisper. Her mind reeled as she thought of a possible reason Shamgar would want to speak with her. Perhaps it *was* about Lapi. Dimly, she noticed that Barak had stepped forward.

"Does this have to do with my cousin Lapidoth?"

Elder Reuben's brows drew together. "He is not with you?"

Barak's voice rose in alarm. "No, he's been on assignment. Has he gone missing?"

Elder Reuben placed a hand on Barak's arm. "I have no knowledge of Lapidoth's assignment. Shamgar wants to meet with Deborah because he's heard of her fame and requests to meet the prophetess herself."

Deborah's mind focused on the single word *prophetess*. "I am not a . . . prophetess," she said. The very word on her tongue felt blasphemous.

Both elders looked at her now. There was no mockery in their expressions, only earnestness.

"We will let Shamgar be the judge of that," the younger man said. "When Shamgar summons a person, obedience is not only expected but is also required."

"I understand that, but I'm afraid he believes I am something I am not," Deborah said. She shouldn't be arguing with the elders of their village. These were men who were esteemed and honored. They made decisions for her people and handed down punishments to criminals. They answered to Shamgar, who answered only to God.

Surely Shamgar didn't believe exaggerated fables told of her—stories that had been embellished until every kernel of truth had been lost.

"Did you not drive away two dozen Canaanite soldiers from our valley?" Elder Reuben said. Deborah opened her mouth to explain the sequence of events and how it was the entire family, plus Barak and Lapi, helping, but the elder continued. "Did you not heal a sheep that should have died from a snake bite?"

"I prayed over the sheep, and the Lord—"

"And did not God use the signal of smoke that led you to Barak's family when, in fact, they had built no fire?" Elder Reuben cut her off as if he weren't interested in her explanations.

Deborah closed her mouth. Everyone was watching her. It was true that she couldn't explain away the sighting of the smoke plumes. Lapi had insisted that she'd saved Barak's life, but Deborah knew there was only one Being in charge of fate—and that was God Himself.

Something whispered to her mind, words that were not her own: *Signs shall be given unto them to know I am.*

Deborah swallowed against the tightness of her throat. Her chest burned with heat, and moisture pricked at her eyes. She looked at her father and saw no doubt or mistrust. Then she met the elders' gazes. "I am honored by the request from Shamgar."

It was as if Deborah had removed a large rock from the middle of a stream, and the words of the elders gushed straight through her, their conversation faster than she could focus on. Her mind was not in the present but in the past, as one memory after another crowded her thoughts. Other instances, possibly miracles, possibly signs from God that she'd shared with no one.

She'd fallen asleep once while minding the sheep and had been awakened with a touch on her shoulder. When she opened her eyes, no one was near her, no sheep nor man. But she'd awakened just in time to rescue one of the lambs from sliding down the steep ridge.

Another memory that she'd nearly forgotten, or had simply suppressed, rose to her mind. When her mother had been gone for a few months, Deborah had endured frequent bouts of despair. But early one morning, she'd awakened to whispered words in her mind. They hadn't been her words but the words of someone else—she wondered if her father had spoken them at some point. But now she was certain the words had been from God Himself: *All will be well.*

That morning, her deep grief had been lifted, and Deborah's despair had begun to fade little by little. Eventually, she had been able to remember her mother with love and gratitude.

"Come into the tent, and we'll get you refreshment before your return journey to the village," her father said, and Deborah's memories dissipated, and her mind returned to the present. "Tomorrow, I will bring Deborah to the village to meet with Shamgar."

She stared at her father as the reality of the meeting sank in, but he'd already turned his back and was accompanying the elders inside. Barak and Chaim followed. Only Abner held back, and he wrapped an arm about her shoulders. "Are you all right?"

Deborah focused on the comforting weight of her brother's arm. She didn't feel like crying anymore; peace and calm flowed through her. This surprised her most. She shouldn't be able to accept what the elders had said about her . . . yet, with her returning memories, perhaps the elders were right. And perhaps she'd been remiss in acknowledging God's hand in her life, in so many details over the years. She had not properly credited His influence, and for that, she felt an equal weight of guilt and wonder. "I will be," Deborah said at last. "I think I will stay out here for a few moments, if it's all right that Evie serves the refreshment."

Abner nodded, then squeezed her shoulder. "Whatever happens in your meeting with Shamgar, remember that you've been a blessing in all our lives, sister." He released her then and headed toward the tent entrance.

Deborah stared after her brother; Abner had never said anything like that to her. And this alone made her emotions surface. She exhaled, knowing that the next time she faced the elders, she needed to have her decision made. At the same time, she realized she didn't really have a choice. The Judge of Israel wanted to speak with her. What would Shamgar see when he laid eyes upon a simple shepherd girl who had never traveled outside her valley?

Deborah walked out of the courtyard and moved to the grove of pomegranate trees. The sheep had crowded beneath the shade to escape the worst of the heat. But Deborah barely noticed that warmth since her thoughts were so consumed with what the next day might bring. She ran her fingers along one of the tree trunks, feeling the roughness of the bark. Trees and bark could be touched and felt, but the things of God could only be felt inside. Yet, her experiences were as real as her hand against the bark of this tree.

She continued past the pomegranate grove and walked toward the edge of their settlement where acacia trees provided some shade among the wild grasses.

The sound of a horse's hooves and cattle brought Deborah out of her stream of thought. She looked toward the road that led to the village, and the sight before her eyes made her breath catch. A horse and rider were heading toward the homestead, along with at least a dozen cows and sheep. The rider was a fair distance away, but she knew it was Lapi.

There was only one reason he'd be herding animals to Ramah. He was paying her bride price.

Her pulse drummed as he approached, and then she saw that a woman rode behind Lapi.

Kiva.

Deborah hurried from the acacia grove and crossed in front of the stables so she could greet them.

The horse and cattle grew closer, and in the moment that Lapi spotted Deborah, she thought her heart might stop at his smile. His dark hair had come out of its tie, blown back by the wind. She'd forgotten how capable his hands were and how effortlessly he maneuvered a horse.

The sheep bleated, and the cows picked up their pace. Surely they'd seen the grove of acacias and wild grass. Lapi shooed the animals toward it, but they didn't need much encouragement.

Lapi reined the horse to a stop only a few paces from where she stood, his dark eyes intent on hers, making her stomach feel weightless. Kiva slid off the horse. Her hair was bound tightly with a scarf, and a second scarf acted as a half-veil, but the wind had pulled it back, and Deborah noticed the dark-red scar that ran the length of her cheek.

"You are Deborah?" Kiva asked.

"Yes," Deborah said, smiling.

"I am Kiva," she said.

"I guessed that," Deborah said. "Welcome to Ramah. It appears that you've had an eventful journey, traveling with so many animals."

Kiva smiled, and Deborah saw that the scar had not marred her beauty in the least.

Lapi dismounted the horse, and with his eyes intent on Deborah, he said, "Is everyone well?"

"Everyone is well," Deborah said.

They gazed at each other for a long moment, and Deborah had so much to ask him, but she didn't want to do it in front of Kiva.

"Where are Barak and Evie?" Kiva asked, breaking into the silent conversation.

Deborah blinked, then looked at Kiva. "They are all inside my father's tent on the other side of the barn by the pomegranate trees. The village elders are visiting."

"I will meet you there, Kiva," Lapi said.

Kiva smiled at her cousin, then hurried past Deborah, heading for the tent.

"Are *you* well?" Lapi asked Deborah in a low voice. He remained by the horse, as if unsure whether to approach her.

So many emotions collided through her as she held his gaze. She didn't know how to answer his question. Now that he'd returned, she *was* well. He'd returned. With the bride price. She closed the distance between them and slipped her arms about his waist. She rested her head against his warm and sturdy chest. They had some privacy this far from the homestead, but Deborah knew with Kiva going into the tent, her alone time with Lapi would be limited. Once her family discovered Lapi and Kiva had arrived, and with a small herd, no less, there would be many questions.

Without hesitation, Lapi wrapped his arms about her, enclosing her in his embrace. She might have been bold in her actions, but Lapi wasn't complaining or pulling away. His skin was warm against hers, his arms strong around her, and his sage-and-earth scent exactly how she remembered it.

"You brought a lot of cattle," she said.

"I didn't want your father to change his mind." She heard the smile in his voice.

"How did you . . . purchase so many?"

"I haven't had anything to spend my earnings on," he said.

She sighed against him. "I think even my brothers will be impressed."

Lapi chuckled and drew away to look into her eyes. He lifted a hand to brush her hair from her neck. His fingers continued to trace the side of her neck, then the edge of her jaw. "I could not imagine spending another day apart from you. We traveled as fast as we could."

"Well, you're here now."

Lapi's mouth lifted into another smile. "Will you marry me?"

She furrowed her brows. "I already accepted your proposal."

Lapi moved his hand to her shoulder, lingering there. "*Tonight.* Marry me tonight."

Deborah laughed. "What?" Then she sobered at the somber look in his eyes. "I have nothing ready, and my brothers don't even know. The elders would have to—"

"The elders are here, are they not?" Lapi cut in, his warm fingers brushing against her collar bone.

Deborah lowered her gaze. "Much has happened."

"Tell me," Lapi said.

She stepped back, away from his touch, and Lapi dropped his hand. She hated the distance between them already, but she had to think clearly. "The elders have told me that Shamgar wants to meet with me tomorrow. He's coming to the village and has requested an audience."

Lapi didn't look shocked, and he didn't question or argue. He simply nodded. "I am not surprised, Deborah. You are a gifted woman."

"But . . . what am I to *say* to Shamgar? What does he expect?"

Lapi reached for her hand and linked their fingers. "You will know soon enough. Until then, we can only trust in God."

Tears burned Deborah's eyes. "That's your answer?"

One side of his mouth lifted into a half smile, and he leaned close. In a low voice, he said, "Marry me tonight. Tomorrow we will go see what Shamgar has to say, *together*. I will support you as your husband, wherever that takes us."

Everything was moving so fast, changing. "What about your training?"

"I can train anywhere, and if you want to live near your family, I can travel from this valley."

Deborah closed her eyes, her fingers clinging to Lapi's. Could they do this? Marry tonight? Present themselves as a married couple before Shamgar? She knew Lapi was waiting for her answer, patient as always, and when she opened her eyes, there he was. Waiting. "All right," she said. "But only if my father approves."

Lapi smiled fully now. "Let's go find out."

Chapter Fifteen

Deborah entered the tent ahead of Lapi, stepping into the cool interior, her pulse racing at the thought of the conversation that was about to take place. She was about to commit to the meeting with Shamgar, then tell her father she and Lapi wanted to marry tonight. Her life as a lone shepherdess was about to change.

At Lapi's entrance behind her, Barak scrambled to his feet from the circle of men and crossed to embrace his cousin. The two men patted backs, then Deborah's father, brothers, and the elders also greeted Lapi.

"Kiva looks well," Barak said as soon as all the greetings were finished. "Tell us how her stay with Jael went."

Deborah hovered on the outside of the circle as Lapi told them about fetching Kiva after he'd finished his training assignment. "She and Jael had become close friends, and Jael told me Kiva was more help to her than the other way around."

Barak's smile showed his approval.

"Jael is a Gentile," Lapi continued, "yet she holds no prejudice against our people."

"I am glad to hear it," Deborah's father said. "Our lives would be more peaceful if everyone had Jael's outlook."

Deborah barely heard the conversation about Kiva and Jael, so focused were her thoughts on how to tell her father the news. She couldn't delay much longer. The elders could decide to leave at any moment, and she'd much prefer her brothers find out sooner than later.

She waited until there was a lull in the conversation and said, "Father, may I speak with you?"

Her father snapped his gaze to her, and she could see the worried look in his eyes—as if he wondered if she would turn down the opportunity to meet with Shamgar. "Of course," he said, his tone cautious. He rose to his feet.

"You too, Abner and Chaim," Deborah said, trying to hide the tremble in her voice. It would be harder to tell her brothers since they had no knowledge of the betrothal.

The men followed her into the courtyard, and Deborah continued to walk past the barn. Once they reached the other side of the barn, Deborah waved a hand toward the far grove.

"Whose cattle?" Chaim asked immediately.

Her father's knowing look connected with Deborah's, and she nodded.

"Lapi brought Deborah's bride price," her father said.

Chaim's eyes flew to his father. "What?" Then he looked at Deborah. "Is this true?"

Deborah nodded.

"But he is not of our tribe," Chaim said, directing the statement at their father.

Tobiah exhaled. "Deborah is meant for greater things than living in a small village tucked away from the rest of our people. Lapi will be the man to watch over her as she fulfills her future."

Abner's brow furrowed, but he said nothing yet.

"I have agreed to marry Lapi," Deborah said. "As you can see, he brought more than the requested bride price. And with Father's blessing, we'd like to marry tonight. When I meet with Shamgar tomorrow, I want Lapi at my side, as my husband."

Until now, Deborah had never seen all three of the men in her family completely speechless.

Chaim responded first, and his tone wasn't pleasant. "Has Lapi done something? Has he forced you into this?" His voice rose with each word. "I should have known—I saw the way he watched you—"

"No," Deborah interrupted. "He's an honorable man and has done nothing but propose marriage. And Father gave us his blessing as long as Lapi could meet the bride price, which is what he's done."

Chaim focused on their father. "*You* kept this from us? For how long? And what about our tribe?"

Her father sighed. "Deborah belongs to Israel, not just one small tribe in a village. You and your brother are responsible for carrying on our lineage. And Lapi is a good man, Chaim."

Chaim folded his arms. "What kind of life can he provide her? Did you think of that?"

"Let the man speak for himself," Abner finally said.

Lapi came out of the tent and watched from the entrance. He didn't seem worried about being discovered listening to the argument.

"We will live where Deborah can fulfill her duty to Israel," Lapi said, walking toward them, "and I will support her." He stopped next to her father. "The meeting with Shamgar tomorrow might determine that for both of us."

Deborah stared at Lapi. What did he mean about fulfilling *her* duty? Did he know something about Shamgar that she didn't?

Her father turned to Deborah. "Presenting yourself as a married woman will provide you with added support and consideration."

Chaim scoffed. "This is all too sudden."

"They're right, Chaim," Abner said. "Deborah needs the protection of a husband, not just an aging father and two cantankerous brothers."

"I won't take offense at that," her father said, amusement in his voice.

But Chaim still glowered, and Deborah winced as Lapi stepped toward him.

"I'd like your blessing, Chaim," Lapi said, holding out his hand.

Chaim's eyes shifted away from Lapi's outstretched hand.

Lapi dropped his hand, but he remained standing in front of Chaim.

Chaim finally met his gaze. "You have no family, *no* land. You're no better than a nomad."

"And *you* live off your father still," Lapi said in a low, even tone. "Yet, I have brought a bride price worth more than anyone in the village could pay."

Deborah held her breath.

Chaim's jaw flexed, and he didn't respond for a moment. Finally, he looked at Deborah. "Is this what you want, sister?"

Deborah's heart thumped, but she said, "Yes."

The muscle in Chaim's jaw flexed, then he looked at Lapi. "I will give you my blessing if you swear on your life that you will care for Deborah the remainder of your days."

"On my life, I promise." Lapi withdrew the small knife strapped to his thigh.

Before Deborah realized what his intentions were so that she could stop him, Lapi pressed the blade against his palm, drawing blood.

Deborah gasped, but it was too late.

Lapi held out his hand to Chaim again. "My blood binds my oath."

It was the first time Deborah had seen Chaim look upon Lapi favorably. Her brother grasped Lapi's bleeding hand, then placed his other hand on Lapi's shoulder. "Welcome to the family, brother."

Deborah didn't know if she should berate both men or embrace them. But it seemed the animosity had melted away with Lapi's blood oath.

"Well," her father said, clapping his hands together. "We have a wedding to prepare for. I'll inform the elders that we are in need of their services." His gaze cut to Abner. "Prepare our fattest calf. Our family is growing, and we have much to celebrate. The wedding will be at sunset."

Abner left, and her father said, "I will now speak to the elders."

Chaim followed him into the tent.

Deborah was left alone with Lapi, and she turned over his injured hand. The cut had stopped bleeding, but it was still an angry red. "You shouldn't have done this," she said.

"I do not want to be a wedge between you and your family."

Deborah exhaled and looked up at him. There was no regret or pain in his eyes, only warmth and . . . love. She could not believe she'd be marrying this man in a few hours.

"Is it true?" a woman's voice said.

Evie came out of the tent, carrying Hannah on her hip. Kiva and Gilad were right behind her.

Deborah released Lapi's hand. "It's true," she said, feeling like laughing.

Evie embraced her, followed by Kiva.

"We have so much to prepare for," Evie said. "What are you going to wear?"

"I . . . don't know." Deborah hadn't had a chance to consider details such as her wedding clothing.

"I have something you can borrow," Evie said.

Before Deborah knew it, the women were leading her to Barak's homestead, and Lapi was left behind. Deborah looked back at him. He stood, watching them walk away, a slight smile on his face. Deborah's heart skipped. Tonight, they'd be married, and she could hardly believe it.

The events of the next hours were a blur, and Deborah wondered if she'd remember much of it in the years to come.

Evie let Deborah borrow a fine linen mantle that she'd worn on her own wedding day. Then, while Barak watched over the children, the three women went to fetch water from the stream to heat for Deborah's bathing ritual.

Inside Evie's small home, Deborah washed in the flower-scented water, then wrapped up in a square of linen. Both Evie and Kiva rubbed oils into Deborah's skin. It turned out that Kiva was talented at plaiting, and she plaited Deborah's long hair into an intricate design. Even though Deborah would be wearing a veil, the elegant hairdo made her feel like royalty.

While Kiva painted henna on Deborah's nails, Deborah said, "Tell us what it was like living on the plains."

Kiva smiled in that soft way of hers. "Windy."

Deborah and Evie laughed.

"Truly," Kiva continued. "The wind blows day and night. I suppose one gets used to it, although I never quite did. Jael taught me how to do plaits because that's the only hope for having long hair survive, unless we decided to cut it like a man's."

"That would not please our husbands much," Evie said.

"No," Kiva said. "I can't imagine Barak or Lapi caring much for a woman with shorn hair."

Deborah felt her face flush at the thought of how Lapi had touched her hair that afternoon. She had to agree with Kiva.

"Or scars," Kiva whispered.

Deborah placed a hand on Kiva's arm. "You are beautiful, Kiva."

The young woman's eyes teared up, and Evie moved to her side and wrapped an arm around her. "Deborah's right, you know, and she's a prophetess." Evie winked at Deborah.

Kiva smiled and wiped at her eyes.

"I don't know if I'm a prophetess," Deborah said, "but I speak the truth. Don't let an evil man like Sisera take away your value. Let the scar be a reminder of your brother's love for you."

Kiva nodded and looked down at her twisting hands. "It's hard to comprehend how some men can be so cruel."

"Most men are good," Evie said. "Look around us—Barak and Lapi, Deborah's father, and her brothers."

"If you can look past Chaim's stubborn nature, he could be considered a decent man," Deborah said with a laugh.

Kiva's face pinked, and Deborah decided not to comment on it. Had Kiva noticed Chaim as more than a stubborn and grumpy man? Deborah hid her smile and examined the nails Kiva had finished. She'd never felt so indulged in her life. Her heart swelled with gratitude toward these two women. It was like she had two sisters now, something she'd never experienced.

"It's time." Evie rose to her feet and held out her hand to Deborah.

"Already?" Deborah could see that the light inside the tent had shifted from pale yellow to deep orange. The sun was setting, and she had a marriage to attend. She grasped Evie's hand and stood.

Evie and Kiva adjusted the sheer veil over Deborah's face, and the three women exited the tent. The sun had sunk low against the horizon, and the colors of the valley had shifted from summer green to pale gold, edged by burnt orange. The women walked arm in arm back to Deborah's father's homestead.

As they neared, the scent of roasting meat reached them, and Deborah's stomach tightened. She hadn't eaten since that morning, and in addition to her anticipation about standing with Lapi beneath a marriage huppa, her pulse kept jumping.

When they reached the courtyard, Deborah's breath caught at the sight. A marriage huppa had been erected from acacia branches and leaves. Barak stood near the stone wall with Gilad, and the little boy started running toward his mother as soon as he saw her. "Look what Papa and I made," Gilad cried out. "It's for the wedding!"

His mother captured him in her arms and laughed. "I love it, Gilad."

Deborah loved it too.

Gilad's yelling had apparently alerted everyone else to the arrival of the women, and the other men came out of the tent. First, her father, then her brothers. Deborah searched Chaim's gaze, and sure enough, there was contentment there. This brought relief to Deborah, and she also found amusement when Chaim's eyes fixed on Kiva. Deborah didn't miss the interest she saw in his eyes.

Next, the elders came out of the tent, followed by Lapi.

All thoughts of others fled from Deborah's mind. Lapi had changed his clothing and now wore an indigo tunic that made his hair and eyes look even darker. He wore a prayer shawl that she guessed was her father's, and the sight of the traditional garment that would be a part of the ceremony made her heart hitch. Lapi's hair had been washed and combed back from his face, making the angles of his jaw more prominent, and he wore a groom's headpiece.

When he looked over at her, Deborah couldn't help but smile through her veil. Lapi's expression tugged at her heart as she saw the joy in his face—joy that matched her own.

She walked to the marriage huppa and stood beneath it, and soon, Lapi stood across from her, with Elder Reuben in front of them. The elder began the ceremonial words of the kiddushin, and a warm chill spread through Deborah.

"Lapidoth, will you take Deborah as your wife, according to the law of Moses?"

"Yes," Lapi said, his voice low and gentle.

Elder Reuben next looked at Deborah. "Deborah, daughter of Tobiah, will you accept Lapidoth as your husband, according to the law of Moses?"

A tremor ran through Deborah, and she said, "Yes."

She felt Lapi's smile all the way through her veil.

Evie stepped forward, holding a cup of date-palm wine. Lapi took the first sip, then he handed the cup to Deborah. Their fingers brushed as she took the cup. She maneuvered it beneath her veil, then sipped the sweet wine. Finally, she handed the cup back to Evie.

Lapi reached into his robe and brought out a ceremonial ring that Deborah instantly recognized. It had been her mother's. She looked over at her father, who had tears in his eyes. He nodded and gave her a watery smile, and Deborah blinked against the stinging in her eyes. Then she held out her hand and watched as Lapi slid the ring onto her finger. The smoothness and warmth of the band was like its own comfort.

Lapi's next words were soft. "Behold, thou art consecrated unto me with this ring, according to the law of Moses."

The elder nodded and said, "From the beginning, God created male and female."

Now it was time for Deborah to walk around Lapi seven times, symbolizing the seven days of Creation and how Joshua was commanded to walk around Jericho seven times until the walls fell. She began to walk and found that her tears had decided to come anyway. At the end of seven cycles, she stopped in front of Lapi. He lifted her veil and placed the hem on his shoulder. The evening air touched her face, and a warm shiver brushed her skin.

Meeting Lapi's dark-brown eyes sent another shiver through her. He took the corners of his prayer shawl and placed them on Deborah's shoulder.

"What God hath joined together, let no man put asunder," Elder Reuben said.

Next came the garlands, and Evie and Kiva put them on top of Deborah's and Lapi's heads. Then Kiva held out a bowl of blessed water. Lapi dipped his hands into the water, then Deborah did the same.

Elder Reuben then began the prayer. "O, Lord, please bless this union with the fruit of the vine. Bring them joy and sanctification. O, Lord, our God, we humble ourselves in gratitude before Thee. O, Creator of all things, we ask Thy blessing upon this husband and wife. We ask for the blessing of children born to this marriage. We ask Thee for the blessing of companionship and joy to be bestowed upon them. We praise Thy name, O, Lord, our God. Amen."

"Amen," Deborah whispered.

"Amen," each person at the ceremony repeated, and Deborah looked to each person as he or she repeated their amen. Deborah's love for her family only increased. And now she had an even larger family.

When her gaze reconnected with Lapi's, she wondered if he would kiss her. It was tradition but not always done. When he leaned close, she shut her eyes, expected to feel his mouth upon hers, but he kissed her cheek, then pulled away and grasped her hands. He raised their hands together, and everyone cheered.

Deborah tried not to feel disappointed. She'd seen the love and care in Lapi's eyes, even though he hadn't told her he loved her. They'd shared enough affectionate moments that she didn't doubt that kissing him would be wonderful. Yet . . .

She smiled as her father stepped forward to embrace her. Next, she embraced each of her brothers, followed by Evie, Barak, and Kiva. Even Gilad wanted to hug her.

"Come, eat," Evie called out. "Abner has prepared the most delicious meat."

Chapter Sixteen

"Where are we going?" Deborah asked as Lapi led her by the hand toward the stables. Everyone in their family had eaten and drunk their fill at the wedding supper, and the elders had headed back to the village.

Now, night had long since fallen, and the summer moon and stars were the only light by which to navigate. Riding on Lapi's horse over the rocky terrain wasn't the best choice. What if the horse twisted a leg?

Lapi's hand was strong and warm in hers and, oh, so persuasive. Besides, he was her husband now, and Deborah's heart was already beating fast as her thoughts raced forward to sharing all things with him now that they were married.

"It's a secret." Lapi kept his voice just above a whisper. "Here, climb up."

He set his hands on her waist and helped her onto the horse. Then he swung up behind her. Despite not knowing where they were going, a thrill ran through her as Lapi's arms encircled hers. His breath tickled her cheek, and his sage scent enveloped her.

She let herself relax in his hold; after all, she trusted him completely. And he seemed to have a plan in mind. But her curiosity grew as he guided the horse south, away from the homestead and past Barak's place. She remained silent when the horse had to navigate rocky areas in the moonlight.

"Here we are," Lapi said, and Deborah looked around.

The ridge was now behind them, and to the left was a sloping hill. Otherwise, she could see only acacia trees and a small meadow beyond. Then she saw that a tent had been set up in the meadow.

Lapi helped her down from the horse, and his hands lingered on her waist, making her feel suddenly nervous. She'd be spending the night alone with her new husband for the very first time.

"Is this our new home?" she teased, hoping to tamp down some of her nervousness.

"For a short time." Lapi stepped away from her and tied the horse to a nearby acacia trunk. Then he returned to her side and linked their fingers together. "Come and see."

Deborah walked with him toward the small tent. She didn't know if she, let alone Lapi, could even stand up straight in it.

"Just a moment," Lapi said when they reached the entrance. He released her hand and lifted the tent flap, then he disappeared inside.

Seconds later, a dim glow came from inside, and Lapi peeked out. "It's ready." He held out his hand, and she grasped it.

Lapi guided her inside, and she stepped into the small tent chamber set up with cushions, a mat, several rugs, and a low table with two burning oil lamps. In the center of the table was a platter of dates, olives, melon, and cheese. A jug of wine, or water, sat upon the table next to two cups.

It was like an oasis.

"I love it," Deborah said, her voice sounding more breathless than she had intended.

"Good." Lapi steered her to one of the cushions, and she settled into the softness. "I didn't want us to be disturbed."

"We always seem to be surrounded by people," she said.

"Your family is great," Lapi said, "but they're pretty much everywhere."

Deborah laughed. "That's a nice way to put it."

Lapi smiled, then he reached up and drew off her mantle.

The simple gesture made Deborah's heart skip.

"Are you hungry or thirsty?" he asked.

"No." Her nerves were too tight for her to eat or drink much, but she didn't want to admit that to Lapi.

"I'm not either," Lapi said. "I think Evie used up every bit of food your father had."

"I've no doubt." Deborah reached for Lapi's hand and turned it over. It was still wrapped in a bandage. "All the men in my family are stubborn, including you."

Lapi's mouth turned up at the corners.

She liked seeing him smile, and without realizing what she was doing, she raised her other hand to run her fingers along his jaw.

He captured her fingers in his hand, then pressed them to his lips.

The heat of his mouth on her skin startled her.

"I feel like I've waited forever to have you to myself," Lapi whispered, then he pressed his mouth against the beating pulse of her wrist. "And now I can finally call you my own."

She could only nod as her heart raced.

"Deborah." Lapi pressed her hand against his chest. She felt the steady thrum of his heartbeat matching her own. "I hope you know how much you mean to me. You're precious beyond any words."

"Does that mean you love me?" she asked half teasingly but also wanting to know his reaction.

He looked right at her, and his dark eyes seemed to bore into her soul. "I love you more than I thought possible to love another person."

She blinked against the sudden sting in her eyes.

Lapi didn't miss anything. "Does that mean you love me too?"

She wiped at her eyes, then she whispered, "Yes. I love you too."

The edges of his mouth lifted, and he leaned forward. Deborah was ready—ready for him to kiss her. But instead, he began to work out the plaits of her hair that had been so carefully woven. He was close, yet he still hadn't kissed her. Deborah closed her eyes as warm sensations traveled through her while Lapi's fingers worked through her hair until it was completely free and hung in waves down her back and over her shoulders. He lifted a long tress and brought it to his face, then inhaled.

Deborah could not describe the tingling that spread through her as their eyes connected. The intensity was back in his gaze. He released her hair, then slid his hand behind her neck.

She wasn't exactly sure if she was still breathing.

"I'm sorry I didn't kiss you at the ceremony," he whispered, lowering his face to hers. "But I wanted our first kiss to be private."

She exhaled. "That's all right," she somehow managed to say.

Then he closed the distance between them and brushed his mouth against hers. So gentle, so soft. His lips were warm, and she felt herself melting into him, becoming lost at the moment she wanted more. She quickly forgot her earlier disappointment, and she rested her hands on Lapi's shoulders. She kissed him back, hoping she could make him feel as she did because kissing him was sweeter than she'd imagined.

His hands moved up her back as he drew her close, and a warm shiver traveled all the way to her toes. She had trouble remembering anything in her past or thinking of anything in her future. This moment, this night, was only between her and her husband. And at last, she was his, and he was hers.

Deborah wasn't sure when she'd fallen asleep, but hours later, she awoke with a start. She was cocooned in Lapi's arms. He still slept, his arms surrounding her, so whatever had awakened her hadn't disturbed him. She listened to his steady breathing for a few moments, marveling again at the changes in her life and the events that had brought this man to her side.

The only other sounds she heard were the usual night sounds outside the tent. Then the soft nicker from the horse alerted Deborah. Was someone outside? She lifted Lapi's arm and sat up, keeping the covers close to her body for warmth against the cool summer evening.

Suddenly, dread pulsed through her stomach. The feeling shocked Deborah, and she didn't know what to make of it. But her pulse had started to race, and she knew something wasn't right. But what?

She listened for any other sounds but heard nothing above Lapi's breathing.

She couldn't imagine why she felt so fearful. Moving quietly, she rose to her feet and made her way to the entrance of the tent. Her eyes adjusted to the moonlit meadow. There was no wind, no movement of any kind. The horse was still tied to the tree at the edge of the meadow, but it was awake.

Deborah's breath caught when she saw a bit of grass shift and then a dark form slither slowly toward the horse.

The horse nickered, swinging its head toward the snake.

Deborah reached for the knife strapped to her calf, then realized she'd removed it the night before. It was somewhere in the tent.

"Lapi, wake up," she said as she scrambled to find the knife.

He sat up abruptly. "What's going on?"

"There's a snake going toward the horse, and I can't find my knife."

Lapi moved to the entrance of the tent, his own knife in his hand. He moved past Deborah, and before she could ask him how he found his knife so quickly, he'd already thrown it.

The knife struck its target in the head, and Deborah stared as the snake writhed where it had been pinned. The horse whinnied and pranced backward. Lapi left the tent entrance and strode around the snake to reach for the horse. He calmed the great animal with a few words. Then he walked toward the dead snake.

In a swift movement, he grasped the hilt of his knife, lifted the snake, and flung it into a rocky patch. He spent a few moments walking about the meadow, checking for any other snakes. Then he returned to Deborah's side, his knife still in his hand.

"Are you all right?" Lapi asked, stopping in front of her.

"I am." She stared at him. "How did you . . . ?" Deborah couldn't finish her sentence.

He grabbed the waterskin inside the tent entrance and washed off the knife blade. Then he grasped her hand and pulled her into the tent with him.

"Come on. I'm not finished sleeping," he said.

She tugged him to a stop. "Lapi, you just woke from a dead sleep and killed a snake. How did that happen?"

He paused and looked down at her, his eyes scanning her face and hair. He slid his arm about her waist and drew her close, then placed a soft kiss on her mouth. Withdrawing slightly, he leaned his forehead against hers, and said, "I think the question is, How did you hear a snake in the grass?"

"I don't know," she said. "I woke up for some reason and had a strange feeling."

His brows lifted. "What sort of feeling?"

"Dread," she said. "Like something was wrong, but I didn't know what."

"So you looked outside the tent just in time to save the horse's life?" he whispered.

She really had no answer, no explanation.

"You're remarkable," he said and kissed her neck.

"I think you're remarkable," she whispered back. "I don't think you were even fully awake, but still, your aim was true. Is that part of the training you do? Knife-throwing in your sleep?"

Lapi chuckled, his chest rumbling against hers. "No, but it should be. I'm fortunate that I'm a good aim but more fortunate to have you for a wife."

Deborah smiled, then stifled a yawn.

"See? We need more sleep," Lapi said.

But Deborah stayed awake the rest of the night; Lapi seemed to have no trouble falling back asleep. Her thoughts alternated between what might have happened if she hadn't awakened and the events of the upcoming day when she was to travel to the village to meet Shamgar.

Would Lapi include the story about the snake with all the other experiences that had happened to her?

As the interior of the tent began to lighten with the approaching dawn, Deborah's mind turned to prayer. This prayer was not a prayer of thanksgiving but of supplication.

O, Lord, my God. Please guide and direct my paths so that I might live a life pleasing unto Thee . . .

The prayer strengthened her resolve to meet with Shamgar. Perhaps the Judge would have insights into her experiences and he'd be able to clarify them for her. Lapi stirred next to her, and she watched with amusement as he slowly opened his eyes. He'd awakened much more quickly in the middle of the night when she'd told him about the snake.

"Good morning," he said, pulling her against him and giving her a long kiss. When he pulled back, he said, "Did you sleep?"

"No." She closed her eyes and nestled against his warm chest. "There's too much to think about."

"Only good things, I hope."

She didn't answer, but now she was starting to relax with Lapi's arms about her again. She would love to doze in his arms, but dawn had arrived, and her father would be waiting for her at his homestead so they could make an early start for the village.

"Are you hungry?" she asked.

Lapi ran his fingers along her cheek, then along her jaw. "Mmm-hmm."

"All right," she said, reluctantly drawing away from him. "I need to be a good wife and prepare something for my husband, although it will only be what you set out last night."

Lapi kissed her again. "I like the sound of that."

"Which? Fixing food, or that you're my husband?"

"Both."

Deborah laughed. She disentangled herself from him to prepare food and get ready for the day. The sooner she met with Shamgar, the sooner her questions would be answered.

As Deborah prepared the meal, her nervousness about meeting the religious leader returned.

After they'd eaten, they climbed onto the horse and rode to the homestead. She was surprised to see that no one was out working.

"I think everyone's still asleep," Lapi said as he reined the horse to a stop by the stables. "Maybe they kept drinking wine after we left." He helped Deborah down from the horse, and in their brief instant alone, he pulled her into a hug. Even though they were married now, it felt like a stolen moment.

"You've arrived," her father said.

Deborah drew away from Lapi, her face heating.

Her father only smiled. "Abner is coming, but the others will be sleeping off their drink from last night."

As if Abner had heard his father, he arrived at the stable, rubbing the back of his neck. "I might be awake, but I'm not fit for conversation yet."

"That doesn't surprise me," Deborah teased.

Lapi squeezed her hand, and the men prepared their horses for the journey to the village. Deborah rode on Lapi's horse with him, his arms around her once again. She was well used to his embrace now, but she cherished every moment with him.

As they rode away from the rising sun, the valley colors shifted from morning grays and blues to warmer yellows and greens. The heat rose as well, made hotter by the lack of wind.

By the time they reached the village, the cart merchants were setting up their wares and produce in the market square. It had been many months since Deborah had attended the market. She'd been more than content to let her father do the purchasing while she had kept to her quiet life of tending sheep.

As they dismounted their horse, Deborah noticed more than one vendor looking her way. She recognized a few of them, but others she guessed were passing through, traveling from village to village.

The elders were nowhere in sight, but perhaps it was still early for them. She was wondering where Shamgar would be holding court when her father said, "We'll be meeting with the elders at the gates of the town."

"Come," her father said. "There are too many curious gazes here. I suppose I should have brought my daughter to the market more often."

The stares didn't exactly bother Deborah, but when one merchant stepped in front of them as they crossed the square, she was surprised at the man's boldness.

"Is this your daughter?" the bearded man asked.

"Yes," her father said simply.

The merchant looked from her father to Abner and Lapi. "Are the stories true? She can wrestle a lion like a man?"

Her father chuckled. "No. I'm afraid that story is not true."

The merchant looked Deborah over from head to foot, and she wished she had brought her veil. She was married and accompanied by her family, yet this merchant made no secret about his curiosity.

"And my daughter's married," her father continued, his tone less amused. He pushed past the merchant.

Lapi stared down the merchant as they continued across the market.

"He's harmless," Abner observed. The first thing he'd said since they'd left the homestead.

"He gossips like a woman," her father said. Then he looked chagrined. "Not like *you*, Deborah."

"I don't know any gossip to tell; plus who would I gossip to?" Deborah said. "My brothers are too grumpy and my father too busy. And the sheep don't care."

Lapi laughed, surprising her. "What about Evie?"

Deborah didn't have a chance to respond because just then, she spotted a man standing beneath a grove of trees near the main gates. She knew immediately it was Shamgar. No other man in the village had his countenance. He wore a lustrous, deep-green robe, a garment finer than any she'd ever seen before. His beard was dark, and he was not as old as she thought he might be. His posture was straight, and he seemed in good health. Not the stooped, graying man she'd imagined. He was speaking to Elder Reuben as they stood beneath a palm tree.

Even from across the market square, she sensed Shamgar's authority and rank. And when his gaze landed on her, it was as if he knew who she was, even though they hadn't met.

Deborah approached Shamgar and Elder Reuben with her family.

Shamgar watched their approach, his gaze taking in the rest of the family, then returning to Deborah. She couldn't explain the flood of emotions that coursed through her as their eyes connected. It was as if she knew him, like he was an uncle or grandfather.

They entered the grove, and Shamgar held out his hand. Several jeweled rings decorated his fingers, but Deborah wasn't off-put by the display of wealth. The jewels designated the status of his position.

"Deborah, daughter of Tobiah," Shamgar said before Elder Reuben could make introductions. "I have been anxious to meet you."

She was stunned, and she bowed her head, suddenly wondering if she had been too bold by staring at him. She felt like dropping to her knees, as if this man were a king or other member of royalty.

"Look at me, Deborah," Shamgar said. "The only bowing you must do is before our Lord God."

Deborah exhaled and looked back up at the Judge. His eyes were not a typical brown but more of a green—the color of pomegranate leaves. The fine wrinkles about his eyes and mouth only made him look more distinguished.

"It is an honor to meet you," she said in a trembling voice.

His lips moved into a slight smile. "We have much to discuss. But first, tell me who you travel with."

Deborah took a shaky breath and introduced her father, brother, and finally Lapi.

Shamgar nodded and greeted each man, seeming respectful toward each one in turn. "Come to the back courtyard while the heat holds off. The elders have provided mats upon which we might sit and converse. I want to hear all about you, Deborah."

Deborah reached for Lapi's hand, hoping the public intimacy wouldn't be offensive, but she needed his support. He squeezed her hand and walked with her. Mats had indeed been situated in a circle, and along with her family, three other elders joined them.

Elder Reuben served date-palm wine and honey cakes to everyone, and for once, Deborah was on the receiving end of hospitality.

The next two hours passed as Deborah recounted recent events and recalled things that she hadn't even shared with her father. The men all listened in silence, while Shamgar interrupted with questions here and there. When Deborah had spoken all that she could think of to say, Shamgar fell into a long silence. Only the buzzing of flies that had found the sweet wine sounded in the heat of the late morning.

Finally, Shamgar held out his hand, and instinctively, Deborah knew he meant for her to take it. She placed her hand in his, and he turned over her palm. Shamgar slid off one of his rings and set it in her palm.

"Deborah of Ramah," he said. "Israel needs a spiritual leader to pull it out of its fallen state. If it is God's will, I'll live many years yet. But should I die tomorrow or in ten years, my successor needs to be someone who has God's ear. Today, I have a declaration to make, before these elders and these witnesses. Upon my death, you will become the next Judge of Israel. You will be known as Deborah, prophetess and Fourth Judge of Israel."

Part Two

In the days of Shamgar the son of Anath, in the days of Jael, the highways were unoccupied, and the travellers walked through byways.
The inhabitants of the villages ceased, they ceased in Israel, until that I Deborah arose, that I arose a mother in Israel.
—Judges 5:6–7, KJV

Chapter Seventeen

Fifteen Years Later

Barak paced between the two hundred men arranged in ranks as they stood at attention in the early dawn light. One hundred men on the west faced one hundred men on the east, with only a dozen steps separating the two sides. Today, these men would enact a mock battle and use the strategies they'd been taught over the past few weeks. The uninhabited stretch of land where they now stood was a desert wasteland. No water, no trees, and no interference from Canaanite spies.

"Remember who you fight for," Barak called out, keeping his head down as he strode between the two lines of men.

"Israel!" came the collective shout of two hundred voices.

Barak looked up, his eyes focusing on a young man of about sixteen. Fourteen was the qualifying age to join in training, but boys as young as twelve had tried to get past the restriction. This young man barely had stubble on his chin, and his black eyes met Barak's, his gaze steady. Good. There was no fear in them.

The younger the recruits, the more they wanted to defeat the Canaanites, for the young Israelites had lived their entire lives under oppression. All these men had been witnesses to Canaanite atrocities, which seemed to grow in depravity with each passing decade. King Jabin had taken wives and concubines at will, some of them ripped from their Israelite husbands and children. Sacrifices to the Canaanite god, Baal, had been made with the fatted calves and sheep from Israelite homesteads. Taxes increased each year and, upon threat of death, were collected.

Some of these men had family members unjustly imprisoned or forced into the king's workforce, which was another form of slavery. Some had had children stolen in the middle of the night, then used as sport in arena games in which the children were forced to defend themselves against wild beasts. Other men had witnessed their virgin daughters kidnapped and taken to the temples to work as temple prostitutes.

"Remember who we fight against," Barak bellowed, continuing his brisk stride.

"Canaan!" the men shouted.

The wind had been soft that morning, but with the rising sun, it increased in strength, causing Barak's scarlet robe to billow behind him as he walked. The scarlet color would enable him to move among the fighters without becoming a target himself.

Barak slowed when he saw Nathan, a man of about fifty, who had three missing fingers. Lost in a fight when a group of Canaanite soldiers took the man's daughter to live in one of their Baal temples. The girl was never seen again. But the missing fingers didn't stop Nathan from becoming the fiercest fighter Barak had ever trained.

Since Nathan's daughter's disappearance, he'd dedicated his life to preparing for his day of vengeance.

And Barak couldn't blame him. He himself still bore the scar on his palm from his encounter with Sisera some fifteen years ago. Sometimes he woke in the middle of the night with a throbbing ache, and though he knew the pain wasn't real, his flesh still remembered that fateful morning. Barak looked at more faces of the assembled men as he walked down the line. One man was stooped with age, but he could hit a target with his bow and arrow with unparalleled precision. A boy no more than seventeen could throw a knife with deadly force, hitting his target every time.

Pride in these men and their hard work buoyed Barak as he thought of the years and years he'd dedicated to training under the direction of Shamgar, the Third Judge of Israel. The Judge was said to be deathly ill, but Barak couldn't think of that now or of what the future might be if Shamgar died. What it would mean for Barak's family, for Lapi and Deborah, for all of them.

Barak turned and walked to the other end, feeling like Moses, who had parted the Red Sea. Except he wasn't walking on a seabed, and his sandaled feet kicked up plumes of dust from the desert ground. "Remember who you pray to!" he shouted.

"The God of Israel!"

The men's voices echoed through Barak's heart, speeding up his pulse. When he reached the head of the assembled men, he turned to face the two long lines. These men might not have armor of metal or chariots of iron, but their bodies were hard-muscled, their grit unwavering, and their faces those of warriors ready to fight for liberation.

Barak unsheathed the sword that hung from his waist and raised it overhead. "Ready . . . Attack!"

The men withdrew their own swords, knives, spears, and bows and arrows and roared their final shout. Each man leapt forward to face the opponent across from him. Swords and spears that had been wrapped with cloth clashed with dull thuds. Other men thrust their knives with covered blades, mimicking death blows. Finally, arrows with dull tips sailed through the air. Shouts and grunts mingled with the rising dust, and the wind did nothing to dry their perspiration.

Barak lowered his sword and replaced it in the sheath about his waist. Then he watched the fighting, the lunging, thrusting, clashing, and hand-to-hand combat for a few moments before he stepped between two of the men. "Micah, you would be dead by now if your opponent were a Canaanite. *Never* turn your back. If you drop your knife, keep your eyes on your enemy at all times while you use your hands to find the knife."

Micah, a man of twenty-something years, with curly, dark hair, nodded. Perspiration bathed his face and neck, and he wiped at his brow, then lunged again for the man opposite him. But his opponent easily dodged Micah's too-slow and too-predictable movements.

"Again," Barak commanded. "This time, look him in the eye as you drive your knife into his heart."

Micah lunged with a scream, and this time, his opponent, an older, wiry man caught Micah's wrist.

"Again!" Barak said.

Men's lives would be lost; this Barak knew. It was inevitable, and a part of war, but the time had come to prepare diligently. In their last meeting, Shamgar had directed Barak to start training in larger groups and to role-play mass fights. So Barak had scouted out desolate places in the desert, then sent his son of nineteen years, Gilad, to each village with the message and location of the gatherings. Men were to travel only at night and never be gone over market days, when the Canaanites came into the village to collect taxes and whatever else they felt like pillaging—from goods to animals to children and women.

King Jabin's attitude that everything belonged to him, beast and fowl, man and woman, had bled into his soldiers' minds and actions.

No one was safe. Not anymore.

An arrow sailed past Barak, missing his ear, and struck another man's chest dead center. Barak turned to see Nathan grinning, bow gripped in his good hand.

"How many Canaanites dead?" Barak called out.

"Eight!" Nathan said in triumph. Then he reached behind his back to fetch his next dull arrow and nocked it against his bow. Seconds later, the arrow sailed through the air. Barak followed its progress, and as the arrow thunked an unsuspecting Israelite in the back, Barak was reminded of another person who was a dead shot with a bow and arrow.

Deborah.

It had been over a year since he'd seen his cousin Lapi and Deborah. And it had been months since he'd seen Evie and his two daughters: Hannah, now in her fifteenth year, and Rachel, who'd been born two years after Hannah.

"Hold your ground, Johanan!" Barak shouted. "Crouch lower; thrust your knife upward into the man's gut!"

Johanan was about in his twentieth year but looked to be in his thirteenth. His scrawny stature could be used to his advantage, if he'd but listen to Barak's advice.

Johanan crouched, and sure enough, as his taller opponent loomed over him, Johanan had a clear path to the man's gut.

"Good!" Barak said. He didn't hand out compliments readily, but the days had been long and hot, and today would be no exception. It was the last day of training for this group before the two hundred would be sent back to their villages. A few days would pass before the next group would arrive.

Barak knew they couldn't continue this mass training for much longer. It was only a matter of time before the Canaanites would discover this secret training ground. Barak continued through the fighting men, his scarlet cloak getting caught on the end of a spear more than once, when he spotted two men on the ground. The young man on top clearly had the advantage and was proceeding to strangle the man on the ground.

The strangulation looked quite real because the defeated man was red in the face and calling mercy.

"Gilad! Release him!" Barak ordered. "You know the rule of mercy."

His son, long and lanky with his youth, immediately opened his grip, then rose to his feet.

The man on the ground was Ezra—a fair-haired youth with unusual blue eyes. He scrambled to his feet, took one look at Barak, then moved away, presumably in search of another opponent who wasn't the wild-tempered Gilad.

"What is this?" Barak said, folding his arms.

"He's a coward," Gilad said, spitting on the ground, then wiping at his face. The young man took after Barak in his build, but his straight, brown hair and deep-set eyes were like his mother's. "He refused to fight me. Said he wanted an easier opponent. So I took him down to show him what it would be like if he really had to fear for his life."

Barak couldn't exactly argue with his son, yet he knew Ezra would learn fast enough if a real battle came. Fight-or-flight would be the only option, and it appeared Ezra might choose flight.

"You know he has no father," Barak said. "He provides for his mother, and sometimes sons in that situation are more willing to compromise instead of fight."

Gilad scrubbed at his sweaty hair and rotated his shoulders. "Compromise and letting the Canaanites walk all over us is why we're treated like dirt beneath the Canaanites' feet. If we allow cowards in our midst, we might as well go home now."

On one hand, Barak was proud of his son's declaration because it was entirely correct. On the other hand, he couldn't have his own men fighting each other. It would create dissension among the Israelites. Not that Barak planned on letting Gilad get anywhere near a real battle. Gilad just didn't know that yet.

"Ezra is intelligent enough, and he's been well-trained," Barak said. "We can't always train a man's heart and soul. That's up to each individual."

Gilad rolled his eyes. "You sound like Aunt Deborah."

"She's a wise woman."

"And she's a dead aim with a bow and arrow," Gilad said with a lopsided grin. "Too bad women can't join our ranks. We could get rid of men like Ezra."

"God intended for women to bear and nurture children—"

Gilad groaned and held up a hand. "Please, it's too hot for a lecture."

Barak shook his head. "Then let's see what you've been working on." He withdrew his sword.

"At last." Gilad grinned.

Barak chuckled. They'd sparred a few times but only to demonstrate single moves to show others.

Gilad picked up his sword from the ground.

"Don't tell me you dropped your weapon to strangle Ezra," Barak said.

Gilad looked sheepish but said, "I'll make up for it." He lunged at his father.

Barak easily dodged his son. Gilad was well on his way to becoming a fine fighter, but he had a major flaw. He showed too much emotion in his eyes, which gave away the direction he was about to lunge.

"Keep your eyes on me," Barak said. "Empty your mind. Don't give away your next move in your expression."

Gilad swallowed, then sidestepped and lunged again.

"Much better," Barak said, although it took little effort to dodge the thrust. Barak could spar in his sleep, and in fact, his wife had complained that he'd kicked her a time or two in the middle of the night.

A whistle sounded, capturing Barak's attention. He held up his hand to ward off Gilad's next advance and turned toward the sound. Nathan was waving his hand, trying to get Barak's attention. Beyond Nathan, Barak spotted a small caravan traveling toward the training ground.

Immediately, Barak's skin broke into perspiration. His first thought was that a contingent of Canaanite soldiers had discovered them, and his second thought was a realization: he'd recognize that man on horseback anywhere. *Lapi.* But what was he doing here? And who was he with?

Barak strode across the ground, ignoring the fighting going on around him. The closer he grew, the more details he made out. Lapi was riding with his wife, Deborah, and behind them was another horse carrying their two boys. Young Tobiah, who must be about thirteen now, and Abram, who was about ten.

The boys had early signs that they'd be as broad as their father, and from what Barak remembered of his last encounter with his cousin's children, both boys were quick and agile.

Barak was relieved that the caravan wasn't one of Canaanites, but his curiosity grew as different reasons for his cousin's appearance tumbled about his mind.

"Cousin," Lapi said as his horse neared.

Behind him, Deborah smiled as she clung to her husband's waist. "Hello, Barak," she said pleasantly.

Why were his relatives so cheerful? Barak wondered. Didn't they know he was doing some serious training?

Gilad caught up to him and called his greetings to everyone.

Lapi climbed off his horse, then handed Deborah down.

Barak embraced them both. It was good to see them, but he was still confused. "I did not expect visitors," Barak said. Deborah had changed little in fifteen years, and her dark eyes were quick and intelligent. He had no doubt she could still fell a lioness with a single arrow while a group of Canaanite soldiers stalked her.

"We've come to help," Lapi said.

Barak schooled his features to keep his shock from showing.

Lapi continued as if he didn't notice his cousin's surprise. "Deborah and I can take on training groups, and our sons can join in with Gilad."

"You do know the age restriction is fourteen," Barak said. "Gilad is a man now and no longer a playmate to your boys."

Lapi didn't seem offended at the comment. "We understand that, but when have you ever turned down help?"

"I'm not turning it down," Barak said. "I thought you were busy with the homestead. It's been years since you've traveled and trained." When Tobiah died a few years ago, Lapi decided to stay on the homestead and take over a good portion of the work. Abner lived in the village with his own wife and children, where they farmed a parcel of land. Chaim had married Kiva, and they farmed on the property adjacent to Barak's own in Kedesh-naphtali.

"Abner is covering our duties for a few weeks," Lapi said. "We're here to help you now."

Barak was still stunned. He didn't know what to say. He looked over at their boys, who were already involved in some conversation with Gilad that included showing off their knives. He stepped closer to Lapi and Deborah. "Is everyone well? Have you any news from home?"

By "home," he meant Kedesh-naphtali, where Evie and his daughters lived, along with his aged father, Abinoam.

"We've had no recent news," Deborah said, placing a hand on Barak's arm. "We are glad to find you well, Barak." She scanned the fighting men. "This area looks to be an ideal place for your training."

Barak narrowed his eyes. "Tell me what's going on, cousin," he said in a low voice.

Deborah paused, then said, "Two nights ago I had a dream." She glanced at Lapi, who nodded at her to continue. "I saw a battle—an immense battle. When I woke up, I was drenched in sweat, and the battle images wouldn't leave my mind."

Lapi moved closer to his wife and draped an arm about her shoulders.

"I still cannot shake the sense of urgency," she continued, her voice nearly a whisper now. "We must prepare our people, and our men must be ready to fight."

Barak stared at Deborah. He knew this. Shamgar had said this as well. But Deborah's words stirred something deep inside him and caused the hairs on the back of his neck to rise. "This is why you've come?"

Deborah nodded. "This is why we've come. Whatever you're doing, we will double all efforts."

Barak swallowed, his throat suddenly dry, his heart pounding. "Then I will accept your help."

Chapter Eighteen

Deborah blinked away the last threads of a disturbing dream she'd had. One she didn't want to believe or remember. In it, a group of elders was riding with all haste to deliver bad news. She didn't know where they were going or what the news was, but it pressed dread into her heart. Deborah exhaled as her thoughts came into focus.

She was still at Barak's training camp, and her husband slept by her side, where they'd spread their bed rolls out on the open ground. Dawn was only a hint of gray on the horizon, the bird songs had yet to erupt, and Deborah wondered if there were birds in this part of the land. So desolate was the terrain that Barak had assigned two men to fetch water from a distant stream before dawn each morning. She heard their footsteps now as they passed through the camp.

Turning her head, she spotted their dark forms moving in the gray light. No one slept in tents—the sight of tents would attract too much notice. So they slept on bedrolls, covering themselves with blankets the color of sand. If one were to look down at the camp from a mountain pinnacle, one might think the ground was strewn with boulders.

As if sensing she was awake, Lapi stirred next to her. He always woke up fully alert, and it often amused Deborah. After fifteen years of marriage, she knew everything about her husband, down to the smallest detail. Unless she had a disturbing dream, she liked to wake slowly, reviewing the upcoming tasks for the day before she rose from her bed mat.

Lapi's arm wrapped around her torso, and he pulled her against him.

Everyone else seemed to still be asleep. Deborah's face heated. She didn't want one of these men to wake up and see her in her husband's arms. She was already missing their privacy enough, and Lapi's affection made it harder.

She turned to face Lapi, propping herself up on her elbow. "Did you sleep well?"

"Not really," Lapi said, his eyes amused. He'd noticed her blushing. "But I'm not complaining. I'm the only man here who has his wife with him."

Deborah smoothed some hair back from his face. A hint of gray had started at his temples this past year, and it was about the only thing that marked his aging. Otherwise, he looked like the same man she'd married.

He caught her wrist and kissed her fingers where she wore two rings—her wedding ring and the ring Shamgar had given her years ago.

"Lapi," she said with a soft laugh. "We're surrounded by strangers."

"*Sleeping* strangers," he whispered, then moved closer and kissed her mouth.

She closed her eyes, reveling in the closeness with her husband. Today, they'd be training separately again, and she likely wouldn't see him until evening. It was their second week in Barak's training camp, and she'd been working with groups of four or five men, teaching them technique with a bow and arrow. Lapi had taken over knife-throwing training, and Barak made sure all the men knew how to forge and strengthen their own weapons.

An Israelite had to be clever in where they stored their weaponry because the Canaanites were known to confiscate weapon stockpiles. And despite the danger, should the training camp be discovered, Deborah knew she was in the right place. She still thought about the dread she'd felt in her recurring dream, so being involved with the training helped her feel that she was contributing.

When she pulled away from Lapi's arms, determined to start her day, he sighed. "All right, I'll walk with you to the stream," he said.

"Thank you." She caught his half smile before he rose to his feet. The stream was far enough away that Lapi didn't want her traveling alone, even though there had been no sign of anyone else for as far as they could see.

After she'd washed in the cool stream water, she and Lapi returned to camp to eat some of the dried meat and flatbread left over from the previous night's meal. Barak had assigned a group of men to prepare the meals—which were simple but edible.

Her two sons still slept while the rest of the men of the camp were waking up and preparing for another day of training. Deborah crossed to her sons' bedrolls and looked down at them for a few moments. She marveled at their existence, that she'd brought them into the world. Their personalities were different, but they'd come from the same parents.

Young Tobiah wasn't so young anymore. At nearly fourteen, he was becoming the image of his father. And Abram would soon catch up to his older brother in height. Tobiah was the more outspoken one, much like his Uncle Chaim, and Abram was quieter but steady—like Lapi.

Deborah nudged each of their shoulders, waking them gently.

Abram awakened instantly and sat up.

Tobiah turned over with a moan. "The sun's not up yet."

"Gilad is already setting up targets," Deborah said, goading him.

This seemed to penetrate Tobiah's sleepiness. He turned over. "Where?"

Deborah laughed and pointed north. A few minutes later, her two sons were jogging over to their cousin, eager to begin another day of training. A far cry from their quiet life of herding at the homestead.

Lapi joined Deborah, linking their fingers together. "They both told me last night they wanted to fight if there's a war."

"I hope you told them no," Deborah said.

"Of course I did," Lapi said, no hesitation in his voice. He pressed a kiss against her temple, then released her hand as Barak strode toward them.

Out of all the men, Barak had seemed to age the most. His short-cropped hair and beard were now streaked with a generous amount of gray. This morning, he wore a dark turban and his usual scarlet robe. Although age showed in his hair and lined his face, his body was still straight and strong, his shoulders muscled, and his arms and hands skilled in the hand-to-hand combat he taught the men.

"Good morning," he said, his greeting friendly but brief. "I want them running today, Deborah."

"Running?"

"Running and shooting at targets," Barak clarified. "Give out punishments to those who miss their targets."

Deborah nodded.

Next Barak looked at Lapi. "Keep your sons out of my training session."

Lapi's brows shot up. "What are you talking about?"

"They joined in yesterday afternoon, and they are both talented wrestlers, but they're still too young. I don't want a broken arm on my conscience."

Lapi glanced over at Deborah, but she just shrugged. She had been too busy with her own instruction to notice what her boys had done.

"I'll speak with them," Lapi said.

"We only have three more days with this group," Barak continued, his tone still clipped. "We need every moment we can get so that they have a strong enough foundation to build upon once each of the men returns to his home."

"We will work them hard today," Deborah said. She lowered her voice. "We're here to help *you*, Barak. And remember, God is on our side. We are all in this together."

Barak focused on her, exhaling. The lines about his eyes eased somewhat. "You're right, but I feel like all I'm doing is shouting and giving orders. And then I see something like that happen." He pointed to where two men were clearly in an argument.

Deborah rested a hand on Barak's shoulder. "Before training starts today, remind them why they are here. Why they are training. What our future will look like if we follow God and prepare ourselves to receive His blessings. We all need reminders. These men do too."

Barak nodded. "You're right. I'll gather everyone together before training begins and issue the reminders."

By the time the training started, Deborah's skin prickled with perspiration. The sun would be merciless today, and there didn't appear to be any promise of clouds. Deborah led her group of twelve men to the location where her targets were. Every day, she'd been given a different group of men to train. Barak's philosophy was that the men could learn new skills according to the teachings of each instructor.

"First, we will learn to inspect our bows and arrows for quality and accuracy," Deborah said, walking among the men and teaching those who needed help.

When she stopped before an older man with a few missing fingers on one hand, she recognized him as someone she'd seen hit target after target. "What is your name?" she asked.

"I am Nathan of Bethel," he said, lowering his head, then offering a bow.

She watched him with amusement. "Do not bow to me, Nathan. We are all equals in the sight of God."

Nathan straightened and smiled, revealing a broken tooth. This man had been through some physical challenges. "Oh, but you are next in line to be Judge, Deborah of Ramah."

Deborah's face heated. From time to time, someone would speak to her this way. It was usually an older person—someone who'd been around when the rumors about her experiences had been roaming about the countryside.

Now, Nathan had the complete attention of the other men, who'd all stopped what they were doing to look at her.

"Only God knows who will be the next Judge of Israel," Deborah said in a firm tone. "Right now, we have been commanded by the current Judge of Israel to prepare our minds and bodies to fight for our freedom."

Nathan pressed his lips together, but his eyes were bright upon her with questions and knowledge. Deborah wondered what stories he'd heard and how embellished they'd become. Whatever he'd heard, she had no doubt that after their training session that day, he'd be sharing those stories with some of these men.

Deborah stepped back from the men and lifted her own bow. "We will each shoot five times, then we'll shoot the same target while running."

Surprised looks met her gaze. "There are very few times in battle when you'll be stationary. We must learn to shoot targets while we're moving or while the target is moving."

All heads nodded, and Deborah took aim at the farthest target she'd set up. When she released the arrow and it hit the target dead center, a few of the men clapped, including Nathan.

"No clapping and no praise," Deborah said, focusing on Nathan. "Hitting a target only means you will live to aim again. Celebrations will happen after the Canaanites are defeated."

Nathan bowed again, annoying Deborah, but she decided not to comment on it this time.

"Line up," she said. "After everyone's shot your first round, retrieve your arrows, and I will give instructions based on where your arrow landed."

The men lined up, and Deborah called out, "Now!"

Twelve arrows shot through the air. One of them veered way off course, so only eleven arrows reached the targets. Nathan's arrow hit the center. Deborah was more than impressed, considering the man's handicap.

She moved among the men after they'd fetched their arrows, and corrected postures, hand positions, and strength of grip. When she reached Nathan, who stood at the end of the row, she simply nodded. "Your form is good, and your aim is true."

Nathan said in a low voice, "I'd love to hear about how you took down that rabid lioness when you were running from the Canaanites."

Deborah exhaled and tried to calm her irritation. "I will set the story straight after training is over." She turned before Nathan could say something else; she didn't want the other men listening in and becoming distracted.

After they'd all shot five volleys of arrows, she demonstrated running toward the target, grabbing for an arrow, aiming, then releasing. A second demonstration was running parallel to the target and aiming, then shooting. She hit the center both times.

No one clapped or congratulated her, and she counted that as a good thing, until she turned to face the men. All of them were staring at her, wide-eyed.

Deborah used her free hand to wipe at her brow. "Form a line, and we'll begin the forward run first," she said, ignoring their expressions of awe. "If you miss, run to those bushes and take cover. We need to plan for what happens when we do miss our targets."

Slowly, the men formed a line, and Deborah hoped they would pick it up sooner rather than later. She'd like to teach them to hit moving targets next, but that would depend on their skill at running. The only man to hit the target on his first run was Nathan. This didn't surprise Deborah, but it did surprise her when he looked over at her and saluted her. As if she'd somehow taught him something.

Deborah gave a slight shake of her head, hoping he'd know it was a warning. Nathan didn't need to be in this group, and she feared that the repercussions of what he'd said to her earlier would continue. As it was, the men were looking at her differently. They were watching her closely, listening to her intently, and asking serious questions each day during training.

After everyone had mostly been successful at the running exercise, Deborah allowed them all a break to drink water. She checked the position of the sun and guessed the midday hour was upon them. Gazing across the training ground, she saw that Barak's group was on break, but Lapi's was in some sort of a tournament. Men were sword-fighting one opponent, then switching to another opponent every few seconds.

Deborah found a spot of available shade, then took a long drink from her waterskin. When she finished, she realized Nathan had settled next to her.

"I've meant no offense," Nathan said.

She glanced at him. "I don't want the distraction," she said. "As you can imagine, in the first place, many of the men already have to learn to accept that a woman is training them."

"All they have to do is see you aim and shoot once," Nathan said. "And I know that stories of you have been embellished, but I also know there is truth to them."

Deborah turned her head. What she saw were deep-set, brown eyes, years' worth of wrinkles, and a man who had been a survivor. "What happened to your hand?" she asked.

He blinked, and then he visibly swallowed. In a quiet, dull tone, he said, "They took my daughter to the temple."

There wasn't any other explanation needed. Deborah could almost see it playing out in her mind. The Canaanites noticing a beautiful girl in a market square, then following her home. When the father protested, there was a fight.

"How old was she?"

Nathan rubbed at his face. "Fifteen. I haven't seen her in eight years. No word. No message. Nothing."

Deborah's own throat felt thick. "I am sorry."

Nathan nodded. "One day, Deborah of Ramah, one day, you'll lead us in victory."

Deborah snapped her gaze to him.

Nathan only smiled, revealing his broken tooth. "You aren't the only one who has the ear of the Lord."

The skin on Deborah's arms prickled at Nathan's words, but she had no time to question him because Barak was shouting something to the whole camp.

Deborah scrambled to her feet to get a better view. All the training groups had disbanded and were forming into rows of ten, lining up behind Gilad. Was this a new training drill? Then she saw Lapi running toward her.

"Deborah," he called out. "You must take cover."

She stared at him, recognizing the fear on his face. What was going on?

Nathan joined her side. "I'll protect her," he declared.

Lapi reached Deborah and grasped her arm. "A convoy of men is heading straight for the camp. Barak's guards spotted them on the other side of the hills. It's only a matter of time before they see us."

"Are they Canaanites?" Deborah asked.

"They're not dressed as Canaanite soldiers, but that doesn't mean—"

"They are not soldiers," she said, cutting off her husband's words. "I saw this in my dream last night, but I had hoped it was only a dream."

Lapi stared at her, his dark eyes full of questions. "Why didn't you say something this morning?"

Perhaps she should have, but there was no going back now. "Lapi, I will not hide. I need to be present to meet the messengers."

Lapi's jaw tightened, but their marriage had taught both of them to listen to Deborah's promptings. And now she recognized that her dream had been a prompting, or perhaps a warning. She knew one thing: the riders weren't Canaanites, but that was perhaps the only consolation.

"Then we will wait together," Lapi said.

Deborah nodded. She really didn't have any answers beyond knowing that the messengers were coming. She didn't know what news they might be bringing to such an out-of-the-way location or why there was such urgency. She walked with Lapi to where Barak had organized that last formation of the men. Each man, including both of her sons, stood in rows, weapons at the ready.

Deborah didn't like seeing her sons included, but she would let Lapi inform Barak.

"I thought I told you to hide Deborah," Barak growled out as soon as he saw them approach.

"Peace, cousin," Lapi said to Barak. "They are not Canaanites."

"How do you know—?" Barak cut himself off when he looked at Deborah. "What is going on?" he asked, lowering his voice.

"They're messengers," Deborah said. "I saw them in my dream last night, but I can't tell you anything more."

Barak glanced in the direction of the hills the messengers would need to traverse. "Very well. We will wait in our formation, and we will be ready to receive whatever message they bring." His gaze returned to Deborah. "If there is any danger at all, retreat behind the men."

Deborah swallowed, feeling emotional about Barak's protection of her. Not much had changed in fifteen years. "I will," she promised.

Barak turned to his men and held up a hand for them to hush. "The convoy is made up of Israelites, not Canaanites," he called out. "Remain in your formation and be prepared to answer to my commands. Our guards have done well to prepare us, and now, all we can do is wait until the messengers arrive."

After Barak finished instructing his men, he joined Lapi and Deborah so she was flanked by both, watching and waiting. The minutes passed slowly, interrupted only by buzzing insects and the occasional gust of the desert wind.

Finally, Deborah saw the men and horses crest the hills, then descend toward the plain. Her heart thudded at the sight as she counted over a dozen men. These were no desert men wearing turbans and sand-colored tunics. They wore bright-colored vests.

Deborah's questions multiplied, and she sensed that Barak and Lapi were equally curious as the convoy of elders grew closer and closer. Deborah recognized three of them from her own village. Elder Reuben was among them. He'd become thin in his advanced years, but his mind was still sharp, and his eyes didn't miss anything. They'd had many conversations since that day when Shamgar had visited Ramah. Deborah often shared her impressions and dreams with him, and there had been benefits in doing so since sometimes the Lord warned her of periods of drought or of roaming bands of Canaanite soldiers.

The elders slowed their horses as they neared, their gazes taking in the entirety of the camp and the assembled men. Deborah wondered where the Israelite elders had procured so many horses.

Elder Reuben rode in front, and it seemed the others were taking his lead. When he reined in his horse, so did the others.

Elder Reuben was also the first to dismount. When the other elders had dismounted and joined him, he nodded at Barak and Lapi, then focused on Deborah.

Everyone behind Deborah was absolutely silent. Even the wind had stopped blowing.

"We've come with grave news," he said in the stillness. "Shamgar, son of Anath, Third Judge of Israel, has died."

The words were like an arrow being driven into Deborah's heart. No one moved, and no one spoke.

"We've come to declare God's will," Elder Reuben continued. "And it's God's will that Deborah of Ramah, daughter of Tobiah and wife of Lapidoth, become the Fourth Judge of Israel."

Chapter Nineteen

The words of Elder Reuben repeated over and over in Deborah's mind. She gripped her hands in front of her and looked up at the heavens, directly into the sun. The blinding yellow made her eyes water, and she had to look away. She wasn't dreaming. A group of elders truly stood before her, having traveled all this way to inform her of Shamgar's death.

Neither Barak nor Lapi had moved, and Deborah didn't dare look at them. Would she see disbelief in their eyes? Doubt?

And then she became aware of the buzzing of a single fly that had found her feet, and the sounds of the desert returned one by one. The wind remained lazy, the horses shuffled, someone behind her coughed, and Deborah's thoughts jumped from one question to another. She was gripping her hands so tightly together that she could feel the imprint of the ring Shamgar had given her the day after her wedding.

The silence around them persisted, its weight becoming heavier and more stifling.

"When did Shamgar die?" Barak asked.

Relief ran through Deborah at his words. Someone had spoken.

And Elder Reuben didn't seem offended by the question. "He took his last breath as the moon reached its zenith last night. These elders arrived in our village as dawn broke, and we began the journey here as soon as we procured the horses from Chaim."

Chaim, Deborah thought. He was a part of this.

Elder Reuben moved to the satchel hanging from his horse. He opened it and pulled out a dark-green cloak.

Deborah knew there was more than one cloak of the same color throughout the land of Israel, but in her heart, she knew this was the same cloak she'd seen Shamgar wear that day in Ramah.

She heard the sharp intake of air from her husband and knew that he'd realized the same thing.

Elder Reuben walked toward Deborah, his strides sure, and he held out the cloak to her. She met the elder's eyes and found only confidence and respect.

"This cloak signifies the wishes of Shamgar, the Third Judge of Israel," he said. "By accepting it, you are accepting your calling, according to God's will."

Deborah's eyes pricked with hot moisture as she gazed at the finely woven cloak in the man's hands. She'd never touched or worn anything so fine in her life. She was content living on the homestead with her husband and two sons. She loved the peace and solitude of her valley, the quiet love of her family, and the occasional prompting or personal revelation that made her realize God was only a prayer away.

But this . . . She reached out and touched the edge of the cloak. As expected, the fabric was smooth and blemish free, and it felt like she'd dipped her fingers into warm, melted wax. But it wasn't the feel of the luxurious fabric that had her trembling; it was what it represented. Shamgar had been the Israelites' military leader, their Supreme Judge, and their spiritual prophet.

Deborah was none of these things. Yet, her bosom burned with a heat stronger than she'd ever felt before. She blinked against the burning tears in her eyes until the tears dripped down her cheeks, landing on the fabric of the cloak.

She wished her father were here and her brothers, Abner and Chaim. They'd know what to do when their Deborah was faced with such a decision.

But she was a grown woman now. A married woman with two sons. She was a military trainer who'd spent weeks in the desert teaching men how to fight. And her dream this morning had foretold of this very event, as much as she wished to pretend it was only a dream. She could never deny what she'd seen and felt.

She blinked back the stubborn tears and swallowed against the ache in her throat. "I will accept the call." Her voice was merely a croaked whisper, but the wind seemed to carry it to every man within her perimeter.

Elder Reuben bowed his head, followed by the elders behind him. "It is with honor that we present the cloak of Shamgar, Third Judge of Israel, to you."

Deborah lifted the cloak with both hands, her fingers trembling and her breathing shallow. She held up the garment, and the length of it shimmered to the dusty ground. She would have to hem it; she was not nearly as tall as the previous Judge.

She looked over at Lapi and saw the tears in his dark, dark eyes as he met her gaze. He gave her the barest of nods, and she nodded back. Then she drew the cloak about her shoulders, and the cool fabric draped against her arms, making her feel cocooned in its history. The man who'd last worn this had left a legacy that could never be equaled. And Deborah knew that only with the help of God could she even dare to walk in Shamgar's footsteps.

One by one, the elders stepped forward, introducing themselves and telling her where they were from. Each of them pledged their support and hospitality, should she ever cross into their lands.

Then Elder Reuben bowed again, his expression sober. "We seek your counsel, Judge Deborah," he said. "You are aware of the increase of Canaanite control and abuses throughout our villages. On this day, the Israelites will learn of the death of their one trusted leader. What is the message you want us to take to your people?"

My people. Deborah stared at the elders, then looked over at Barak, then Lapi, and finally the men lined up in their rows. Her sons were among them, but she couldn't pick out their locations right now. They were all waiting for her to speak.

She inhaled slowly, then looked back to the elders. "Tell our people to get on their knees and repent of their iniquities. Tell the people to cleanse their hearts and minds so that they might become a helpmeet to the Lord and His purposes. Tell the people to prepare to fight for our freedom." The words weren't Deborah's own. It was as if in donning the cloak, she'd donned another mantle—one of God's will. Was this what had happened to Shamgar? Had he accepted the call as the Third Judge of Israel, and then after accepting the call, had he had experiences in acting as God's mouthpiece?

She turned to Barak. "Assign Nathan to my archery group. You will continue the training as Shamgar instructed."

Barak placed a hand over his heart. "It would be an honor, Judge Deborah."

The title was new, and Deborah tried to grasp at the reality of it. "Thank you, Barak," she said. She knew she could trust him always, and there was no better man she could ask to lead the Israelite army. For she hoped that one day soon, they could call themselves an army—a victorious army.

And then it was as if she saw the events of the past that led up to this moment: all the impressions and personal revelations. Facing the Canaanite soldiers and finding a way to outwit them. Being led to Barak's family when he was gravely injured. Meeting Shamgar and receiving his ring and declaration. The way her prayers had been answered time and time again. Lapi's willingness to support her calling. The meetings with Elder Reuben over the years and how he'd carry out her counsel. And finally, her prompting to come to Barak's training camp and to oversee a portion of the training herself.

Barak separated himself from the group of elders and set about organizing the next session of training with the men. The mood was somber and subdued, but Deborah sensed that all eyes were still on her.

Her sons walked over to her, their steps hesitant, their gazes wary.

But she held out her hands to them, and moments later, she embraced and kissed each boy.

"Will you still be our mother?" Abram asked.

Deborah smiled and kissed him again. "I will always be your mother. My daily tasks will be different now; that is all."

Abram nodded and stepped away.

She faced Elder Reuben. "As you can see, this will be a significant change for my family. I need to know what is expected of me."

Elder Reuben looked to the other elders, then back to Deborah. "Let us sit, and we can answer any of your questions."

Deborah grasped Lapi's hand. "Come," she told him, then nodded to her boys. "You come too. This will affect us all."

Elder Reuben led them to an outcropping of rocks interspersed with a few acacia trees. They were a decent distance from Barak and the training men. The shade was sparse, but it was better than staying in the direct sunlight. Lapi brought what was left from the morning meal to share with the elders.

Deborah's sons sat at her feet, and Lapi sat on the boulder next to her. As it was, she felt like she was presiding over everyone present, and she wasn't sure how to direct her questions without sounding like she was inept. All of these men were looking to her for leadership and guidance.

"Shamgar presided in Bethel," Elder Reuben said. "But you will want your own place so you can start fresh. A place where the Israelites can come for judgments and a place that will be accessible and can provide accommodations for travelers."

"My valley is near Ramah," Deborah said, thinking of locations that might work.

"That is near Mount Ephraim too?" one of the elders said.

"I can't very well establish myself in Bethel or Ramah," Deborah said. "Each of those already have leaders, and it would be like usurping them."

"What if we establish a camp *between* the two villages?" Lapi asked. "There are several oases with wells, and all we'd need is a good water source."

"There are palm groves there too," Deborah said.

"Plenty of shade, plenty of dates, and plenty of water," Elder Reuben said. "And room for travelers to camp without getting other elders or village authorities involved."

"We will visit the various oases and decide if it will work for Deborah's purposes," Lapi said.

She met his gaze and was grateful for the support she saw in his eyes. In front of the elders, she was holding back her overwhelming emotions, which only made her realize she needed Lapi by her side more than ever.

"When do I need to relocate?" she asked Elder Reuben.

With no hesitation, he said, "Today, if possible. The sooner you are established and receiving the people, the less speculation and contention there will be."

"Contention?" Deborah asked. "What do you mean?"

"Any time a new leader, a new elder, or even a new Judge takes on their role, there will be naysayers," Elder Reuben said.

"Not everyone supported Shamgar," Lapi said in a quiet voice. It wasn't a question but a statement.

"Very true," Elder Reuben said. "That brings us to another issue. You will need guards."

Deborah stared at the elder. "To guard me against my own people?"

"The calling of a Judge brings power and influence, along with wealth," Elder Reuben said. "Although you know that having the ear of God is a heavy burden, indeed, others do not see it that way. They see only the outward manifestations of a person being held in high esteem, being offered gifts and praises."

"I never asked for this calling," Deborah said. "Nor desired it."

"We know," Elder Reuben said. The other elders nodded their agreement. "We all know that, and as spiritual leaders in our villages, we understand it. There are Israelite groups who have fallen into iniquity; some have formed secret agreements with the Canaanites, and others are downright thieves."

"I will provide security," Lapi said. "I will act at the head of the guard and find other men I trust to protect Deborah."

The lump in Deborah's throat grew. "I don't want you to be in danger," she told Lapi quietly. "You have not accepted this call; I have. If something happened to you, what would our sons do?"

Lapi's gaze was unwavering. "If something happened to *you*, my life would be useless. I cannot leave your safety in another person's hands."

Deborah bit her lip. When Lapi was determined about something, there was little chance of her changing his mind. Perhaps he could serve as head of her guard in the beginning, and then he'd see the wisdom in letting someone else take over. Deborah wished she could speak to her husband in private, but there was no privacy on this training ground, and she sensed that her days of privacy would be few from now on.

"Father's right," Young Tobiah said, speaking up for the first time, surprising Deborah. "We have your best interest in mind, and we'd know how to protect you the best."

"*We*?" Deborah said.

"I'm going to be one of your guards, Mother," Tobiah said. "You can't tell me I'm too young either. I'm only a few months away from turning fourteen, and that qualifies me for joining the army."

Deborah gazed into the dark eyes of her son, eyes so much like her husband's. "Very well," she said quietly. "Lapi will be the head of the guard, and he will choose the rest of the guards."

"Might I offer more advice?" Elder Reuben asked.

"Of course," Deborah said.

"When a petitioner arrives to seek judgment in the afternoon, ask them to eat and drink and sleep one night under the stars before approaching you with their complaint," Elder Reuben said. "Food and drink and sleep have a way of calming a man's temper."

Deborah smiled. She well knew that. "It shall be done."

The next hour sped by as Deborah and her family packed their belongings, loaded their horses, and made their farewells to Barak and the others. They'd be traveling with the elders until each elder split off to his village. Then she'd survey the location Lapi had suggested, and within a few days, she planned to be established there.

It was all happening so fast, yet for some reason, Deborah felt a sense of peace.

Before Lapi could help her onto the horse, Nathan approached. He grinned and bowed to Deborah, and before she could tell him to stop bowing to her, he said, "You will make a marvelous Judge, and Israel will soon be delivered under your direction."

This was not something Deborah had already learned, but she smiled at Nathan. "Thank you for your confidence and support. I hope you will receive the blessings you so desire."

Nathan's smile faded. "Thank you, Judge Deborah." He bowed and stepped away from her.

Deborah's heart ached to see the man's pain so clearly displayed in the depths of his eyes.

"Ready?" Lapi asked, his voice soft.

She placed her hand in his, reveling in his steady strength. She needed it more than ever. After she had settled on the horse, Lapi mounted behind her, and his left hand grasped her waist, his hold comforting and secure.

The convoy started its return journey, away from the training camp and away from the place she first learned of her new calling. Her sons' horses flanked hers and Lapi's, with the elders riding both in front and behind them. As Lapi guided their horse, Deborah looked behind them. Barak was hard at work with the men of Israel, preparing for a battle against their greatest enemy.

Chapter Twenty

Four Months Later

Barak shook Nathan's good hand, then clapped the man on the shoulder. "It's been a privilege to work with you," he said. Various groups of men had come and gone through training, while Nathan continued to stay month after month, helping with reorganization in preparation for the next group of Israelites.

Gilad had climbed upon Barak's horse and was scanning the large area of the training ground, looking for any pieces of weaponry left behind that could be repurposed for something else.

"It will be just you and your son for the next two days?" Nathan asked, his lined face squinting against the setting sun that shone directly into his face.

"Yes, we have done it many times now," Barak said. In truth, it was his sixth month here, four months after Deborah had left, and he was weary. He also missed his wife and daughters. He could only trust that while he was doing God's work, his family would be watched over as well.

"How far is your village?" Nathan asked.

"Two days' ride," Barak said. "Too far to visit my family at home."

Nathan nodded. He'd come for another round of training and stayed to help with the cleanup. "It is fortunate that you have your son with you. He is a fine warrior."

Barak exhaled. "He is. But my heart is divided when I see him fight."

Nathan's gaze shifted past Barak, and they both turned to watch Gilad for a few moments. The nineteen-year-old had grown from a boy to a man much too quickly, and more often than not, Gilad reminded Barak of himself.

"Yet, two of you out here, on your own . . ." Nathan's voice trailed off.

Barak gave the man a sharp look. "What are you saying, Nathan? Have you heard something?"

Nathan shook his head. "I haven't heard anything. It's just a feeling."

Barak had been training men for a long time, and many of them had fears and worries. Preparing for battle was like that, but Nathan's tone was different. "A feeling?" he prompted.

"I'm no Deborah," Nathan said. "But I feel things deeply." He shrugged. "Perhaps it's nothing."

As if in response to Nathan's statement, the wind shifted, and the hairs on Barak's arms rose. "Explain your feeling."

"When I think of leaving you and your son in this camp alone, waiting for the next group of men, dread overtakes me," he said. "I feel compelled to remain with you, at least until the next group of men arrives."

Barak nodded, seeing the conviction in Nathan's eyes. "I won't force you to leave, but I don't want to take you away from your duties or your home for longer than necessary. You are proficient in many battle skills, and you probably didn't need all this training."

"Perhaps not as much as the other men, as far as learning the skills," Nathan said. "But I needed to feel the comradery of being with my people, of preparing for the same cause, of feeling like we are of one heart and mind."

Barak could very well understand that.

"I will stay, then," Nathan said. "As long as it takes for the feeling to leave."

"We will welcome your help," Barak said. Perhaps Nathan would be a distraction and the time would go by faster. After this next training session, he planned to travel to his homestead to visit the rest of his family, even if it could be for only a short time.

"We have company." Nathan pointed past Barak, and he turned as a group of riders came over the hill.

With no guards, Barak had had no forewarning. And unlike the group of elders, these men were not Israelites. Their breastplates, which glinted in the light of the sunset, gave them away.

"Gilad!" Barak shouted, not caring that his voice might echo across the plains, because if he could see the Canaanite riders, they could see him as well. Barak turned to look for his son. Gilad had stopped his horse and was focused on the hills too. He'd spotted the riders.

"Leave the horse!" Barak cried out, running in the direction of the outcropping of boulders, beyond which were sunken caves. A location they'd preplanned to flee to if such an occurrence should happen.

Nathan didn't need to be told to follow, and the two men ran across the hard-packed ground, their footsteps mimicking their pounding hearts. Gilad quickly caught up with the two of them, his younger legs much faster.

"Stay low," Barak commanded, his breath coming in pants as they reached the boulders. "We don't want them to see where we descend."

Gilad's eyes were wide but his expression determined as he followed Barak, Nathan close behind. They crouched and crawled their way through the boulders. Barak passed one deep opening and a second. At the third cave opening, he descended. The darkness was complete within seconds, and Barak used his hands and feet to guide him.

"One hand on me," he told Gilad. "Nathan, one hand on Gilad."

Barak's labored breathing started to slow, but his heart rate continued to drum. If only they could stay hidden until night fell. Then they could creep out of the cave and find a way to defend themselves or escape.

The cave narrowed, and even with Barak stooping, he could go no farther. He came to a stop, and Gilad shuffled next to him.

No one spoke for a few moments, then Gilad whispered, "Who do you think it is? A scouting party?"

"No," Nathan whispered. "They were riding too fast. They already knew where they were going."

Barak's mind raced as he thought about how they could have been discovered. Had there been a spy among the Israelites? Or had someone been tortured to give out the information? He winced at the thought, but he knew it had been dangerous from the beginning. Training had always been dangerous, but on this larger scale, even more so.

"We only have an hour until it will be dark enough to leave the cave," Barak said. "Right now, there's nothing we can do and no reason to speculate. We'll just have to wait." He slid to the ground and found a space to sit.

Gilad and Nathan joined him, their knees touching in the darkness. Barak leaned his head back and closed his eyes, trying to calm his breathing and his racing heart.

So much would have to change now. They could no longer use these grounds for training. They'd have to find another place and get the word out again. He hoped they could do it in time so the men who were due in two days didn't fall into whatever trap the Canaanites would surely set now.

He did wonder who this group was. And how fast they'd get word back to King Jabin. What would the king do? Post soldiers at the passes leading to the training ground? Raise taxes in the surrounding villages again? Use someone as an example and kill them?

The sound of a skittering rock made Barak's blood run cold.

Then a shout echoed against the boulders above.

"We know you're hiding," the man shouted in his Canaanite language. "Come out, Barak, my friend."

If Barak's heart stopped, he wouldn't be surprised, for he recognized the man's voice.

Sisera.

Involuntarily, Barak grasped Gilad's arm and hissed, "Don't make a sound, no matter what."

Gilad didn't respond.

Good boy, Barak thought. His son knew the story of Sisera, how Kiva had come to be scarred, and why Barak's hand still pained him. But Barak had never thought he'd see the day where Sisera would be in the same place with Gilad.

The very thought of Sisera meeting Gilad made Barak want to empty his stomach. Cold perspiration broke out on his skin, and Sisera's next words were even more chilling.

"Give yourselves up, and we will show you mercy." Sisera was closer now.

Barak held his breath, trying to decipher every sound coming from above. He could hear the scatter of rocks, the scrape of a sandal against a boulder . . .

"We know there are three of you," Sisera said. "Not enough to contend against the twenty of us."

Barak knew he was sorely outnumbered and would have to find a way to escape.

"And when we find you," Sisera said, his voice farther away now, "you'll wish you'd given yourselves up."

Barak realized he was hearing another sound—a whisper. Nathan was whispering a prayer. Barak should be praying too, but he didn't dare distract himself from the sounds above. "Hush, Nathan. They might hear you."

Nathan's whispering stopped, and the silence that descended felt heavier. Every skitter of rock, every scrape of sandal or shoe, every word spoken above jolted through Barak as if he were experiencing his hand injury over and over.

The hours passed slowly, and Barak had no idea what time it was, but it had to be night now. They hadn't heard the Canaanites for some time, and Barak took that as a good sign.

"I will go above and see what I can," Barak whispered into the darkness. Nathan and Gilad shuffled so Barak could make it past them. He felt his way in the dark, his hands sliding along the cool, dry rocks as he walked along the uneven ground. The dusky scent of the cave was soon replaced by the fresher air of the outside, and Barak knew he was close to the surface.

And then finally, he saw a swath of stars, and the glittering light made Barak breathe easier. Yet his pulse began to rise. Where were the Canaanites? Were they waiting at the cave opening? Would they see him before he saw them?

He lifted his head into the open, and his eyes adjusted quickly to the lesser darkness. The first thing he noticed was the scent of smoke—a campfire—which meant that they weren't trying to hide their location. He looked from one boulder to another, confirming each was a boulder and not a crouching man. Then he scanned the terrain beyond, searching for signs of the Canaanites. Near the camp, their horses were tethered to the desert acacia trees, and beyond . . . The soldiers were making good use of Barak's belongings. The bedrolls had been collected, and the men were gathered in a circle around a small fire.

White smoke rose from the fire in the center of the circle of men, and Barak counted the forms he could see. Two short. Barak had no doubt that the missing two were on the lookout for him or perhaps had already spotted him. Barak ducked back into the cave, waiting to see if an arrow or a knife whooshed by. Nothing happened.

He could hear no conversation and no laughter from the group of men surrounding the fire. He raised his head, then crawled out of the hole, keeping as low as possible. If there was someone waiting for him, he'd rather be the one to fight them off. He didn't want anything to happen to Gilad.

Barak moved through the boulders, staying low, keeping track of how far he was moving from the original cave. He paused when he had a better view of the camp and the Canaanites. Then he scanned the area for possible escape routes. The hills were too far away to reach without notice, and the north stretched into more plains. Again, too visible for travelers.

That left traveling east, which would take them past the camp. Or west. They could travel west until they were able to evade the Canaanites, then wait a day before moving south, and make their way to their villages. Barak could think of only one thing—getting back to Evie and their family—and going into hiding again. If after fifteen years Sisera still remembered his name, Barak's family wasn't safe either.

He didn't see the two guards as he made his way back to the cave. He descended once again, gritting his teeth as his ankle twisted and sent a skittering of rocks beneath him. He bit back a cry and continued to move, more slowly and carefully this time.

When he bumped into Nathan, Barak whispered, "Sorry."

"What did you see?" Gilad asked.

Barak explained all that he'd seen and the danger of guards who were on watch.

"How long should we wait before escaping?" Gilad asked. "Until they're all asleep?"

"I don't think anyone will be sleeping," Barak said.

"I agree," Nathan said. "Besides, they'll post guards all night. If we leave now, we'll have a longer span of darkness to get farther west."

"But they'll expect us to leave, right?" Gilad asked.

"Right," Barak confirmed, swallowing hard. "We'll need to be ready to fight. Does everyone have their knives?"

Both Nathan and Gilad confirmed that they did.

"Good." Barak took a deep breath. "This is our plan. We'll rise to the surface one by one. I'll go first, then Nathan. When we give you the all clear, Gilad, be ready to move fast. We're going to stay low until we clear the larger boulders. Don't run until I give you the signal . . . or if we're spotted."

"We'll need to spread out too," Nathan said. "Divide up so they can't target us all at once."

Barak nodded. "I know Sisera, and he knows me. If anything goes wrong, I will stay behind to negotiate with him. You two continue your escape. We'll plan to meet in Ramah should we get separated. If both of you get separated, don't wait; just keep going."

"I will stay to contend with Sisera," Nathan said. "I have no family now. You have each other, and the rest of your family as well. I have no one. I only fight for Israel."

"No," Barak said. He could never allow another man to fight what was his own fight. "Sisera will use me as some sort of ransom against the Israelites. I'd rather that happen than one of you get caught. He might not be so merciful to you, or he'll torture you as a way to get my compliance."

Nathan didn't argue further, and Barak decided that was agreement enough. "Let's start up to the surface," Barak said. "Follow me."

Barak moved quicker and easier the second time he ascended, and Gilad and Nathan kept close behind. When Barak reached the top of the cave, he listened for a few moments before raising his head from the hole. All seemed to be as before. The soldiers looked to be in their same spots, and he counted the same number surrounding the fire. He climbed out of the cave and crouched among the boulders. Then he clicked his tongue a couple of times, signaling for Nathan to join him.

Moments later, Nathan emerged out of the hole. He moved to a boulder on the other side of the cave and gave Barak a nod. They stayed quiet for several more moments, then Barak clicked his tongue again, and Gilad emerged.

Barak didn't wait any longer. If there were guards watching the area, it would be a lot harder for three men to go undetected than one. They had to move now. Barak led the way, keeping low and moving around the boulders that made up the western landscape of the training grounds. With every step, his heart both soared to victory and plummeted with another moment exposed to possible discovery by the Canaanites.

He began counting paces once they cleared the boulders and headed toward a thicket of acacia trees. The forms were dark beneath the moonlight, looking like gnarled limbs twisting toward the sky. Once beyond those, Barak knew they could move upright and start running. The trees would act as a decent barrier between them and the camp.

It wasn't a sound that alerted Barak but a feeling. They were perhaps twenty paces away from the acacia when he felt compelled to warn the others. "Get down," he hissed.

Gilad hit the ground at the same time Barak did. Then Barak heard it. The whoosh of an arrow passing right where his torso had been. Then another whoosh of an arrow, but this one didn't pass by. It thudded into Nathan's back. He'd been a second too late diving to the ground.

Barak twisted to see his friend trying to rise, an arrow protruding from the center of his upper back.

"Keep running," Barak told Gilad, whose eyes were wide in the moonlight at the sight of the fallen Nathan. "I'll catch up."

"We have to help him," Gilad said, his voice high with panic.

"You have to get to the trees," Barak said, fighting not to yell at his son. "Get to the trees now, and I'll help Nathan."

"They're coming!" Gilad said, horror in his voice.

Indeed, the soldiers were climbing over the boulders, and two more arrows were sailing their way. "Duck!"

The arrows missed any human targets, and Barak turned to his son, no longer keeping his voice down. Fifteen paces to go. "Run!" Barak yelled.

Gilad turned, nearly stumbling, and began to run.

Then came the dreaded sound that Barak hoped to never hear in his lifetime. His son's blood-curdling scream. Barak didn't need to look to know that Gilad had been hit by an arrow.

"I've been hit," Nathan yelled in the Canaanite dialect, pushing himself to his feet.

Barak snapped his head to look at the older man. He was walking toward the pursuing Canaanites.

"You fool!" Barak cried out.

"Save your son," Nathan shot back, then continued to call to the Canaanites in their language, "Have mercy on an old man!"

Barak couldn't wait any longer. If the man wanted to walk directly into a horde of Canaanites, then that was his choice. Before Barak could turn to assess what had happened to Gilad, another arrow hit Nathan. This time in the thigh.

Nathan sank to his knees, his arms outstretched. "Have mercy!" he cried. He was trying to distract the soldiers, this Barak knew. And Nathan would go to his grave doing it. Barak's stomach roiled at the sacrifice the man was making, but he had to get to his son too.

He turned on his heel and headed toward the injured Gilad. The boy was limping toward the acacia trees, and Barak saw the arrow that had found its way into Gilad's calf. Not a life-threatening blow, *if* he could keep Gilad from getting hit again.

"You're outnumbered, Barak!" Sisera called behind him.

Ten paces. Barak sprinted, although his upright posture was only making him a bigger target to the archers.

"We gave you a chance to live!" Sisera continued. "Now you'll pay for it."

Five paces.

Barak reached Gilad. "Get on my back," he yelled. "Now!" He crouched in front of his son, and as soon as Gilad's knees locked onto Barak's waist, he straightened and started to run in long, loping steps.

Nathan was still yelling at the Canaanites, somehow still coherent after having two arrows in his body, and Sisera's voice boomed above Nathan's.

Barak didn't look left or right but focused only on the ground as he carried his son. The weight of the body on his back was of no significance, and he ignored the burning in his thighs and calves. Once he got Gilad to safety, Barak could turn back and . . . what?

He had only a knife. No spear he could throw. No bow and arrows to shoot.

"Fire!" Nathan yelled.

Barak felt like he was in a bizarre nightmare. Why was Nathan yelling about fire?

They reached the trees, and the branches scraped Barak's arms and legs as he plowed past the trees.

"Fire," Gilad said, his voice coming in pants. "Let's start a fire!"

"What are you talking about?"

"Burn the trees," Gilad said. "Give us more time."

Barak nearly stumbled as his foot hit a root.

"I have chert," Gilad said.

Barak's thoughts collided. He wanted to run and put as much distance between himself and Sisera as possible. But his breathing was ragged, his legs trembling, and he knew he was losing ground.

Barak took three more steps, then sank to his knees. "Get the chert," he rasped.

Gilad slid from his back with a grunt, then he handed over a pouch. The moonlight was spotty in the grove, and Barak fumbled inside the pouch until he grasped the chert. With trembling hands, he struck the chert against a rock as Gilad scrambled about for some tinder. When they had a spark, Barak blew on it, igniting a flame.

He added more tinder, then anything dry that he could. With the fire still a young thing, Barak turned to Gilad. He used his turban to tie Gilad's leg above the protruding arrow, then he told him to bite down on the pouch. Gilad did so as Barak worked the arrow out of Gilad's calf.

His son's scream was stifled, but Barak kept his focus, and miraculously, Gilad fainted.

"Let's get out of here," Barak said, even though Gilad couldn't hear him. Barak lifted him in his arms, knowing he could only get so far. But right now, adrenaline was helping him with his grown son's weight.

As Barak hurried through the grove, he no longer felt the scrape of the branches or the burning in his muscles. He no longer heard Nathan's cries or Sisera's threats. All he knew was that the fire was growing, and the smell of smoke was the best thing he could hope for right now.

If he didn't live to see the sun rise another day, he'd at least done all that he could.

Chapter Twenty-One

Deborah peeked through the tent flap. A large group of people had assembled themselves outside her tent. It was a new moon, and although she should be getting used to the petitioners who sought her for counsel, she still marveled at the Israelites who came seeking—both young and old, male and female, those who were healthy, sick, wealthy, or destitute.

Lapi had taken his assignment to be her protector seriously. He'd always been her protector, yet this was now on a grander scale. He'd brought Abner and Chaim in on rotating months, and two other men also worked as guards. He'd even had Young Tobiah take on some shifts—something Deborah didn't like, but Lapi insisted that their son was a man now and needed a man's responsibilities.

Deborah shifted her gaze from the gathered petitioners to where Lapi stood beneath the large palm tree—the location where she'd sit and hand down judgments. Lapi was speaking with someone Deborah didn't recognize. At least, not at first. When Lapi changed his stance, Deborah was surprised to see Elder Reuben. He wasn't due for a few weeks.

By the look on his face, the news he was delivering to Lapi wasn't pleasant. Lapi chose that moment to look over at the tent, his expression dark and worried.

Deborah stepped back, letting the tent flap fall. Elder Reuben had been on her mind for a couple of days, and she hadn't thought much of it. Now she wondered if she'd had a prompting that she'd be seeing him soon.

If the news was bad, she sensed Lapi would be entering the tent soon. She looked about the place that had been her home for four months. They'd kept it simple, to three sections only. One was a private room for Lapi and her, the other for their sons. The main area served as a gathering place, plus a cooking room. She hadn't needed the cooking room yet. According to the elders, other people considered it a spiritual calling to serve the Judge. Two elderly sisters lived in another tent nearby, and they did all the cooking for her family. This allowed Deborah to spend more time with the petitioners and finish each day at sunset instead of working into the hours of the night.

"Deborah," Lapi said, and she turned to see him coming into the tent.

Sure enough, Elder Reuben was right behind him.

"What is it?" Deborah asked immediately, skipping over any sort of greeting.

"We've had grave news," Elder Reuben said. "I think we should sit."

Deborah didn't want to sit; she didn't want to wait. But Lapi crossed to her and grasped her hand. So she sat with him on the section of cushions they reserved for guests. Elder Reuben took his place across from them.

"Barak's training grounds have been discovered by the Canaanites," Elder Reuben said.

Deborah could only stare. "How? What happened?"

Elder Reuben looked at Lapi, and Lapi's hand tightened about hers.

"Tell me," she demanded.

"We are not sure if there were spies among us or if it was discovered some other way," Elder Reuben said. "But the soldiers who arrived were led by Sisera, commander of—"

"No," Deborah cried out before Elder Reuben could finish. "What's happened to Barak?" Her eyes burned with tears as she looked at her husband.

"He's disappeared, with Gilad," Lapi said.

"No one has seen them yet," Elder Reuben said in a quiet voice. "We have no reason to believe they are dead, but there is evidence of . . . destruction."

"What kind of destruction?" Deborah whispered.

"We sent scouts to examine the training grounds. They found arrows littering the ground. The Canaanites didn't even bother collecting them, which tells me there was a pursuit." He fell quiet for a moment. "And there was a fire."

"Did they find any . . . bodies?" Deborah whispered the last word.

"No," Elder Reuben said. "The scouts searched the entire area for hours. But they couldn't find evidence of Barak's trail. The rain had washed everything away."

Yesterday morning, there had been a rainstorm. Deborah had been grateful for the moisture, but now she saw that it had only made it harder to find Barak. And . . . harder for the Canaanites to find him as well.

"It seems that the Canaanites don't believe he's dead either," Elder Reuben continued. "King Jabin, at the bequest of Sisera, has put out an edict announcing a reward for Barak's capture. Soldiers are going from village to village requesting information about him. Asking questions."

Deborah closed her eyes. "They will execute Barak when they find him."

Elder Reuben's answer was soft. "Yes."

She rose to her feet and began to pace the chamber. "Where is his family?"

"Still in their village, as far as we know," Elder Reuben said.

Deborah looked over at Lapi and saw the same thoughts in his eyes that were going through her mind.

"We need to bring his family into our protection," Lapi said. "Can some scouts be spared to bring Barak's family here?"

"It will be dangerous for whoever takes on that task," Elder Reuben said.

"You must go," Deborah said to Lapi. "We can't send men Evie doesn't know. She will refuse to leave. If you go, she will understand the necessity and come with you."

"But who will guard *you*, Deborah?" Elder Reuben said. "I wouldn't be surprised if the Canaanites know about your role at the training grounds. And as the new Judge of Israel, they might come here and demand that you find him."

"We must find him regardless," Deborah said, meeting her husband's gaze. "If he's alive, we need to find him."

Lapi rose to his feet and crossed to Deborah. He grasped her hands. "What are you planning?"

"I will ask God what I should do, and then I'll do it."

Lapi nodded. "You found him once. But I don't want to leave you unguarded."

Deborah squeezed his hands. "My brothers will come and watch over me; besides, we have our sons too. You go fetch Evie and her girls. We can't delay either task."

Lapi hesitated. She knew he wasn't going to argue with her, but he would think through every scenario before acting. Finally, he said, "As soon as Abner and Chaim arrive, I will be ready to leave."

Deborah should have felt nervous about sending her husband on such an errand. Surely he'd be stopped and questioned by the Canaanites, and once he was with Evie and her family, the danger would only be worse. But all Deborah felt was determination and conviction that this was the right course. This was the feeling she'd learned to trust and to understand that this was one of God's ways of communicating with her.

The next hours sped by as she met with the petitioners beneath the palm tree while her heart was focused on what might have happened to Barak and Gilad and if she'd see them again.

When the heat of the late afternoon was at its worst, Deborah took a meal break and met Lapi inside the tent. Her sons came inside too, full of questions about Barak and Gilad and how they wanted to join a search party.

Deborah lifted a hand. "Nothing will happen until Abner and Chaim arrive," she said. "We can't all run off into the wilderness. There are Canaanite spies out in full force, and you would be followed immediately."

In fact, two of the petitioners who'd come this afternoon hadn't approached Deborah yet, and she sensed they were either Canaanites trying to appear as Israelites, or Israelites who were spies.

"We are here, sister," a man's voice cut in.

Her brothers, Abner and Chaim, stepped through the entrance of the tent. Deborah hurried toward them and embraced them both. Abner chuckled and squeezed her tight. Chaim was more sober and kissed her cheek, then turned to Lapi. "Do you need me to travel with you to Barak's village?"

"I'll travel alone," Lapi said. "I'll draw less notice that way, and I don't want to leave Deborah here without knowing you and Abner will watch over her."

Chaim nodded, his jaw tightening.

Abner spoke next. "When Elder Reuben brought the news, I wondered if Barak would make his way back to our old homestead."

Deborah nodded. "I've considered that too."

"But you don't *know*," Abner stated.

"No, I don't," Deborah said, and she knew her brother was asking if she'd received a revelation from God about Barak's whereabouts. God didn't work the same in every case. Perhaps He would show her a stream of smoke again, but it could be entirely different this time. *If* it was His will that Barak and Gilad be found.

The men, including her sons, all watched her.

"Have you had any other . . . impressions?" Chaim asked.

Deborah took a deep breath. "Nothing specific," she admitted. "But I feel peace." Again, she didn't know if the peace was because they'd soon find Barak alive and healthy or because it was God's will that Barak was now in His care.

"Yet, you think we should look for Barak?" Chaim pressed.

There was no doubt about that in her mind. "Yes, I do. How and when has not been revealed to me." She looked to Abner and said, "Thank you for coming so quickly. Both of you. Lapi has been anxious to get started on his mission. Once we know Evie and her girls are safe, we will all rest easier."

As Lapi made his final preparations to leave, Deborah felt worry set in. She had to tell herself to focus on the peaceful conviction she'd felt earlier. She walked with Lapi around the tent to the stables, where he had readied his horse.

"Travel safe," she said, reaching up and kissing him.

Lapi pulled her in close. "I don't like leaving you."

"I don't like missing you," she said, gazing into the brown eyes of the man she loved. "May God watch over you."

Lapi ran his fingers along her cheek. "I will return as soon as possible. Although I think this is only the beginning of the troubles we'll be facing."

Deborah nodded. "I agree, but in the end, we can only have faith."

Lapi kissed her again, then he mounted his horse. Deborah watched as he rode away from the stables, his broad shoulders squared, his posture erect.

Then Deborah looked to the line of petitioners that had already formed. The two men she was suspicious of lingered at the back of the line. They never seemed to move forward but merely kept an eye on things. Well, Deborah had nothing to hide. Her counseling might be done individually, but it could also apply to many more people should they choose to listen.

She walked toward her spot beneath the palm tree and sat.

A man stepped forward, and Deborah noticed the burn scars on his hands and arms. She immediately thought of the fire Elder Reuben had told her about. She blinked away the memory and focused on the man's complaint against his neighbor and their issues over their property division. Since the neighbor hadn't come to petition his own side, Deborah could only give her advice, followed by her blessing and counsel for love and peace. "You will be neighbors the rest of your lives," she said. "Would you rather live with good feelings toward your neighbor instead of ill will?"

The man nodded, looking chagrined.

"You are correct in feeling what you do, but if you do not approach your neighbor with the intent to compromise, and listen to his reasonings, then there is little chance of peace between the two of you."

The line continued, and Deborah listened, spoke, listened some more, but all the while, her mind kept straying to her husband and how his journey fared. She had to trust in God that he would be safe, or else why would she have felt such a peaceful conviction? It was practically a physical thing, to keep reminding herself to hold that trust strong.

By the time the sun set, Deborah was exhausted, more so than usual. She felt as if she'd been holding herself together emotionally when all she wanted to do was sink onto her knees in prayer and supplication for her husband's safe travels and Barak's and Gilad's health and safety. Barak had lived a life of service, and surely God still needed him. And what about his son, Gilad? The young man was merely nineteen and had an entire life to live out.

Abner took Deborah's place and told the petitioners there would be no more counseling until the next morning. Deborah was grateful for his interference and surmised he'd noticed her exhaustion. Abner walked Deborah back to her tent. "Your sons have prepared hot water for you to wash in," he said.

Deborah stepped into the gathering room and found that her sons had arranged the meal and were standing proudly by the table. "You boys are spoiling me," she said with a smile.

Young Tobiah laughed. "We only set out the meal. The other women prepared it, as usual."

Abram motioned toward a basin of steaming water. "You can bathe your feet first," he said. "We won't mind the wait."

Deborah turned to Abner. "Bring Chaim, and we'll eat as a family."

"He'll not want to leave his post."

"I know," Deborah said. "Tell him to come anyway."

While Abner was gone, Deborah soaked her feet for a few minutes. This simple act made her feel better and less anxious. By the time she'd dried her feet, Chaim stepped into the tent.

As expected, his brows were drawn together in displeasure.

"Sit, brother," Deborah said cheerfully. "You can leave as soon as you've eaten, but I want to break bread with my family tonight."

Chaim nodded, not saying anything, and that was a probably a good thing. When he was quiet, Deborah knew he was working hard not to be contentious.

Abner offered the prayer of gratitude for the food, then the meal began. Deborah appreciated the time and preparation that went into these meals others made, but she did miss the routine of cooking and feeding her family. She'd taken satisfaction early in her marriage in preparing food and watching her husband enjoy eating it, and his appreciation that followed.

She'd felt the same things with her sons—being able to perform such a physical service and seeing the immediate results of that service. And now her service had changed, and others were serving her. As the men discussed Barak and the Canaanites in low tones, Deborah didn't interject her thoughts but merely observed the men in her life—men who had dedicated so much time to her well-being so she could fulfill her calling.

She was grateful her sons were mostly independent now and that they were so supportive. She knew they followed their father's example. When she thought of her initial resistance to marrying Lapi, she wanted to laugh at her past foolishness. It seemed God had been more than patient, as had Lapi, because God had known the type of husband Deborah needed.

Deborah closed her eyes as the men talked. She wondered where Barak and Gilad could be right now, if they were healthy, if they were hungry. Where would they have gone? What sort of living conditions were they enduring? She couldn't think of them as deceased. Instead, she considered the various directions they could have traveled when leaving the training grounds. One by one, she ruled out each possibility.

And then she knew. It was rather simple, when she thought about it. And she was surprised it hadn't been the first location she'd thought of.

She opened her eyes and cleared her throat.

One by one, the men turned to look at her, giving her their full attention.

"I know where Barak is," she said. "Who will come with me to fetch him?"

Chapter Twenty-Two

Barak woke to the sound of a woman humming. That couldn't be right. He was in the middle of the wilderness, and he'd heard only the buzz of insects or the call of birds for days. Not even Gilad would be humming. Barak's son was in a poor state, and each morning when Barak awoke, he had to do the hard thing of checking his son's pulse to see if he was still alive.

Barak couldn't quite open his eyes yet, but his mind was becoming more and more alert. He turned his head, knowing that was the direction he'd last seen Gilad lying on his side. He was a strong young man, but after three days in the wilderness suffering a festering wound, he'd grown weak.

Barak had done the best he could in caring for Gilad's wound. But last night before dark had fallen, his son's leg had swollen to twice its normal size.

The woman's humming continued, and Barak wondered if he was in the half-dream-half-awake state. But her voice didn't sound like the women he was familiar with. Not Evie or Deborah or even Kiva. And it wasn't either of his daughters.

Although the effort of opening his eyes was greater than he expected, he dragged open his eyelids. He blinked a couple of times, feeling the dry grit, which only stung his eyes more. Instead of a scraggly desert bush and, beyond that, endless sand and rock, Barak saw a length of fabric. Pale blue. Touched by light. He blinked again. Where was he?

He tried to prop himself up on his elbows, but searing pain shot through his shoulder muscles—the ones he'd strained carrying his son away from the fire they'd set at the training camp. The images from that night still followed Barak: Sisera. The Canaanites. Hiding underground. Running as arrows sailed around them. Nathan's surrender. Barak carrying Gilad deeper into the wilderness, with a raging fire blocking the Canaanites' way.

Barak still wasn't sure if he'd been blessed or cursed that night. Blessed because he and his son were still alive. Or cursed because they were now slowly dying in the wilderness.

The humming stopped, and the silence was more disturbing than the humming. Was Barak now awake? But why was he still seeing the pale-blue curtain? And what was that fragrant scent of something cooking . . . ? *Meat cooking.*

Barak groaned as he rolled onto his side. Pain lanced through his limbs, and he almost gasped as the muscles in his shoulders throbbed. Gilad wasn't lying next to him, where he was supposed to be. And Barak was lying on a mat instead of the desert ground. Where was his son?

"Gilad," he called out, but it only sounded like a raspy whisper.

The scent of cooking wafted around him. If he was smelling cooking meat, did that mean he'd been rescued? Or captured? Was he on Canaanite property, awaiting a trial, only to be accused and found guilty? Would he be given a final meal before his execution?

The scent grew stronger, and Barak's stomach felt like it had flipped over. He couldn't ever remember being so hungry—he felt so desperate that he was delirious. Yet, he couldn't bring himself to sit up, let alone rise to his feet and find the location of the food.

Perhaps he was a prisoner, and he'd be sentenced to smelling the cooking food while he slowly starved to death. He had to move. He had to force himself to get to where the food was. He had to eat, and then he had to find his son and make sure he ate too.

Gilad.

"Where are you, Gilad?" Barak managed to croak again.

What if calling for his son brought the wrong kind of attention? Barak blinked his eyes again, trying to focus on his surroundings. Everything seemed to be a pale blue, except for the mat he lay upon. That was made of dried palm leaves.

Then the humming resumed.

"Hello?" Barak rasped.

There was no response, but he was sure there'd been a break in the humming.

"Can someone help me?" he said, his voice more audible now. He lifted his head, wincing but forcing himself to study the area. More blue.

"You're awake," a woman said. Her voice came from somewhere behind him.

There was no way Barak could look up or twist around.

"Who are you?" Barak said, wishing he had a drink to soothe his scorched throat. "Where am I?"

The woman gave a soft laugh, and then suddenly, she stepped into view.

Barak wouldn't be surprised if he woke up from this strange dream to find that the woman standing above him was in no way real. For she wore a ring he recognized. Which meant she could be only one person: Jael.

"How are you feeling?" Jael said in a soft voice.

She knelt beside him, her dark-brown eyes wide as she watched him carefully, as if he were a desert hare ready to leap away.

"I am . . ." The words stuck in his throat, and he cleared it. "Where's my son? Where's Gilad?"

He hoped Jael's smile meant Gilad was fine.

"Gilad has been very ill," she said.

No, Barak thought. He tried to push himself up, but the pain stole his breath.

"Rest," the woman said, placing a hand on his arm. "There is nothing you can do to help your son."

She must have seen the panic in his eyes, because Jael said, "Gilad lives, but he needs time to recover. You'll be a better help to him once you're well yourself."

"How—how did you find us?" Barak asked, laying his head back down. He was out of breath with the effort.

"Heber found you many miles from our home while out hunting with one of our sons," Jael said. "You were both half-dead. Heber doesn't want any trouble from the Canaanites or the Israelites, but he recognized that you were in dire need of help, so they brought you here."

Barak thought about what a miracle this truly was. To be happened upon by a man he'd met only once. The memories of hiding in the caves from Sisera, then emerging in the night and running from the Canaanites, Nathan's sacrifice, and Gilad's injury. The fire, followed by excruciating days of trying to survive, without leaving any trace to be discovered by the Canaanites.

"Thank you." Emotion welled in his eyes as he thought of the number of times he'd come close to death over the past few days. "From the depths of my soul, I thank you." His voice cracked, and his throat closed off.

Jael nodded, a smile on her face and her own eyes moist with tears. "You have endured grave trials, Barak. All I know is that your God is not finished with you. It seems you still have work to do on this earth."

Her words could not have driven more deeply into his soul, and he knew she was right. There was only one reason God could have spared him again and again. Barak's mission wasn't over.

"Jael," a man's voice said from somewhere outside the tent walls.

"I must go," she told Barak. "Rest, and I will return soon to check on you. I will also bring back a report about your son."

Barak watched the woman leave. She was an angel on earth, of that he had no doubt. First, she'd cared for his sister, Kiva, and now he and his son were being nursed back to health.

Barak closed his eyes and fell into a light sleep, one in which he dreamed of a day that he and his family would live free of fear and persecution by the Canaanites. Free of the ever-present fear of Sisera discovering his activities. Free from the grueling days of teaching men how to fight for their lives.

When Barak next opened his eyes, the inside of the tent was dim with the fallen night. An oil lamp flickered, and the orange glow illuminated the form of a man sitting a few paces away. The man's beard was gray, his cheekbones prominent. He wore a gold circlet in one of his ears.

"Heber," Barak said, testing out his parched voice. It felt stronger now.

Heber seemed to understand Barak's plight, and he moved forward and helped Barak drink from a cup.

The cool water was the best thing Barak could ever remember tasting. Heber was patient in helping him drink, yet Barak hated being so dependent.

"There is barley soup too," Heber said, setting down the cup and picking up a bowl. "It's tepid now but will be nourishing."

"Can you help me sit?" Barak said. "I don't want to make you feed me too."

Heber chuckled and helped Barak sit, then piled a couple of cushions behind Barak for him to lean on.

Barak picked up the bowl of soup. His limbs protested every movement, but he decided to push through the pain—it meant that he'd survived. That he was alive.

After Barak had managed to swallow some of the soup, Heber said, "I'd like to know what happened. When you're ready to tell me the tale."

Barak set the soup down. "You remember when you and your wife so kindly cared for my sister, Kiva?"

Heber's brows drew together. "Yes, but it has been years since that incident."

"It has been fifteen years, to be exact," Barak said, "but some things a man never forgets. Not me, and not Sisera."

Heber's brows shot up at this. "Your condition has to do with the commander Sisera?" Before Barak could speak again, Heber said, "You were running the Israelite training camp, were you not? I should have guessed it . . . and I should have known the Canaanites would discover it eventually."

It was Barak's turn to stare now. "How did you know about it?"

Heber smiled. "I'm a desert man, remember. Not much gets past my notice."

"Well, I am grateful, then," Barak said, "that you found me."

The man shrugged as if it weren't a big deal that he'd saved Barak's and his son's lives. "Did you fight a duel with Sisera?"

"Not quite," Barak said, and he proceeded to tell Heber how the Canaanites rode their horses over the hills to the training camp where Barak, Nathan, and Gilad had been preparing for the next group.

Heber listened, captivated, asking questions from time to time. He seemed both horrified and impressed at the turn of events, especially when Barak told him about Nathan trying to distract the soldiers and losing his own life in the process.

"I met Nathan of Bethel once," Heber said.

This surprised Barak, yet it shouldn't have. After all, Heber had said himself that he was a desert man.

"He was in an archery contest there when my sons and I were passing through. We heard of the contest, and we were curious enough to go watch."

"I'm assuming Nathan won?" Barak said.

Heber chuckled. "You assume right. He was impressive to watch."

Barak nodded, and both men fell silent, the memory of a hero on their minds. A man who had lived through terrible trials yet had put others before his own life.

"There is another who I've heard is a good archer," Heber said in a quiet voice.

"Oh?" Barak said, wondering where Heber was going with this conversation.

"I believe there is a family connection to you as well," Heber continued. "Deborah, the new Judge of Israel."

Barak exhaled as he thought about Deborah and her new calling. The Canaanites would already know about the death of Shamgar and the rise of Deborah. Was she safe? Would Sisera dare disrupt her ascension? "She is married to my cousin Lapidoth, whom you met," Barak told Heber.

"Yes, I remember Lapidoth," Heber said. "He was a quiet but loyal man."

"He will be searching for me," Barak said, "even though he should be staying with Deborah and protecting her. I'll find him and warn him about Sisera."

Heber poured more water into the cup and handed it over to Barak. As Barak drank, Heber watched, then said, "You and Gilad need to fully recover before you leave. Think about what you've escaped. Sisera probably has soldiers looking for you in every village. He's not going to let you escape a third time."

"No," Barak agreed. "Not after seeing what they did to Nathan. But I don't want anyone else put in danger on my behalf."

Heber took the cup that Barak returned. "We live in dangerous times," Heber said. "That hasn't changed with your altercation with Sisera, but it does let Sisera know the Israelites are planning an attack or, at the very least, are going to defend themselves on a grander scale."

"That is what Shamgar wanted us to prepare for," Barak said. "His instruction was the very reason we set up the mass training ground in the first place. But now he is gone."

"What does Deborah say?" Heber asked.

Barak leaned forward. Pain lanced through him, but he'd rather sit up for a while than give in and lie down again. "She trained with us, even worked with Nathan on target shooting with a bow and arrow. Without asking her, I've no doubt she will instruct me along the same lines that Shamgar did."

"I believe you're right," Heber said in a thoughtful tone. "I have never understood the Canaanites' oppression of your people. I know there are two sides and two opinions in everything, yet I have seen and heard of tragedies that should not have been borne. Take Nathan, for example. His daughter was an innocent. There was no reason for the Canaanites to capture his daughter and force her to the temples."

Barak might be an invalid, but this talk was making his anger rise. And it both exhausted him and sent a surge of adrenaline through him. "There have been many wrongs, and my family has been grateful for your help, even though you do not pledge allegiance to either side."

"Don't think I am without opinion," Heber clarified. "If someone is unfairly treated, I will step in and do what I can. No matter their race or religion."

"You are a unique man," Barak said. "And I consider it a blessing to know you."

Heber smiled. "Then, my friend, go back to sleep. Rest well. For tomorrow, I believe your son will want to see you."

A warm buzz ran through Barak. "Do you think so?"

Heber chuckled. "Most definitely." He refilled Barak's cup with the cool water and set it by his mat. Then Heber gathered the bowl that had contained the barley broth. "Good night, my friend."

When Barak was left alone again, the pain still pulsed through his body, but his stomach was satisfied, and he knew that as soon as the sun rose, he would move forward with his next plans. And that included seeing his son at last.

Chapter Twenty-Three

Deborah rode in front of Abner and Chaim, with Young Tobiah in the rear. They'd first delivered Abram to Kiva's home. Elder Reuben would take up residence at Deborah's new homestead and await the arrival of Lapi and Evie, then inform them of Deborah's mission.

Deborah hoped she wasn't leading her brothers and son into disappointment. But when the idea came of Barak going to the plains of Zaanaim, and more specifically the homestead of Heber the Kenite and his wife, Jael, Deborah couldn't shake the thought. The impression had been accompanied by a surety that she'd come to recognize as personal revelation. And no matter how many times she'd tried to talk herself out of trusting those impressions, they'd proven correct time and time again.

So, here they were, riding toward the plains of Zaanaim, keeping off the main roads to avoid other travelers. Deborah had changed out of the Judges' robes she'd inherited from Shamgar and instead wore a plain traveling cloak. She'd also covered her head with a dark-green mantle and had a veil at the ready should she need it.

If they encountered any Canaanite soldiers, she fully planned to act as the reticent Israelite woman. She didn't want the Canaanites to follow them and find Barak. The sun was now high in the sky, and the wind was the only saving grace against the unbearable heat. They should spend time resting beneath one of the palm groves, but Deborah was too anxious. She not only had to find Barak, but she also had to secure him a safe place to live. And she didn't want to be gone too long from Lapi or Abram.

She slowed her horse to ride by Young Tobiah. "How are you doing, son?" she asked.

Tobiah looked over at her, a gleam in his eyes. He looked so much like his father that Deborah had to smile.

"I'm glad we're finally doing something," he said. "Not that I don't want to help Father at our new homestead, but seeing all the travelers coming and going makes me feel like I'm wasting my days."

She drew her horse closer to his and laid a hand on his arm. "You've never wasted a day. And once we've reduced the threat of the Canaanites, I'll not need so many guards."

"Do you think we'll fight them soon?" Tobiah asked.

Before Deborah could respond, Abner said in a low voice, "There's someone up ahead."

Deborah lifted her gaze, and the hairs on the back of her neck rose. Two men were coming toward them, riding on horses, leaning forward on their beasts as if they were trying to counter the wind. Most likely, they weren't Israelites, although they didn't appear to be Canaanite soldiers either.

Deborah immediately pulled her veil in place and said to Tobiah, "Remember what I told you should we encounter strangers."

"I remember," he said. "Say nothing."

"Correct." Through the thin fabric of her veil, Deborah watched the horsemen approach. They were desert men, and their arms were tanned and lean with muscle. They each rode with a waterskin strapped over their bare torsos. Their sand-colored turbans flapped in the wind, and they made no signs of slowing as they approached.

Perhaps they'd pass by Deborah's group.

As they neared, it was clear that one man was older, the other man younger—only sixteen or seventeen. Deborah held her breath as the men continued past and beyond. But they didn't ride out of sight. Instead, they slowed and turned their horses and started to follow.

"What are they doing?" Tobiah whispered, looking behind them.

"I don't know," Deborah said. They were still a couple of hours' ride from the plains of Zaanaim, and this area of the country wasn't well traveled. Perhaps the desert men were just curious. The fact that there hadn't been any greeting on their part told Deborah they probably spoke another language.

Abner stopped his horse and turned it around to face the approaching desert men. Chaim turned too, and Deborah had no choice but to stop with Tobiah.

The desert men didn't seem surprised, and they continued confidently, then stopped mere paces from Abner.

Instead of looking at Abner or Chaim, the older desert man focused on Deborah. His face was tanned and scarred, his beard a mixture of gray and black. He wore a gold circular on one of his ears and several chains and leather necklaces about his neck, which was more jewelry than what many Israelite women wore.

And despite her veil, Deborah felt as if the man could clearly see her face.

"You are Deborah, the Fourth Judge of Israel?"

Deborah nearly gasped. Abner and Chaim moved their horses in front of hers, coming between her and the desert men.

The older one raised his hand. "I am Heber the Kenite. We are no enemy of Israel."

Deborah tugged off her veil. "I am Deborah," she said. "We are searching for Barak Kedesh-naphtali. Have you heard of his fate?"

Heber exchanged glances with the younger man, who Deborah now assumed was his son. Both had the same deep-set eyes and long, narrow nose. "We do know of his fate," Heber said at last. "We discovered Barak and Gilad two days ago."

Deborah's heart leapt at the news of Gilad, but were they both still alive?

Before she could ask the question, the younger man said, "They are recovering slowly. When we found them, they were nearly dead."

The statement was blunt, but one that Deborah appreciated, especially since these two men seemed to be rescuers. Not to mention part of the family who'd cared for Kiva when she'd been scarred by Sisera.

Deborah urged her horse forward, and her brothers separated, allowing her through. "Then we are indeed fortunate to meet you on our way to your homestead. For we have been traveling these past two days in order to speak with your family."

The two desert men stared at her. "You knew Barak would come here?" Heber asked. "Did he plan this?"

"No," Deborah said. "There was never any agreement that should he have to flee from the Canaanites, he would come to the plains of Zaanaim. I had a feeling that this might be a location he'd try to escape to."

Heber's brows lifted. "Barak was right. He said you'd be searching for him." He held up a hand. "I have heard many stories about Deborah over the years, and this will yet be another story that will spread across the land."

He nodded to Abner and Chaim. "You are her brothers? Barak told me about you as well."

"How do we know you are Heber the Kenite?" Chaim interrupted, his voice gruff.

Heber nodded. "Ah. Perhaps I can offer you some information that only I would know."

Deborah wanted to argue with Chaim, but she let the conversation between the men continue.

"Barak's sister was here many years ago," he said. "My wife is Jael, and she was given a ring from a woman in Barak's village. Vania was her name."

Chaim nodded, appearing satisfied.

"Follow me, then," Heber said. "We'll take you back to our homestead. Jael will want to celebrate your arrival. I hope you are all hungry."

Tobiah laughed, and Deborah looked over at her son. Relief washed over his face.

Deborah set off after Heber with no hesitation. Abner and Chaim followed, then Tobiah and Heber's son.

They rode with the desert wind along the plains of Zaanaim. After about an hour, Heber directed them to a well, and he drew water for the horses to drink. Deborah felt impatient to reach Barak, so when they mounted their horses again, she was relieved.

She didn't know what she expected to see when they arrived at Heber's homestead, but the place looked like its own small village. Several structures had been built, along with a sprawling tent with multiple chambers if the peaks and valleys were any indication. A large pen of goats sat on the north side, while a stable with more horses occupied the south.

A woman stood beneath the tent's canopy that stretched over the entrance. Her long tunic was a pale blue, and her light-brown hair was plaited, hanging over one shoulder. Her bare arms were covered with at least a dozen silver bracelets, and two anklets shone at her ankles. When her gaze met Deborah's, the woman offered a tentative smile.

"Jael," Heber said. "This is Deborah. She's come for Barak and Gilad."

The woman's smile broadened.

Heber continued the introductions, and Jael walked toward Deborah. "Come inside," she said, then looked at the men. "All of you. Bathe your feet and take refreshment. Barak will be pleased to see all of you."

"My husband and son will feed and water your horses while you rest from your journey," Jael continued. "Barak told me he'd been praying to be reunited with his family. It seems the Israelite God listened to him."

"We are indebted for your hospitality," Deborah said as Jael linked their arms together.

Jael had no hesitation in drawing Deborah into the tent chamber. A younger woman, who appeared to be Jael's handmaiden, fetched and carried water so the men could wash.

Jael led Deborah into another inner chamber. The tent walls were hung with colorful swaths of linen, and a large, intricately woven rug covered the ground. A large basin sat in the middle of the chamber, next to a smaller basin. "This is my bathing room," Jael said. "If you want to bathe tonight, I will have the basin filled with hot water."

She ushered Deborah to a cushion where she could sit and dip her feet into the smaller basin. Another handmaiden came in and dumped heated water into the basin, then added sprigs of dried flowers and several drops of imported orange oil.

"Soak your feet," Jael said. "It's not everyone I'll share my orange oil with."

Deborah smiled. "You are very generous. Kiva told me how you treated her like royalty."

"How is the dear woman?" Jael asked. "I heard she at last married."

Deborah was surprised this woman had heard such news. "Yes, she married my brother Chaim. He's with me."

"So that's the Chaim she married," Jael mused.

"How did you hear about Kiva's marriage?"

"Heber had instructions from me to discreetly inquire during his travels," Jael said. "Kiva feared she'd never marry and have children. It broke my heart that she'd received such a poor fate. But now, all is well."

"She has one son and three daughters," Deborah said. "She seems to be the only one who can bring out a soft side in Chaim. My entire family is grateful for your care of her."

"I was happy to help her," Jael said. "She told me many things about your people and your religious beliefs. Although I found them interesting, I could never be such a devout worshiper." She waved a hand about the luxurious chamber. "We might live an isolated life, but I enjoy fine linens, trinkets, and jewelry. I'm afraid I'm too idolatrous."

Deborah shook her head. "I may be a Judge among my people, but I am not here to judge you. I wish that more of my people would have as much generosity and love in their hearts as you do. I wish the Canaanites did as well. Just imagine if everyone was a Jael. We'd have no need for battles."

Jael laughed. "I think one Jael is enough for this world. And I wish there didn't have to be battles or strife or hot tempers dictating our lives. There's a reason my husband lives separate from his Kenite people."

"Making those types of choices can be difficult," Deborah said. "But sometimes a battle is necessary, especially when one people thinks they have the right to oppress another."

Jael rose to her feet and fetched a cloth for Deborah to dry her feet. "No one has that right. I don't care which God someone believes in. At moments, I can understand different sides to the same problem. There are good men who are Canaanites, and there are good men who are Israelites. There are also evil men who are evil despite what they profess to believe in or fight for."

"You are right," Deborah said in a soft voice.

"Sisera is one of those men," Jael said, her voice thick with emotion. "Of course, words of atrocities reach us, but when I saw the gash on Kiva's face . . . It was astounding to think such a young, innocent girl could be his target."

As Deborah dried her feet, she thought of the day she'd first met Kiva. She had been a sad, beautiful sight. And now, the girl's scar continued to remind the entire family of the power of the Canaanites.

Jael took the cloth and rose to set it in a basket on the other side of the chamber. "Barak told us of Nathan's sacrifice."

Deborah lifted her head to stare at Jael. "Nathan of Bethel?"

"Yes, he was with Barak and Gilad when the Canaanites came to the training ground. Did you know him?"

Deborah rose to her feet. "I do know him. What happened?"

Jael exhaled. "He was killed by those soldiers who invaded the camp. He was the distraction that enabled Barak and Gilad to flee to safety."

Deborah thought of the man she'd told not to bow to her. How he'd said she was not the only one with God's ear and how he'd predicted she would soon be the next Judge of Israel. How he'd endured many hardships, losing his daughter and becoming maimed in the process. And now he was . . .

"Take me to Barak," she told Jael.

Chapter Twenty-Four

Barak had heard the conversations coming from the other side of the tent walls, but he thought he was dreaming when he heard Deborah's voice and then . . . Abner's? Whatever tea Jael had prepared for Barak had made him sleepy. It was a comfortable drowsy though, and whenever he awoke, he felt much better.

He blinked his eyes open and guessed it was nearly sunset. The interior of the chamber he'd been put in with Gilad was a warm gold-brown, and the oil lamps had yet to be lit.

"Father," Gilad said, turning onto his side on his mat. He'd been placed just a few paces from Barak the night before. "I think Deborah is here."

"You heard her voice too?" Barak asked. Whether or not Deborah had truly arrived, Barak was grateful to be looking at his son—alive and well. In another day or two, they'd be able to travel, but Barak hadn't been able to come up with a plan to reunite with his wife. He didn't want to put her in danger, but he felt desperate to see her.

Someone laughed. *Jael.* Barak had come to recognize her laughter—which was frequent.

"Here we are," Jael said, her voice clear.

Barak shifted so he could see the entrance to the chamber. Jael entered carrying an oil lamp that cast a slightly brighter glow about the room. She was followed by Deborah.

"Barak," Deborah said, smiling and rushing to him. Before he could do more than sit up, she knelt and grasped his hands. "How are you?" She scanned him as if she were searching for any sign of injury. Except for bruises, all of Barak's aches and pains were inside.

"Much better," Barak said. "I can't believe you're here. How did you know where to find us?"

Deborah only smiled, then turned her attention to Gilad. "And how are you?" She rested her hand on his arm.

Gilad grinned. "I'm alive."

Deborah chuckled. "I can see that."

Abner and Chaim, along with Tobiah, came into the chamber. Barak's heart soared at the pleasure of seeing these men.

"Lapi has gone to fetch your family and bring them to Bethel," Abner said.

Barak nodded, too emotional to speak as he thought of yet another family member making a sacrifice on his behalf.

"We've every reason to believe that Evie, your daughters, and your father are well," Deborah added. "Lapi was insistent that he travel on his own to bring less attention. By the time we return, Evie should be there."

Barak could only hope so.

He watched Deborah as she talked to Gilad and marveled over the changes that had taken place. She carried an air of authority with her, one of assurance. She'd always been a strong woman, but her leadership was plain for all to see.

His thoughts were drawn to a recurring impression he continued to have, one that he didn't want to act on. First of all, he'd barely escaped Sisera with his life, as well as Gilad's, and in truth, he was tired. So when he couldn't shake the thoughts from his mind about how it was time to gather the Israelites and go battle against the Canaanites, he hoped the thought was only of his own imagination.

He would keep silent for now since he couldn't bear the idea of enduring more trials with his family. He didn't want to be separated from them for a long time again.

"Supper is ready," Jael said, coming into the chamber again. "Barak, are you up to joining us in the gathering room?"

"Yes," Barak said, looking over at Gilad. "We can assist you, son."

Moments later, they were all situated before a large meal set upon a long, low table. Barak settled onto a cushion, gingerly moving his body. His aches and pains were still present, but not nearly as severe as they had been. And Gilad was slowly regaining his strength, even protesting when Abner picked him up and carried him to the gathering room.

Barak ate with gratitude as the conversation flowed about him and the others discussed the Canaanites, the duties Deborah faced, and what the future might bring. Heber and Jael asked plenty of questions, which everyone was eager to answer.

The only thing that would make this meal better was the presence of the rest of their family members. And Barak wished he could make time stand still because everyone was safe and accounted for.

"We should depart tomorrow or the next day," Deborah was saying. "Once both Barak and Gilad are fit to travel."

Abner frowned at this. "Your absence will be missed and speculated upon. Barak and Gilad might be able to hide out but not the Judge of Israel."

"He's right," Chaim said, looking over at Barak. "I could stay and travel back with Barak and Gilad." He shifted his gaze to Deborah. "Abner and Tobiah will return you to Ramah."

Deborah exhaled. "We should all stay together. I feel very strongly about that. Separating again, after coming so far, will only make things more complicated."

Barak fully expected Chaim to argue with his sister as he'd so often done in the past. Instead, he hesitated, then nodded. "We will wait, then."

"We are fit to travel," Barak said, glancing over at his son. "We will plan on leaving at dawn."

"Are you sure?" Jael said. "Gilad can barely walk."

"I can travel," Gilad said, straightening. "I might need some help."

"We'll carry you if necessary," Abner said, and Gilad smiled. "Your mother will want to see you."

Barak couldn't argue with that, and it seemed no one else could either. By the time everyone had eaten their fill, the travelers were more than ready to get some sleep. Barak told Jael he didn't want any tea so that he'd be more alert when dawn arrived.

As a consequence, he slept little, and he finally rose a couple of hours before dawn. He made his way quietly through the tent chambers until he reached the main entrance that led outside. There, he found a place to sit and watch the sun rise.

He'd been in this place a few days now, but this was the first time he'd been outside. The cool morning air felt refreshing, and he even enjoyed listening to the insects as they began their morning calls. The horizon was a mixture of violet and gray, still a ways off from the orange the rising sun would bring.

Again, the words he'd been ignoring came to his mind.

Go and draw toward Mount Tabor.

A location that was just north of the main Canaanite camp.

And take with thee ten thousand men of the children of Naphtali and the children of Zebulun.

Barak scrubbed a hand over his hair. It had grown beyond its usual length during the months he'd spent at the training camp. He'd have to ask Evie to cut his hair again, and suddenly, he was looking forward to nothing else.

Ten thousand men . . . He'd probably trained only a quarter of that number, and even if he added in the training Lapi had done, they weren't even close to five thousand.

And I will draw unto thee to the river Kishon, Sisera, the captain of Jabin's army, with his chariots and his multitude; and I will deliver him into thine hand.

Barak knew this part of the impression couldn't have come from his own imagination. As much as he wanted to deny the words, only God could command such a feat—bringing the entire army of Jabin and then . . . *delivering them into the Israelites' hands?*

Images of war passed through Barak's mind. Even if he knew going into the battle that the Israelites would prevail, how many lives would be lost? How many women would become widows? His own wife had nearly become a widow. And it tore at Barak's heart to think of a time when he might not look forward to seeing her again.

He couldn't do it. Not now anyway, and perhaps a war would never happen. Skirmishes, yes, but not something that might separate Barak from his family forever. He pushed to his feet and stood, with his hands on his hips. He stood there a long time, unmoving, until the sun's rise shifted the violet-blue sky to a golden yellow.

It was time to return home.

Upon entering the tent, he found that the servants had stirred, and one of them was preparing the morning meal. Through the tent walls, he could hear the murmur of voices, although he didn't know to whom they belonged. He went to help Gilad get ready for the journey. Each time he saw his son, a rush of emotion struck him, reminding him anew how he needed to focus on his blessings.

Heber had lent Gilad clothing since his had been beyond repair.

"Do I look like a desert man?" Gilad said, his smile lighting his face. In addition to his sand-colored kilt, he wore a braided leather band around his arm, given to him by Heber's son.

"Near enough, and it might serve you well," Barak said.

"How can we repay Heber and his wife?" Gilad asked, and it was a question Barak had asked himself.

"Deborah brought them some trinkets," Barak said. "So we will have to find a way to repay her."

"Will she let us repay her?" Gilad asked, getting to the heart of the matter.

"Probably not." Barak rested his hand on his son's shoulders. "We can't pay her back in trinkets, but there might be other ways."

Gilad nodded. "I could fight in her army."

"You?" This took Barak by surprise. "What do you mean?"

"Tobiah said that all the young men have doubled their training efforts since Deborah became Judge."

Barak exhaled. "What exactly did Tobiah say?"

Now Gilad looked worried, as if he'd said something he shouldn't have.

"Tell me, son," Barak continued. "I must know what people are talking about. I am one of the commanders, after all."

"It's more secret than the training you were doing because it's among the younger men and even some boys." Gilad looked away from him.

Ten thousand men.

Barak blinked. "Surely Deborah wouldn't approve of boys going into battle." Boys who would hopefully be grown men if war should ever erupt.

"Whenever Deborah settles disputes among the people, she tells them to remember who their real enemy is," Gilad said, his voice hesitant. "Not their neighbors but the—"

"Canaanites," Barak finished. He clenched his jaw, looking at the young man before him, a son he loved with all his heart. Barak would do anything to save his son but not if it meant sending him into battle against the Canaanites.

"I will speak with Deborah and find out what is really going on," he said, wondering if Deborah was already doing her part to build an army while he'd been sequestered to the training grounds.

Laughter erupted from the other side of the tent walls, and the sound of conversation rose. Barak and Gilad joined the others for the morning meal. When it came time to bid farewell to their hosts and rescuers, Barak's heart was full. He didn't know if he'd ever see these people again, but they'd been a blessing in his life.

As they rode away from the plains of Zaanaim, Barak's heart was full of gratitude—gratitude for Heber and Jael and their hospitality and gratitude for Deborah and her sacrifice in coming to find him. He watched Gilad ride next to Tobiah and marveled at how this next generation had so much more resolve and courage.

When they'd traveled through most of the morning, Barak drew his horse next to Deborah's and told her what Gilad had said about the boys and younger men training on their own.

"It's true," Deborah said, looking over at Barak, her dark eyes steady. "They've watched their fathers and mothers and grandparents endure abuse year after year from the Canaanites. They want to rise up as a whole, not in small skirmishes that never result in any changes."

Barak swallowed. "They are young, yet surely it would be like walking into a death trap if they were to go against the Canaanites as a large group."

Deborah didn't even blink. "That's exactly what must happen, Barak. Shamgar said so as well. I believe he was given a glimpse of the future and what we must do about it."

Barak went silent, thinking of how Shamgar had been the one to ask him to begin training in larger groups and with more intense purpose. That risk had proven almost fatal to Barak and his son though. And Nathan had lost his life.

"I know what you're thinking," Deborah said in a soft voice, slowing her horse to put more distance between the two of them and the others.

Barak remained quiet, waiting for her to continue.

"The Canaanites have stockpiles of weapons, chariots, and horses for every soldier," Deborah said. "They are a mighty force, yes. But we have one thing they don't."

Barak knew what she was going to say before she said it.

Regardless, when she spoke, the hairs on his arms stood up.

"God is with us," she said with simple conviction.

And God had told *him* to take ten thousand men to stand before the Canaanites.

The burn in Barak's eyes made him look away from Deborah's gaze. Surely she noticed his emotion, that he'd become a wreck of a man when he'd nearly lost his son. That the only reason he was even alive was because a desert man had happened to find him.

Deborah was finished with her counsel, and they continued to ride side by side in silence as their two sons rode ahead, keeping up a lively conversation. The boys had their whole lives in front of them, and Barak worried that they would be cut short . . . and then how could he ever go on?

Chapter Twenty-Five

As the traveling group neared Ramah, the night was still young. Deborah was grateful the heat had been cut in half, and she looked forward to seeing her husband and youngest son. At least, she could only hope that Lapi had already arrived home and was waiting for her.

Deborah felt blessed that they hadn't encountered any Canaanites on their journey. They'd stayed off the main roads, and she'd kept her face covered in case any of the Israelite villages they'd passed contained spies.

Now the waxing moon and stars lit the remainder of the way. Since the distance was not far, Deborah and her brothers decided they'd continue to travel and hope the horses would remain sure-footed on the path. Up ahead, Deborah spotted the last grove of palms before their tent would come into view. Her pulse sped up at the thought of seeing Lapi, her son Abram, and Evie and her daughters. The reunion would be sweet.

Tobiah and Gilad urged their horses to a faster canter, and they passed by the grove first, but instead of continuing, they both reined their mounts to a stop.

Deborah continued to ride until she saw what they saw. Behind her somewhere, Abner, Chaim, and Barak also stopped.

Chaim breathed out a curse, but Deborah could only stare.

Even in the half light of the moon, it was obvious that something or someone had destroyed their tent and the surrounding shelters. The wind shifted just then, and the acrid scent of burnt goat hair gusted to the traveling party. The tent panels were made of goat hair, which could mean only one thing: lives were at stake.

For a moment, she couldn't move. She couldn't comprehend such a tragedy. And then she cried out and slapped the reins of her horse. She galloped toward the burnt structures. One of the men behind her called out to her, but she would not stop. Her horse slowed, complained, reluctant to approach the dark mass that still smoked.

"Lapi," Deborah gasped.

Where was he? Abram? The maidservants? All the people who had come to be judged?

Someone else yelled, and she was dimly aware that her brothers were calling out for Lapi as well. Deborah dismounted her horse, grasped her long tunic, and began to walk toward the smoldering rubble. She scanned the area, seeing a wall-hanging half charred, a burnt basin, melted cushions.

She brought her hands to her mouth, trying to make sense of what she was seeing. How could this happen? God had led her to find Barak, and then she returned to this . . . ?

Abner grabbed her arm. "Don't get any closer," he said, his voice firm. "You might burn your feet."

She let him pull her back, but her eyes kept going over the rubble. Next, she looked toward the cragged hills. And that was when she saw it.

"Look," she said in a trembling voice. "Someone's out there."

"She's right," Barak said, joining them.

"I'll go check it out," Chaim cut in. "Everyone stay here, and stay together."

But Deborah wasn't listening. She pulled away from Abner and hurried around the smoldering tent. Whoever it was, she was going to find out. If it was a Canaanite, she'd be prepared with her knife, and if it was an Israelite, she'd demand answers. She removed the knife strapped to her leg as she hurried toward the flickering form. As she grew closer, she could see there was more than one person—there were several sitting among the rocks, and the light was an oil lamp.

There were men, women, and children, it seemed. Israelites.

Relief poured through Deborah, and she called out to them. "Hello? Can you tell me what happened?"

"Mother?"

Deborah froze. Several paces away, someone rose. She'd recognize the hair and shoulders anywhere, even in the near darkness. "Abram."

Abram ran, and moments later, Deborah was clutching her son to her. "Where's your father?"

"He was helping another family, and—"

"Deborah?" the sound of Lapi's voice was like a jolt to her heart.

She turned from Abram, still holding onto his arm. Her husband jumped over rocks and came down the hillside to get to her. He pulled her into his arms and held her so tight she gasped for air.

"Lapi." She clutched at his clothing and held on. "What happened?"

"The Canaanites started a fire early this morning when most of us were sleeping," Lapi said.

"Why?" she asked, but it was a question no one could answer. Deborah drew back and looked up at him. "Was anyone injured? Where's Evie and her daughters?"

"They're here." Lapi set his hands on her shoulder. "No one was injured. Most of the patrons left, but several remained and are camping nearby, waiting for your return. They will want to hear from you in the morning."

Deborah nodded, feeling numb. At least no one had been hurt in the fire. Abram joined Tobiah, the two of them sharing their stories. She turned to search for Barak. He'd already made his way around the burnt rubble and was coming toward them.

Deborah watched the two cousins embrace, and after Lapi's brief explanation of the fire, he led Barak past a few camps of those who remained. When Barak finally spotted his family and hurried to greet them, tears pricked Deborah's eyes as she watched Barak hold Evie close.

Lapi returned to Deborah and wrapped an arm about her shoulders. "How did you find Barak?"

"It was almost like he found us," Deborah said. "Well, at least Heber the Kenite did. He came across Barak and Gilad in the wilderness and saved their lives."

Lapi exhaled and tightened his hold on her shoulders. "We can't go on like this," he said.

And Deborah knew what he was talking about. "Have other fires been started that you've heard of?"

"No, but we might find out more as the days go by." Lapi fell silent, and the two of them watched Gilad join his family.

Deborah leaned her head against her husband's shoulder. "Our days of peace have come to an end."

"They've been at an end for a long time."

It was a long time before Deborah found any rest. She moved among the people, asking after their welfare, and when she was satisfied, she rejoined Lapi and her sons. They'd set up a decent makeshift camp, and Abram assured her that her judging spot beneath the palm was unmarred from the fire. As Deborah lay beside her husband, she nestled against him, reveling in the warmth and steady strength of his body. Her silent prayers began as the sounds of the camps quieted.

Then, finally, Lapi's breathing evened out, and she knew he was asleep.

Deborah slept fitfully all night, in that state of being half-awake for most of it yet too exhausted to move or have any coherent thoughts. When the warming air foretold the approach of dawn, she began to stir. And that was when the words came to her mind.

Opening her eyes, she didn't move for a moment, feeling the full impact of the message the Lord had given.

I have commanded Barak the son of Abinoam out of Kedesh-naph-tali to go and draw toward Mount Tabor and take with him ten thousand men of the children of Naphtali and the children of Zebulun.

She blinked. The sun was a sliver against the eastern horizon, and Deborah placed a hand over her eyes as the sun glinted across her face. Still, the words echoed in her mind.

I will draw unto Barak to the river Kishon, Sisera, the captain of Jabin's army, with his chariots and his multitude, and I will deliver him unto Barak's hand.

Deborah knew the enormity of this revelation would affect all Israelites—men, women, and children. And her body and heart seemed to swell with the realization. God had already told Barak . . . yet he had said nothing to her. Deborah lowered her hand, keeping her eyes closed for a moment longer as the sun now bathed her face.

The scent of cooking fires mingled with the scorched smell of the burnt tents and the morning dew. A contrast in smells. She moaned. She'd have to speak to Barak. They could delay no longer. God already had a plan.

Deborah turned over. Lapi still slept by her side. He must have taken off his robe in the night and slept only in his half tunic. His bare chest and shoulders would warm with the sun, and she had no doubt the warmth would wake him soon. Beyond him, both sons slept as well. Her family had been through an ordeal of late, and now that they were reunited, everyone needed rest. She observed the sleeping men in her family, and her heart filled with love, as well as regret for what news she must impart to them. But first, she needed to speak with Barak.

She picked up her waterskin, took a drink, then rose to her feet. She was already fully dressed, and since her extra clothing had been destroyed along with the burnt tent, she had nothing else to change into. Scanning the campground, she looked for Barak's family and anything that might identify them. She assumed they all still slept.

Over by the destroyed tent, Chaim and Abner picked their way through the burnt remains, looking for anything that could be salvaged. Deborah walked down the slope beneath where they'd camped and joined her brothers.

"Do either of you know where Barak camped last night?" she said.

Both brothers glanced at each other, then turned to face Deborah.

Chaim made to speak, then stopped and looked away. Abner blew out a breath of frustration but said nothing.

"What?" Deborah rested her hands on her hips. "What is it you're not telling me?"

Chaim scratched the back of his neck, then said, "Barak set off with his family before dawn. He said that he didn't want to be around anyone for a while. They went back to his lands in Kedesh-naphtali."

Deborah stared at her brother, unsure how to respond.

Abner sighed. "We told him to consult with you first, but he looked at us as if we'd told him to drown his favorite horse."

Why had Barak fled when he'd received specific instruction from God? Couldn't he see that the fire was only another indicator that it was time for the Israelites to rise up against the Canaanites? "How long ago did he leave?" Deborah asked.

Chaim scoffed. "What? You're going to chase him down?"

Deborah narrowed her gaze.

"Abner and I can help with the clean-up," Chaim said. "Let the man rest. He nearly died last week."

It was Abner who spoke next. "You've had instruction from God, haven't you?"

Before she could respond, someone spoke behind her.

"What's going on?" Lapi said.

Deborah turned. Her husband must have walked to the burnt site the moment he'd awakened. He hadn't even pulled on a robe over his half tunic.

"Barak left with his family to return to Kedesh, and I need to stop him," she said.

Lapi's brows rose, but he didn't question her or argue with her. He looked to Abner, then Chaim, then back to Deborah. "We will go get him, then," he said with finality.

"I'm coming too," Deborah said.

Again, Lapi didn't argue. "I'll get the horses ready." He looked to Abner. "Keep track of our boys while we're gone. We should return by midday."

Deborah grasped Lapi's hand. "Thank you."

He nodded, then strode to where they'd tethered the horses the night before.

When Lapi was out of earshot, Abner said, "We're going to war, aren't we?"

Deborah didn't answer; she didn't need to. Neither Abner nor Chaim looked surprised. Chaim turned away and began to sift through more of the debris. What he was looking for Deborah didn't know. Perhaps he was just processing what Abner had concluded.

Deborah left her brothers then and joined her husband. He helped her mount a horse, and despite the hunger pangs in her stomach, she didn't want to delay another moment. As they rode in the direction Barak had gone, gray clouds gathered above, moving across the sky as if they were guiding Deborah and Lapi.

They rode for more than two hours. The clouds continued to darken, and the wind increased before Lapi said, "I think I see them."

He pointed up ahead, and Deborah lifted her veil. Beyond the darkening landscape, she saw the forms of a traveling family. Relief buzzed through her, and she increased the pace of her horse.

It didn't take long for Barak to look back and spy them following. Deborah wondered what was going through his mind as he realized she was the one approaching. He fully turned his horse, left his family, and rode toward her.

Lapi slowed, letting Deborah travel on her own in order to speak with Barak privately.

When Deborah and Barak reached each other, she reined in her horse and lifted her veil. Barak scanned her face, and she sensed that he wasn't completely clueless as to why she'd come.

"The Lord spoke to me this morning," Deborah said.

Barak's jaw tightened.

"Why did you leave?" she continued, although she could probably guess.

"I needed a few days away from everything and everyone."

Deborah exhaled. "I understand. But the time is now, Barak. Has not the Lord God of Israel commanded you to go to Mount Tabor?"

Barak didn't blink, didn't move. His tone was raspy when he said, "Yes."

"God wants you to take ten thousand Israelites."

Barak swallowed. "Where will I find so many men?"

"God will provide a way," Deborah said softly. "Put the call out, and they will come."

He ran a hand over his face and looked away for a moment. Then he said in a low tone, "I have seen and felt what it would be like to lose my son, my family, and I don't know if I can be the commander you want me to be, Deborah. I have tasted fear, and I cannot rid myself of it."

"You thought that a few days away from everything would restore your courage?" Deborah pressed.

"Yes," he said in a faint voice.

Deborah well understood fear, but she could not ignore God's command.

"The Lord said He will draw Sisera to the river," she said, "and deliver the Canaanites into your hands."

Barak exhaled. "How many Israelite men and boys will die?"

Deborah remained silent. She didn't have an answer.

He looked over his shoulder at his waiting family, then back at Deborah. "When the Canaanites assemble with their horses and chariots and armor and weapons, do you not think half our army will flee? Even if we can assemble ten thousand?"

"They respect you," Deborah said. "Many of them have either trained with you or they have heard of your life's work."

Barak gazed down at his scarred palm. "More than anyone, I want Sisera to pay for what he's done to my family and to our people. But I can't lead ten thousand men to their deaths."

Deborah moved her horse closer so she could grasp Barak's arm. "God will be with you."

Barak's eyes were rimmed in red as if he were on the verge of tears or exhaustion or both. "Will you go with me?"

Deborah stared at him, wondering if she'd heard right.

"If you go with me, Deborah, then I will do this," he said, his voice cracking. "But if you will not, then I cannot ask ten thousand men to follow me to their deaths."

She opened her mouth, then closed it. Women did not go into battle with their men. If the Israelites knew she was with Barak, leading him, they would credit her for the victory. Did Barak not want to see this through? Take his revenge and redeem their people?

But his watery gaze told her that he was earnest in his request.

"I will go with you, but you must know that when Sisera is defeated, it will be at the hand of a woman."

Barak bowed his head. "Then it shall be since I cannot do it without you."

They were silent for a long moment as the wind tugged at their clothing and the clouds darkened to deep gray, keeping away the sun's warmth. The coolness should have been refreshing, but instead, it sent a rush of urgency through Deborah.

As the first raindrops fell, landing on her cheeks, she knew without a doubt that the time had come. The time was now.

Chapter Twenty-Six

Barak rested his hands on his wife's shoulders as she stood before him in the private chamber of the tent they were sharing with Abner's family on the outskirts of Bethel. Despite the dim gray of the early-morning light, he saw her dark eyes glisten. The tremble in her voice told him her words were braver than her heart.

"God will be with you," Evie whispered. "Deborah will be with you. And *I* will be praying for you."

It seemed that Barak had spent most of his married life apart from Evie. She'd raised and taught their children while he'd been raising soldiers. They might have shared a private chamber the past couple of weeks, but they'd been surrounded by people every moment of the day. Deborah had sent out secret edicts to every Israelite community, calling the tribes of Zebulun and Naphtali to stand against the Canaanites.

The meeting place was north of Bethel. Men, women, and children had arrived by caravan, setting up camp, awaiting the day of the march.

Barak was at a loss of what to say to his wife, knowing these might be the last words they shared. Evie, as always, understood him. She stepped forward and slipped her arms about his waist, then rested her head against his chest.

Her familiar scent of wildflowers surrounded Barak. He pulled her closer as his throat tightened, and his eyes burned with tears. "I love you, Evie," he whispered.

"I love you too," she said. "I will see you soon. Have faith, my husband."

Barak's throat was too tight to answer.

A horn blared from somewhere outside the tent, signaling the beginning of the march. Gilad had been made the designated horn blower, an assignment Barak hoped would keep him out of any fighting.

Evie had already said her goodbyes to Gilad, so now it was time for Barak to leave the private chamber and take his place at the front of the procession with Deborah.

"It's time," his wife said because his grasp on her hadn't loosened in any measure. "Go in peace." She drew away and lifted both hands to his face. "Barak, your name will be heralded for generations to come. What you are sacrificing will bring freedom to our children, our grandchildren, and all their descendants."

Barak nodded, and Evie wiped a tear from his cheek that he hadn't realized had fallen. He threaded his hands through her hair and pulled her close again, then kissed her. She kissed him back, a tender kiss wrought with years of marriage. Then she grasped his hands and squeezed. He released her. Stepped back. Turned. Walked through the connecting chambers of the tent until he reached the entrance.

Outside, the place was a hive of activity. Men were saying goodbye to tearful families, and Barak felt the lump in his throat all over again. Gilad blasted another long note on his horn, and more men joined the assembled soldiers. They'd all been instructed to bring a weapon, a waterskin, and a food satchel. How many days this might take, Barak didn't know, and who might return . . . he didn't know that either.

Deborah was already sitting on her horse, her bow and arrows strapped across her torso. Lapi's horse was right next to hers, and Lapi also wore a bow and arrows, as well as a long dagger strapped to his waist.

Not too far from the pair sat Gilad upon a horse. Barak knew his son had strapped a knife to each thigh, and Barak hoped Gilad wouldn't have to use either weapon.

Deborah turned, and their gazes connected. She gave him a single nod, and he strode the last few paces to his horse, then climbed up. Heart pounding, Barak clicked his tongue and urged the beast forward. He moved past the men, who parted for him. The Israelites would mostly be traveling by foot, a three-day journey until they reached Mount Tabor. First, they'd have to cross the river Kishon, which was really a stream, then they'd wait between the river and the mount for the Canaanites to arrive.

Barak reached Deborah and Lapi, then he nodded to Gilad to blow the final three blasts, signaling the official beginning of the march. As the horn rent the air, Barak's heart thundered. This was it. From this moment, there was no turning back.

Barak urged his horse forward, followed by Deborah. Next came the commanders of one thousand, the commanders of one hundred, and the commanders of fifty, who all rode horses, followed by the walking regiment.

With each movement of the horse beneath him, Barak's pulse increased. By the time they traveled past the next village, the Canaanite spies would report that the Israelites had started their march. In fact, Sisera might already be waiting for them somewhere, planning to waylay them from the cliffs or block their passage with hundreds of chariots.

Barak looked back at Gilad. He sat erect on his horse, proud to be able to ride instead of walk. There were plenty of boys among the men. Deborah had forbidden Abram to travel with them, but Tobiah was not too far back. When the first arrivals of men included boys younger then fourteen, Deborah had finally relented to allow Tobiah to come with the army.

The lesser commanders kept watch on the marching men, and Barak could not even fathom counting them all, yet they had been counted. Song broke out among a small group, and soon, voices raised to the heavens, echoing against each other as they repeated praises to the Lord.

* * *

On the third day of travel, as they neared the river Kishon, Barak slowed the pace, keeping his eyes peeled for any sign of interference, such as a smaller band of soldiers that might cause trouble. But the morning was quiet. Almost too quiet.

He studied every brush, every tree, searching for signs of recent travel. Gilad joined him, and the two of them searched in silence. As the sun reached the valley floor, like a gold net cast across a dry seabed, Barak caught sight of the river.

"There's the river Kishon," he said, pointing ahead.

This time of year, the stream was very low and easy to cross. The horses plunged in, and water splashed all around Barak, soaking his feet and cooling his skin. Gilad laughed when his horse soaked him, and Barak smiled at the sight. But then his smile dimmed. Watching Gilad reminded him that his wife was waiting for them to return to her. If only Barak could make that promise.

Have faith, she'd told him.

Barak faced north again and continued to ride, his focus on the south slope of Mount Tabor, which rose before them.

Deborah rode up next to him. "We are here."

Barak nodded and scanned the terrain. Between the river and the mount, there was no place to hide. The Canaanites would be able to spot the ten thousand no matter which direction they approached. "We'll set up camp at the base of the mount and keep guard," Barak said. "I want Lapi to take over as captain of the guards." Deborah didn't argue, so Barak continued. "How long do you think it will take the Canaanites to arrive?"

"Not long. They are riding from Hazor."

Barak's jaw tightened, but he nodded. "We will be ready, then."

He watched Deborah turn her horse and rejoin Lapi.

Barak snapped his reins and rode over to the lesser commanders to give them orders to begin setting up camp.

The next hours sped past as the heat surged until, finally, the afternoon shifted into evening. With each passing moment and hour, Barak felt the anticipation increase. It was no surprise when Lapi joined him in the makeshift tent that would act as headquarters.

"Come with me," Lapi said.

Barak knew his cousin well enough to know Lapi wouldn't explain until Barak could see for himself. The two men strode through the camp and continued up the mount. It wasn't long before Lapi stopped and turned, then pointed.

Barak followed his lead. In the distance, a few dozen men had gathered, their chariots marking them as Canaanites. The group was much too small to be any sort of threat. But Barak would not be fooled.

"So it won't be long," Barak said.

"Right," Lapi agreed. "And they'll come ready. Our preparations haven't exactly been secret."

"There are too many spies among us for any hope of secrecy," Barak said.

Lapi rested a hand on Barak's shoulder. "You've prepared a long time for this—most of your life."

The words didn't bring much comfort. "Tonight, Deborah will speak to the men," Barak said. "She's the true leader. She has the ear of God, and we all know we have no chance of defeating the Canaanites without divine help."

"As it should be," Lapi said. "God is our deliverer in all things, and in this, we must accept God's will. We live or die according to His will anyway. If He's commanded us to stand against the Canaanites, He will not abandon us."

Barak had witnessed enough miracles and blessings in his life that he knew he could never deny the existence of God. But what if part of His plan meant the Israelites had to obey and stand against their enemy only to lose and become a humbler people?

"The people listen to Deborah," Barak said quietly. "She speaks to their hearts and souls." He turned to Lapi and clasped his hand. "If it be God's will that I perish against the Canaanites, I'll die knowing I was an obedient servant to God."

"You're more than that, cousin," Lapi said. "Don't forget that we are together in this. Together, we'll fight. And together we'll either fall or triumph."

Barak gazed back over the terrain, past the ten thousand Israelites, past the river Kishon, to the west where the sky had deepened to violet. Sisera was out there, somewhere. At this very moment, he could be receiving the news of the Israelite gathering.

As Barak and Lapi descended the mount, setting off toward the camp, Barak imagined Sisera's astonishment at his first sight of the vast number of Israelites ready for battle—men who were tired of being oppressed. Barak headed for his shelter, parting ways with Lapi for the time being. As he walked among the Israelites, who were setting up camp and sharpening their weapons, he stopped to talk to several men. He asked about their homes and livelihoods. They told Barak of their hardships—ones not of their own doing—hardships directly related to interactions and confrontations with the Canaanites.

Barak thought of Nathan more than once as he listened to various men's stories. The stories kept coming until Barak didn't know if his mind could hold any more. He'd most likely not sleep tonight as it was.

By the time he reached his shelter, he had heard enough stories to anger him for a lifetime. He proceeded with eating some dried bread and cured meat, then he donned his red cloak and joined Deborah, Lapi, and Tobiah at their cooking fire. When Deborah offered him food, he declined. He couldn't eat more than what he already had.

Barak listened to Deborah and the men talk about the march. He gave his opinion only when Lapi talked about the rotating guard. "Double them up," Barak said. "We want all eyes on the surrounding territory. We need at least one desert man in each pair."

"Agreed," Lapi said.

The group fell silent as the sounds of the camp surrounded them. Barak stared at the small, crackling fire. Even now, Sisera could be issuing commands, gathering his men, beginning his march.

Barak had a feeling that tonight, these moments gathered around the fire, would be the only calm before everything changed. He rose to his feet and shook out his red cloak. He wanted to be clearly visible to Sisera when he arrived at Tabor.

"I'll be upon the mount, keeping watch," Barak said.

"I can send men in your place," Lapi offered.

"No," Barak said. "I'm not sleeping anyway."

Soon, he was climbing the mount again, ignoring any natural trails. The moonlight cast enough of a glow for him to pick his way through the scrub brush and rocks. He found an alcove that afforded him a view of the Israelite camp as well as the river. Campfires still burned, not making any secret of their location to the Canaanites.

Sounds of men's voices reached him as conversations ebbed throughout the evening hours. But still, Barak couldn't sleep. He watched for any sign of the greater Canaanite army. He thought of his son, who was part of the camp, how he might be forced to fight. Barak could only pray that Gilad's life would be spared. He thought of Evie and his daughters, wondering if he'd ever see them again.

He rose and paced the ground in front of the alcove. Moving was better. Moving made his heart feel less heavy. All these men had joined him, trusted him, and he had to trust too. Trust in Deborah, trust in the Lord.

Barak continued to pace for what felt like hours, and finally, he sat again. But he was still awake to witness the deep violet of the horizon melt away to azure blue, then lighten again. As the first orange and pink hues appeared, Barak saw someone climbing the mountain below him. It took only seconds to realize it was Deborah.

She didn't seem to be in a hurry, so he waited where he was. Perhaps she hadn't slept either. Her hair was covered with a deep-green mantle, and she kept it clutched at her throat so it wouldn't tug away in the wind. Only then did Barak realize how much the wind was blowing. The temperature was also dropping, and Barak scanned the sky. Clouds raced across the vast expanse, and despite the wind, the air felt heavy.

Deborah was closer now, and when she looked up, their gazes met.

Without a word from her, Barak suddenly knew what she'd come to say.

She stopped before him, the wind stirring her clothing and mantle. "This is the day that God will deliver Sisera into thine hand."

Barak let the words settle into his heart and mind. *Today.*

He shifted his gaze to the river Kishon. He couldn't see masses of Canaanite soldiers, but he felt them approaching. It was as if the very earth had started to vibrate . . . and then he saw dark forms appear against the shimmering horizon. Chariots.

Deborah turned as well.

Neither of them spoke as they watched hundreds of chariots take shape, first as a mass group, then as individual chariots, horses, and riders. Barak realized the sound he'd thought was his thumping heart was the sound of the approaching chariots. Although the Canaanites were on the other side of the river and much too far away to feel the impact of their arrival, the ground beneath Barak's feet seemed to rumble with the approaching chariots.

At the camp below, the Israelites were stirring; surely they'd felt the rumbling as well. And then Barak spotted the guards that had been posted near the river. They were riding their horses back to camp, ready to alert everyone.

"Time to go," Barak said as a gust of wind tugged at his cloak. The cold air was like a freezing river against his skin, and Barak felt the numbing chill in his bones.

"May God be with us," Deborah murmured, her voice trembling.

She started down the mount, Barak following. By the time they reached the base of the mount, the clouds had darkened overhead, threatening the rising sun. A peal of thunder ripped through the sky, and Barak's heart jolted.

He wanted to return to the mount, to force back time. But there was no going back now. The Canaanites were amassing across the river—their numbers increasing by the moment like a horde of locusts.

Lapi met them at the base of the mount, leading Deborah's horse. Lapi's hair was tied back, and his bow and arrows were already strapped on. He reined his horse to a stop once he reached them. "You've seen the chariots?"

"Yes," Barak said. "Tell all the commanders to mount their horses and meet me at headquarters."

Deborah swung up onto her horse and moved to Lapi's side. They gripped hands briefly, then Lapi steered his horse back to camp to issue instructions, and Deborah followed him at a slower pace.

Barak hurried through the camp on foot. The Israelites were dousing cooking fires, strapping on weapons, and calling out instructions to each other. When Barak reached his tent, he found his sword where he'd left it.

He strapped another dagger to his leg, then slung on a bow and arrow set. He mounted his horse and waited for the lesser commanders to join him.

As the men arrived one by one, Barak met their gazes—most of them were determined, fierce, ready. One commander was pale, and Barak wondered if the man had just been sick.

"Assemble your ranks," Barak said. "Men with swords and spears at the front, men with bows and arrows at the rear. Send fifty archers up the mount."

Chapter Twenty-Seven

Once the Israelites had assembled according to rank, Barak noted that the Canaanites had started crossing the river Kishon. Their great horses and iron chariots splashed through the water. Beyond, the sky darkened even more, and thunder continued to rumble.

Barak rode his horse along the front line, calling out, "Who do we fight for?"

"Israel!" the men shouted, their voices echoing against the mount behind them.

Barak spurred his horse faster, his scarlet cloak billowing behind him as he held up his sword. "Who do we fight against?"

"Our oppressors, the Canaanites!" the men roared.

The sound buzzed through Barak, and he turned his horse and rode in the other direction. A gust of wind momentarily stole his breath.

Thunder pealed overhead once again, and when it died, Deborah rode her horse to the front of the line and cried out, "Who is on our side?"

"The God of Israel!"

The sound of men's voices faded with another peal of thunder. Deborah reined her horse in and turned to face the Canaanites, sitting like a queen upon her mount. Her back erect, her chin lifted, she commanded the attention and respect of all Israelites.

The Canaanites continued to advance, and Barak continued to ride his horse in front of the line while scanning for Sisera's imposing form. Barak knew Deborah would not wait much longer. The Israelites had to strike first. The closer the Canaanites stayed to the river, the better since the Israelites would have the advantage of the mountain at their back.

The first raindrops fell, splattering Barak's cheeks.

Deborah looked over at Barak and nodded.

"Archers ready!" Barak called, keeping his sword raised as he slowed his horse to a canter.

The front rows of men with swords and spears knelt on the damp earth, while the archers nocked their arrows. Deborah followed suit, readying her own bow and arrow as the chariots continued advancing; at least half of them had crossed the river by now.

Still, Barak didn't see Sisera's imposing form. Why was he not out in front of his army, leading them like the commander he was?

Then a chariot broke away from the main line of chariots that had crossed the river. But the soldier who stood upright while another drove the chariot was not Sisera. Who was coming with a message? Did the Canaanites want to negotiate? No . . . they never negotiated.

Barak rode up to Deborah at the same time Lapi joined her. The three of them stared at the approaching chariot.

"Is it Sisera?" Deborah asked.

"No," Lapi said, taking out an arrow and nocking it against his bow. He aimed the arrow at the chariot. "Perhaps an assassin."

"Wait," Barak said as the chariot continued straight toward him. "It's . . . Nathan."

The rider was thin and wiry, and with the bow and arrow strapped across his bare, sunburnt torso, Barak knew without a doubt it was Nathan.

"He's alive!" Deborah said, shock in her voice.

Barak sat mesmerized at the sight of Nathan barreling toward them. The man had bright welts across his chest and arms, one eye was blackened, and his head had been shaved. Nathan slowed the chariot, his gaze fixed on Barak as he neared. Then he came to a complete stop and unslung his bow. With deft quickness, Nathan nocked the arrow and pointed it straight at Barak's heart.

Barak didn't flinch.

Both Deborah and Lapi now had arrows aimed at Nathan. If the man released his arrow, he'd be killed before Barak was struck.

Nathan's eyes were wide, his chest heaved, but his hands were ever steady.

"We thought you were dead," a voice said behind Barak.

"Stay back, Gilad," Barak said through clenched teeth, not taking his gaze from Nathan.

"I wished I would have died," Nathan said in his gravelly voice. "Sisera tortured and threatened me for days, promising me a life of wealth if I would but give him the information he wanted. Fortunately, that all changed last night when he received word of the ten thousand Israelites who had gathered in Tabor."

"Fortunately?" Barak asked.

The gleam in Nathan's eyes made Barak realize Nathan was no traitor.

Lapi must have sensed the same thing, for he said, "It seems you brought the wind and rain with you."

Nathan smiled as the rain pelted his face. "I do not think the Canaanites caused this weather." He cut a glance to Deborah. "God's wrath has arrived."

"Where is Sisera?" Barak asked.

"Disguised among the ranks," Nathan said. "He promised me freedom if I but put an arrow through your heart, Barak."

Barak nodded. "You will be forfeiting your life if you do."

Nathan glanced at the surrounding archers. "I suppose Sisera knew this would happen, and the freedom he promised me was freedom in death. But no matter what torturous acts he put me through, he could never win over my heart or mind." Keeping his arrow still directed at Barak, Nathan continued. "If you will have me, I would like to shoot the first arrow at the Canaanites."

Barak wiped the rain from his face and nodded. "You have already defied death once, and it would be my pleasure to give you that honor."

Nathan grinned as he lowered his bow and took up the reins of the horse and chariot, then wheeled around until he was facing the Canaanites. The Canaanite army had fully crossed the river, and they were now assembled in a huge line of chariots, dozens deep, standing in the mud. Barak estimated nearly one thousand chariots in all were facing the Israelite foot soldiers.

"Archers ready!" Barak called out, holding up his sword again in the driving rain.

As soon as Nathan sent his arrow sailing into the air, directly toward the first line of Canaanites, Barak lowered his sword, giving his signal. Hundreds of arrows flew through the air, many of them striking the Canaanites' armor and chariots.

The Canaanite chariots started forward in one motion, men yelling, horses plunging into the mud, and arrows taking to the air.

Nathan braced himself in his chariot and sent arrow after arrow toward the Canaanites. Deborah and Lapi stayed on their horses, joining in with the archers.

Barak held his position as men started to fall ahead of him and behind. He still couldn't see Sisera, but Barak would find him. The thunder boomed overhead, and it acted like a signal for the heavens to completely open and drench the soldiers.

Barak had never witnessed such a heavy rain in all his days, and when he gave the signal for the foot soldiers to advance with their spears and swords, it was difficult to make out the faces of the men a few feet in front of him. He pressed forward with the foot soldiers as the deluge continued, flooding the Kishon river. The overfilled river built into a fierce rapid, and horses slipped, and chariots turned over.

Canaanites scrambled from their chariots only to be caught underfoot by the rushing water or knocked to the ground by a floating chariot. But the Canaanites continued to advance, pushing back the Israelite army.

"Find higher ground!" Barak shouted, and his command was repeated throughout the army. The Israelites scrambled for the higher ground of the mount, and the archers on the mount shot at the Canaanites.

Barak maneuvered his horse out of the chaos and watched as nature decimated the Canaanite army with a finality he could never have dreamed up. More than half the chariots had been swept away. The Israelites were making the greatest headway as they fought valiantly, cutting down their enemy.

Barak wiped rain from his face and searched for Sisera among the Canaanites, who continued to join in the main part of the battle. Wave after wave of the Canaanites came forward, and those who escaped the flooding were faced with vengeful Israelites, who seemed to possess unending strength.

Two Canaanites on foot charged toward Barak, their swords raised. Barak fought back until one of the Canaanites suddenly collapsed, an arrow in his back. A few paces away, Nathan advanced on the second Canaanite. He took aim and let an arrow do the rest of the work Barak had started.

Nathan turned to face another foe as another peal of thunder sounded. Not too far from Barak, a chariot careened out of control as its horse slipped in the mud. Barak turned to defend himself against the rider, who'd jumped out, sword in hand.

Barak froze. The warrior was none other than Sisera. His clothing was soaked through, and he wore no helmet. His shorn head sported a gash on one side that was bleeding. The rain made quick work of washing the blood away, but Sisera paid no attention to his wound. He'd seen Barak.

If Barak hadn't been numb from the cold rain already, he would have felt the impact of the hatred more deeply. Rage mixed with desperation filled Sisera's glare.

The man didn't move, just gripped his sword as he stared at Barak. Thunder rumbled again, and lightning streaked the sky.

Barak fully expected Sisera to charge him. This was the commander's chance, but Sisera took a step back, then another.

"Sisera!" Barak called out.

A chariot barreled past Sisera, nearly hitting him, but he didn't even flinch. The river behind him was only getting larger, flowing faster, and more chariots were swept away, man and beast screaming in the process.

Barak slid off his horse and sent the beast back to camp. The mud was too slick, and he feared he'd lose his horse too. He slogged through the thick mud, making his way toward Sisera. "Our day of reckoning has arrived, Sisera! Stand and fight me like a man."

"What evil have you brought upon us all, Barak?" Sisera's voice faltered, and a fear showed naked upon his face. He continued to move backward as if he wanted to evade Barak.

"You have brought God's displeasure upon your own head," Barak said. Energy surged through him, and he leapt toward Sisera, sword at the ready.

But Sisera turned. And ran.

Barak stared at the commander's form as he half ran, half staggered through the mud and rain, pushing his way past fighting men. Sisera ran east, away from the main battle.

"You would leave your men to fight?" Barak shouted. "Like the coward you are."

Sisera ran as if being chased by a rabid predator, and as Barak gave chase and skirted around fighting men and others who'd lost their lives, he heard a deep rumbling, greater than any thunder had been so far. He turned to see a wall of water moving along the path of the river, catching both men and horses in its power and swiping them off their feet.

Barak stared in horror and wonder as the water swallowed up chariots and men alike. The Canaanites tried to outrun the water, but many of them were caught up or tripped and fell upon their own swords. It was like watching a giant hand sweeping ants from the face of the earth.

Barak couldn't move, couldn't breathe as the chaos unfolded in front of him. Most of the Israelites had a head start on their enemies and headed for the mount. The flooding extended toward the Israelite camp, and those who reached the mount were able to get away from the rushing water.

The wall of water continued east, leaving only destruction in its wake. What had once been the river Kishon was now a lake. Upturned chariots, dead animals, and their owners floated in the water.

Barak looked for Sisera, but the commander was gone. Had he been swept away by the water too?

The thunder faded, and remarkably, the day brightened. The clouds shifted, revealing the sun. Groups of Canaanites who'd survived were making their way back to the other side of the river, and Barak scanned for Gilad, Deborah, Lapi, Nathan, and the others. He spotted Deborah and her green mantle headdress near the mount. It looked like Lapi wasn't far from her.

Barak strode in the direction of Deborah, passing many bodies along the way. He kept his gaze averted, knowing that what he'd already seen would stay in his nightmares for a long time. When he reached Deborah, she said, "We saw you pursuing Sisera. Where did he go?"

"East," Barak said. "I don't know if he has a hideout he's going to or what."

"The plains of Zaanaim are east," Deborah said.

"He will likely take refuge among the desert dwellers," Barak said. "I hope no one will shelter him."

"Abner has your horse, and I will gather the other commanders," Deborah said. "We cannot delay."

"No," Barak agreed. "Where is Gilad?"

"On the mount with the archers," Deborah said. "He's safe."

Barak's thoughts spun as he debated whether he should track Sisera down or follow the retreating Canaanite army.

"Leave Sisera to his escape for now," Deborah said. "First, we need to finish this battle."

It was like Deborah had read his thoughts. "You're right."

Abner rode up, leading Barak's horse. He was glad the horse was unharmed. Barak mounted, and soon, most of the commanders arrived, along with Nathan. "The Canaanites are fleeing—but we can't let that many get away," Barak said. "They'll re-form an army, and we'll return to our oppressed lives."

"I heard Sisera escaped," Chaim spoke up.

"He won't get far," Barak said. "I'll make sure of that. But we need to stop the others first before they can regain their strength." He looked over at Deborah. "God has helped us get this far."

The commanders all nodded.

"Gather your able men, and let's finish this war," Barak said.

Chapter Twenty-Eight

THE CLEANUP HAD TAKEN DAYS, and Deborah's heart broke a little more each time an Israelite was buried. Lapi had insisted that she establish a judgment seat near the base of Mount Tabor until all the bodies were identified and buried. But Deborah wasn't judging any Israelites this week. She was there to offer comfort for her grieving people.

They both grieved and rejoiced.

Barak and his men had chased down the rest of the Canaanites who had survived the flooding, and not one Canaanite soldier had survived. The ten thousand Israelites had their bittersweet victory.

Messengers had brought the news that King Jabin had gone into exile, probably east to the Hittites, if Deborah could guess. She wasn't about to send anyone in pursuit of the corrupt king. As far as she was concerned, he was out of their lives for good.

The water of the river Kishon had subsided and returned to its normal flow, leaving behind the drowned victims and broken chariots. This was the next task Barak commanded the Israelites to fulfill—to bury their enemies. Barak didn't even want the bones of their enemies to be visible. The only memorial would be to the victorious Israelites.

This morning, Deborah resumed her chosen place in the alcove that provided shade and shelter from the sun. Lapi had risen before the sun in order to help dig the last of the graves. The work was grim and taxing, but the sooner the dead were all buried, the sooner the camp could break up and the Israelites could return to their farms, homes, and families.

As Deborah looked over the valley and all the activity, she wished her father could have lived to see this day of freedom. There was yet a lot of work to do, but hearts were light, souls were joyful, and hope had been restored.

Deborah paused as she saw a small caravan approaching the river Kishon. There were women in the caravan. Even from this distance, Deborah determined that one of the members was also an elder. She descended the mount, and as she reached the base of it, she called to Barak, who was working with Lapi.

When the men raised their heads at her call, she pointed to the approaching caravan.

It took Barak only seconds to identify his wife and daughters.

Deborah smiled as he ran toward them. Despite the grueling war and days of labor that had followed, he still had strength to run. As the caravan neared the river, Barak reached them.

Deborah put her hand up to shield her eyes from the glare of the morning sun. The reunion was sweet and brought tears to her eyes. Among Barak's family was Elder Reuben. Having the elder here to help her counsel with the soldiers and officiate over thanksgiving sacrifices would be helpful.

Lapi joined Deborah, and he wrapped his arms around her shoulders. "I don't think I've ever seen my cousin run so fast."

Deborah laughed. "We have much to rejoice over."

"Yes," Lapi said softly and pressed a kiss against her temple. "If only we knew what happened to Sisera. He could still be a threat to our family."

Deborah nodded. As long as Sisera was unaccounted for, there was no telling what the future might bring.

Suddenly, Lapi stiffened, and his grasp on her shoulder tightened.

"What is it?" Deborah asked.

"Look," Lapi said, pointing to the east. "Someone's coming."

Three people, in fact. Deborah focused on the approaching riders. Two horses carrying three people were racing toward the camp. Deborah stepped away from Lapi as alarm shot through her. "Who do you think it is?"

"I don't know yet . . ." he said, trailing off.

They were desert dwellers, Deborah knew that much, so probably Gentiles. Were they friends or foes? Perhaps messengers. Then Deborah caught another glimpse of the woman behind one of the riders. "Jael," Deborah said. "It's Jael and Heber."

Lapi grasped Deborah's hand, and they started toward the arriving party. Barak had noticed the group, and so had Abner and Chaim. By the time Jael and her husband arrived, along with one of their sons, several people were waiting to greet them.

"We come in peace," Heber said. Perspiration stood out on his face. "We've news about the Canaanite commander, Sisera." He climbed off his horse, then handed his wife down.

"Come," Deborah said. "Take some refreshment and rest in the shade, then you can tell us your news." She was anxious to hear what they'd come to say, yet she wanted to put their guests' well-being first.

The look of gratitude on Heber's face was enough to tell Deborah she'd been right. The three followed Deborah and the others to Barak's tent. Deborah and Evie poured water into cups for everyone, then offered dried figs to their guests.

Heber, Jael, and their son declined the food.

"We would have come earlier," Heber said, "but we were waiting for any message of King Jabin's next move. When we learned last night that he'd gone into exile, I knew it was time to deliver the news about Sisera."

Deborah clasped her hands together, trying to be patient. She hoped Heber would deliver his news sooner rather than later.

"My wife, Jael, will tell you of the events," Heber said.

Jael flushed at the attention, but she was not a demure woman, so she began to talk. "The day of the terrible rainstorm, Sisera arrived at our homestead," she began. "Heber knew who he was right away, and I was leery of welcoming him into our tent. He was exhausted, and there was a gash on his face . . ."

Heber nodded for his wife to continue.

"Sisera told us there was a mighty war and that the Israelites were like ferocious dogs, tearing the Canaanites from limb to limb." She looked down at her folded hands.

Deborah noticed that Jael was clenching her hands so tightly together that they'd gone white.

"I brought him into the tent and directed him to rest on the cushions in our gathering room," Jael said, her voice trembling now. "I didn't want him there." Her gaze lifted and met Barak's. "I knew what he'd done to your sister . . . and then to you and Gilad."

Barak nodded and blinked back tears. Evie reached for his hand.

"Sisera asked for water," Jael said. "And I decided to give him something more substantial. So I gave him milk. For a man who had been so cruel, he was certainly grateful in that moment. So grateful, in fact, that he drank it and fell fast asleep—" Her voice cut off, and she took a couple deep breaths.

"We are not Israelite or Canaanite, you see," Heber said, as if he had to explain why they'd provide hospitality for a man like Sisera.

Deborah was about to say that she didn't hold it against them when Jael blurted out, "I killed him." Tears brimmed in her eyes. "*I killed Sisera.* I could not stand to see him lying there, sleeping, safe from all the horrible things he'd done. An evader of his crimes. So I took a tent peg and a hammer, and I drove the peg through his temple."

No one moved; no one spoke. Everyone stared at Jael.

Then Barak said, "Praise God in heaven. You, woman, have avenged us all."

Jael covered her mouth with her hand as she half sobbed, half laughed.

"Praise God in heaven," Deborah repeated, tears burning in her eyes.

Others in their group laughed, cried, or both. Lapi grasped Deborah's hand, and she leaned her head against his shoulder. Jael answered questions about the location of Sisera's body.

It has come to an end, was all Deborah could think as she closed her eyes for a moment. The years of oppression were over, and now the Israelites could grow into their full potential and destiny.

Barak was talking now, telling Jael that he wanted to view Sisera's body and oversee the burial of it.

Deborah rose to her feet and crossed to Jael, where she bent down and kissed the woman's cheeks. Grasping Jael's hands, Deborah said, "You have done our people a great service. May you and your family be blessed. Today, we celebrate, and tomorrow and every day after, we will celebrate your courage."

Jael nodded, tears in her eyes as she smiled at Deborah.

"Come," Deborah said, still holding the woman's hands. "I will present you to our soldiers and tell them of the good news. It will be a boon to our victory, but most importantly, they will see the power of God in their lives."

Jael rose to her feet and stood with Deborah. "I am neither Israelite nor Canaanite," Jael said, "but your family has become my family."

Emotion tightened Deborah's throat. "And you are the sister I never had."

The women embraced, and then the two of them walked out of the tent and to the base of Mount Tabor.

Deborah waited, standing arm in arm with Jael as the Israelites gathered to hear her announcement. Watching the women of Barak's family join them, along with the soldiers, Deborah couldn't help but remember Barak's shouts to the ten thousand.

Who do we fight for?
Who do we fight against?
Who is on our side?

The answers would be the same the rest of their lives. They would fight for Israel. They would fight against evil and bondage. And God would always be on their side.

The Song of Deborah

Judges 5, KJV

THEN SANG DEBORAH AND BARAK the son of Abinoam on that day, saying,

Praise ye the Lord for the avenging of Israel, when the people willingly offered themselves.

Hear, O ye kings; give ear, O ye princes; I, even I, will sing unto the Lord; I will sing praise to the Lord God of Israel.

Lord, when thou wentest out of Seir, when thou marchedst out of the field of Edom, the earth trembled, and the heavens dropped, the clouds also dropped water.

The mountains melted from before the Lord, even that Sinai from before the Lord God of Israel.

In the days of Shamgar the son of Anath, in the days of Jael, the highways were unoccupied, and the travellers walked through byways.

The inhabitants of the villages ceased, they ceased in Israel, until that I Deborah arose, that I arose a mother in Israel.

They chose new gods; then was war in the gates: was there a shield or spear seen among forty thousand in Israel?

My heart is toward the governors of Israel, that offered themselves willingly among the people. Bless ye the Lord.

Speak, ye that ride on white asses, ye that sit in judgment, and walk by the way.

They that are delivered from the noise of archers in the places of drawing water, there shall they rehearse the righteous acts of the Lord, even the righteous acts toward the inhabitants of his villages in Israel: then shall the people of the Lord go down to the gates.

Awake, awake, Deborah: awake, awake, utter a song: arise, Barak, and lead thy captivity captive, thou son of Abinoam.

Then he made him that remaineth have dominion over the nobles among the people: the Lord made me have dominion over the mighty.

Out of Ephraim was there a root of them against Amalek; after thee, Benjamin, among thy people; out of Machir came down governors, and out of Zebulun they that handle the pen of the writer.

And the princes of Issachar were with Deborah; even Issachar, and also Barak: he was sent on foot into the valley. For the divisions of Reuben there were great thoughts of heart.

Why abodest thou among the sheepfolds, to hear the bleatings of the flocks? For the divisions of Reuben there were great searchings of heart.

Gilead abode beyond Jordan: and why did Dan remain in ships? Asher continued on the sea shore, and abode in his breaches.

Zebulun and Naphtali were a people that jeoparded their lives unto the death in the high places of the field.

The kings came and fought, then fought the kings of Canaan in Taanach by the waters of Megiddo; they took no gain of money.

They fought from heaven; the stars in their courses fought against Sisera.

The river of Kishon swept them away, that ancient river, the river Kishon. O my soul, thou hast trodden down strength.

Then were the horsehoofs broken by the means of the pransings, the pransings of their mighty ones.

Curse ye Meroz, said the angel of the Lord, curse ye bitterly the inhabitants thereof; because they came not to the help of the Lord, to the help of the Lord against the mighty.

Blessed above women shall Jael the wife of Heber the Kenite be, blessed shall she be above women in the tent.

He asked water, and she gave him milk; she brought forth butter in a lordly dish.

She put her hand to the nail, and her right hand to the workmen's hammer; and with the hammer she smote Sisera, she smote off his head, when she had pierced and stricken through his temples.

At her feet he bowed, he fell, he lay down: at her feet he bowed, he fell: where he bowed, there he fell down dead.

The mother of Sisera looked out at a window, and cried through the lattice, Why is his chariot so long in coming? why tarry the wheels of his chariots?

Her wise ladies answered her, yea, she returned answer to herself,

Have they not sped? have they not divided the prey; to every man a damsel or two; to Sisera a prey of divers colours, a prey of divers colours of needlework, of divers colours of needlework on both sides, meet for the necks of them that take the spoil?

So let all thine enemies perish, O Lord: but let them that love him be as the sun when he goeth forth in his might. And the land had rest forty years.

Acknowledgments

I've been looking forward to writing about Deborah, the Fourth Judge in Israel, for some time. Writing historical fiction is daunting, especially biblical fiction, since there is so much scholarship to consider. Fortunately, my scholarly father, S. Kent Brown, was willing to read this manuscript, along with my mother, Gayle Brown. Many thanks to both of my parents. Also, David LeFevre, a long-time acquaintance and scholar, was gracious enough to write up an endorsement and, along the way, give me additional feedback.

I'm grateful to my publisher and all those who have a hand in the production of a book, namely my editor, Samantha Millburn; managing editor Kathy Jenkins; cover designer Christina Marcano; managing director Robby Nichols; and so many more.

Another thanks to my husband, Chris; our four children; and my father-in-law, Lester Moore, who have been supportive since day one. Additional thanks to Julie Daines and Taffy Lovell, writing partners and good friends who are both motivating and inspirational.

About the Author

Heather B. Moore is a *USA Today* best-selling author of more than a dozen historical novels and thrillers written under the pen name H.B. Moore. She writes women's fiction, romance, and inspirational nonfiction under Heather B. Moore. This can all be confusing, so her kids just call her Mom. Heather attended Cairo American College in Egypt and the Anglican School of Jerusalem in Israel and earned a bachelor of science degree from Brigham Young University in Utah. Visit Heather's website here: www.hbmoore.com.